Tim Relf was born in 1968. He
numerous newspapers and mag
Sunday Express and *Front*. *Stag* i
work on his second.

... is a journalist who has written for ... magazines including The Times, the ... is his first novel. He is currently at work on his second.

Stag

Tim Relf

PIATKUS

Visit the Piatkus website!

Piatkus publishes a wide range of best-selling fiction and non-fiction, including books on health, mind, body & spirit, sex, self-help, cookery, biography and the paranormal.

If you want to:
- read descriptions of our popular titles
- buy our books over the Internet
- take advantage of our special offers
- enter our monthly competition
- learn more about your favourite Piatkus authors

VISIT OUR WEBSITE AT: www.piatkus.co.uk

Copyright © 2004

First published in Great Britain in 2004 by
Piatkus Books Ltd of
5 Windmill Street, London W1T 2JA
email: info@piatkus.co.uk

The moral right of the author has been asserted

A catalogue record for this book is available from the British Library

ISBN 0 7449 3493 X

Set in Times by
Phoenix Photosetting, Chatham, Kent

Printed and bound in Great Britain by
Bookmarque Ltd, Croydon, Surrey

Acknowledgements

I'd like to thank my editor, Emma Callagher, and everyone at Piatkus for all their help and advice.

FRIDAY

Prologue

It's late. About eleven, I guess, although I've lost track of time. And no, before you say it, I haven't been drinking. I haven't touched a drop all night. Well, all day anyway. The night is still to come.

It's Matt who's on a different planet. He's out of it. He's not drunk but you wouldn't realise: he's red and flushed and somehow light on his feet. I've never seen him like this before.

'I can't.believe I've done it, Rob,' he says, beaming. 'I've actually got married, I've got a wife.'

We're at a table near the bar and he's got his arm around me, his tie hanging undone. He raises his pint to my Coke, and I get that same old feeling. I want one. A pint, that is, not a wife. I want one, but I guess I always will now. I've just got to deal with it.

Tonight's a start.

No, last weekend was the start.

Tonight is another: the first wedding I've been to without Emma for two years. The last one we went to was her kid sister's. She'd spent the whole day pulling at her dress, complaining that she hated pink; but she looked great. She would have loved this – the church, the speeches, the meal. I feel myself sinking. Claire joins us.

'Should have known where I'd find you,' she says, glancing at the bar. 'Well, don't get too comfortable, you can't avoid dancing all night.'

I'm glad she's here. She wanted to come last weekend but Stevie wouldn't have any of it; he was horrified by the idea of a girl on a stag weekend. She hasn't mentioned Emma yet, but she will, I know that, she's just waiting until we're on our own. And I know that when she does, I'll have exactly the sort of conversation with her that Emma always said I was incapable of – you know, about feelings and things. Maybe it's because there's never been anything sexual between me and Claire – or only once and that didn't count – or because she never takes relationships too seriously or, I suppose, because although she is a girl I've always just seen her as one of the lads, although she hates it when I say that.

Stevie and James join us. Loads of people are here from college, but I like it like this best of all: when it's just the five of us.

There was a pillar between me and the top table so I couldn't see Stevie when he was making his best-man speech, but he was fantastic. Funny and confident, and suggestive without being offensive. Everything, probably, that I wouldn't have been. He scrubs up pretty well. He said what a beautiful bride Katie was and 'Oh yes?' I shouted, and a few people tittered. Now it's over, he's more relaxed. He's on the voddies and Coke. Doubles. His new woman is on the dance floor, giving it some to Abba's 'Dancing Queen' – Emma's favourite song – and I wonder if Stevie has told her about last weekend. Not that she'd hold it against me, she seems really nice.

James heads off for a top-up. It's a big day for him, too. News that he's going to become a dad has spread like wildfire. It still seems bizarre. James, a dad. 'Free bar,' he says, smiling.

'Hidden cost,' the rest of us chorus.

A girl I don't know plonks herself down next to Stevie. See, someone *always* fancies the best man. 'Are you going to tell me now about the stag night then?' she asks.

We look at each other conspiratorially.

We smile.

I wonder if Emma would be enjoying this.

Because I am.

Chapter One

Splitting up's like falling off a horse.

You either conquer your fear and get straight back on (i.e. go out with someone else immediately) or your confidence disappears and you get scared of riding (i.e. end up single for ages).

At least, that's what Matt always says. It's exactly what he'd told me last week, too, after Emma dumped me. 'I'm really sorry, mate,' he'd said, then launched into his horse theory. 'Always said you were punching above your weight there, Rob,' he'd added, laughing, not realising I was crying on the other end of the phone.

Course, other people reckon time on your own is precisely what you do need after splitting up. Time to get over it, lick your wounds, heal.

I can see the sense in both arguments. Not that I get much say in the matter. I mean, I'm hardly Brad Pitt. I've always worked on the principle that if you get an opportunity to go out with someone, you take it, mainly because you never know when another one might come along.

And trains *are* supposed to be good places to meet people. Trains and supermarkets. As we pulled into Stevenage, I put *Captain Corelli* out on the table so anyone who got on might think I was really interesting and well read. Actually, I must have been the only person in the world who couldn't get into this book, but everyone said it was a must-read and Emma loved it. There again, she loved all sorts of books; that was one of the reasons I liked her so much.

No one sat near me. So much for sodding *Captain Corelli*.

I mention about how Emma's love of books was one of the reasons I *liked* her but, of course, I mean *like*. You don't just stop liking someone because you're not going out with them any more, do you. If anything, it's the opposite. As I'd said to Matt on the phone, it was weird but her actually doing it – you know, chucking me – made me want her *more*. Something about the sense of self-preservation that must have made her do it. I admired that.

'You are still on for next weekend though, aren't you?' he'd asked.

'Wouldn't miss it for the world,' I told him, although right then another stag weekend was the last thing I felt like.

'Great,' he replied. 'Dust your riding boots down, then, we'll soon have you back in the saddle.'

Matt, I now remembered, wasn't the ideal person to turn to for advice at a time like this. I had tried Claire but her phone was off.

At Peterborough, a girl wandered into the carriage with a rucksack. She had faded jeans on, great legs, and I got that familiar tug of lust. Please sit down, I thought. *Please.* She checked her ticket and plonked her rucksack on the seat opposite me.

'Sorry,' she said.

'That's OK,' I replied, then got another familiar feeling. It was one I hadn't had for a while, one I'd forgotten: not knowing what to say next. I always did with Emma. I grabbed *Captain Corelli*, wriggled, smiled. She was a student, I reckoned. If she was at Newcastle, we'd have so much to talk about. I wanted to tell her how excited I was to be going back, how it was three years since I'd seen the old place, eleven years since Freshers' Week when I'd bumped into Matt that night in the Union and discovered we were in next-door rooms. Eleven years. I imagined myself telling her about all the things we did when we were there and she would have told me what the city was like now and, who knows, we might have arranged to meet up at some point over the weekend. Things like that happen.

Now that really would be getting straight back on the horse.

But it was the middle of October – probably the second or third week of term – and it was a Friday lunchtime, so it would have been an odd time to be travelling back to college.

I opened a can of Stella. She looked up at me briefly when she heard the ring-pull, then away.

I had another go at my book. Nothing.

Tried the paper. The same.

The free magazine. Ditto.

I couldn't concentrate on anything; it was as if I was being pulled irreversibly back to one thing: Emma. I remembered the party we met at – she was wearing that denim jacket and was with a load of friends – and how I'd gone up to her and said hello. I knew somehow I'd regret it in the morning if I didn't. 'We were just talking about the paint-stripper – I mean the wine,' she'd replied, emptying her glass into a plant pot. 'That'll kill it,' she'd added, smiling. And that was it, I was hooked.

The train raced north. We went through York, where Emma had been at uni. History, she'd done.

That was what I was now. History.

I couldn't have faced staying in London this weekend. I needed to get out, get away, let my hair down. It would have been so weird: waking up and the weekend not involving Emma. And there wouldn't have been time to arrange anything else – most of my friends needed three months' written notice before coming out nowadays. I can get through this weekend, I thought; I'll be surrounded by the lads, and next weekend's the wedding, but what about the one after that and the one after that? You can't be with people all the time. And what about Christmas, Christmas and New Year? Everyone's going on about how important it is to do something special this year, what with it being the Millennium. This, I thought, *this* is what it's like to be single. It means you're always on your own unless you arrange it otherwise.

All week I'd been relieved when Simon or Helen had come back to the flat. It was someone to talk to, someone to listen to. Someone to make noise. Someone, anyone, to stop me going over what happened time and time again, thinking: This time I've *really* blown it.

Funny, I'd always slagged off people who turned the telly on the second they walked in the door, as if they couldn't bear the sound of their own company. This week, it had been the first thing I'd done. I had the stereo on in my room when I was dressing and the radio on in the car when I was driving. Always Radio 4. Anything on Radio 4. Programmes about growing tomatoes, Buddhism, the renaissance of Notting Hill. Whatever. All that highbrow stuff was confusing and all the time I was confused, I couldn't think. I liked the news, too, it reminded me how lucky I was compared to some people. There'd been an earthquake somewhere in India, and I found listening to coverage of it compulsive.

Get straight back on the horse, Matt's voice echoed.

I pretended to read, and looked at the girl opposite me. She was reading.

In the distance – not very old, but rusty already – The Angel of the North.

Time on your own, Rob, that's what you need.

I'm hardly Brad Pitt.

I stared at her. She had blonde hair. Emma's was black. Hers was long. Emma's was short.

She looked up at me, and away. *You're not Emma*, I felt like shouting.

Chapter Two

Emma yawned. 'I'm so tired.'

'Why don't you get an early night?' I suggested.

'No, Rob, what I'm tired of is *this*. Us. You.'

It struck me as odd, her calling me that. She always called me Chip or Bobby or Droopy or, my favourite of all, Ace. It seemed ages since she'd said, simply, Rob.

'It's not as if I haven't mentioned it before,' she said. 'But all we ever do is go round in circles. I could talk about it until I'm black-and-blue in the face, but I don't see why I should have to.'

I sat.

'How do you think the way you've started acting makes me feel?' she said. 'I feel ... incidental.'

'The Sweetest Thing' by U2 – one of my favourite songs – was on in the flat upstairs and it occurred to me I'd never be able to listen to it again now without remembering this.

'I can't see what all the fuss is about,' I said. 'So I like going out? So I like spending time with my friends? What's wrong with that?'

'Nothing. I like the fact that you do. But that's not what I'm talking about, and you know it. What I mean is the way you're never around when I want you to be; and when you are, you're either too hungover to do anything or just want to go and sit in that awful pub.'

'Since when has having a good time become a crime?'

'Don't try and make me out to be some sort of battleaxe. You're always drunk nowadays.'

'No I'm not,' I said. Instinctively.

'Rob, you're *always* drunk.'

'I'm not drunk now.'

'Only because you've had to drive over here.'

Fair point, I suppose.

9

Still, Thursday night. The weekend starts here.

'You're always drunk and it's always me that ends up having to look after you. It's more like having a kid than a boyfriend. It's no fun any more. You never used to be like this.'

The music had stopped upstairs. Someone stomped across the floor – Emma's ceiling – and then it started again, a song I didn't recognise.

'So?' she said. 'How's it going to be?'

Again, my immediate reaction was to stall for time. If I went home with things like this, it would be bad, but it wouldn't be decided, not for definite. I might know what to do tomorrow. Surely everyone must have doubts about this sort of stuff. Don't they?

'What do *you* want?' I asked.

'You know what I want. I want us to get more serious together, maybe get a flat. Or I did. But I'm not going to do it with the way things are, I *can't*. And this isn't about what *I* want. It's you who's got to decide, Rob.'

'I don't want us to split up.'

'But you're not prepared to make any sacrifices to make it work between us, are you?'

'I like things as they are,' I said, as if I hadn't said it countless times that evening. I might as well have said: Purple's my favourite colour.

'Well, I don't. I don't like things the way they've become, anyway.'

I knew I might never get another chance like this, that I'd never meet anyone like Emma again, but I still couldn't say: OK, I'll do it. I'll change. I just couldn't. That would have opened a door on a world I didn't know; it would have made everything alter. Going out was just the tip of the iceberg. Fine, I wouldn't mind doing that a bit less, but I knew how these things worked. It was like dominoes. That would be just the start. She'd want to make me get a mortgage, work harder, sort out a pension. Get a house in the suburbs, a Ford Mondeo, have 2.4 kids. She didn't know what she was saying, but what she was proposing, in fact, was a whole new ball game.

'Why do we have to change?' I asked. 'We're having a good time, aren't we?'

'Do I look as if I'm having a good time?' she sobbed, wiping her eyes. Her wry smile cut into me. I wanted to reach out and touch

10

her, take her arm, stroke the back of her head, the way she liked it. 'I'm afraid, Rob. I'm really, really afraid, OK.'

She looked tired – tired and different, somehow, to the girl I knew, the girl I'd met at that party in Wandsworth. It occurred to me that I had done this to her.

'I'm too old for this,' she said, looking around, her gaze fixing on her flatmate's black-and-white telly. 'I'm thirty. I don't want to be going out with someone who's permanently half-cut and has started acting like they're a student again. You asked me what I wanted. All I really want is the old Rob back, the person you used to be. All I want is my boyfriend back.'

'Less of the old,' I said.

She never said as much, but she was terrified of wasting time. And I couldn't blame her, not after what had happened with her last bloke. She went out with him for nine years – nine – and then he rang her one night and told her it was over. Not that we'd ever really talked about the break-up: it upset me just *thinking* about how upset she must have been.

I tried blaming it on her job – she'd had a couple of quick pro-motions and was frustrated at the time it was taking to get a third – but that wasn't what this was all about, and we both knew it.

'It's down to you now,' she said. 'Well?'

For a second, seeing her cry had brought things into focus. Her tears had torn into me and reduced everything to that singularly sharp spear of pain. It was simple; I couldn't live without her. I *would* go out less. I *would* get pissed a bit less often. But now she had stopped, it was clouding over again, getting muddled, the old feeling of fog coming back. All I could think as I sat there silently, her opposite me, her eyes shining like marbles, was: I don't know *what* to think. I mean, going out less? What else was there to do?

'I just ... I just ...'

'You do realise what you're doing, don't you?'

She wasn't asking if I knew whether this meant we wouldn't be going out any more. More, whether I knew what not going out would entail. No more silly text messages, no more meals in Giovanni's, no more getting her to record stuff when I'd gone out and forgotten to set the video, no more weekends away, no more getting woken up by Capital Radio and lying in her bed, refusing to get up, while she made tea. It would all stop. And I suppose I had-n't given that side of it much thought.

'Yes ... no ... sort of,' I said, crying too.

It seemed unimaginable we could actually split up when we could be like this with each other, this exposed. It was just something to sort out, surely, like car-sharing or cooking.

'Don't cry, baby,' I said, 'please don't.'

'I might as well, I'm going to when you're gone.'

She held her stomach and cried louder – not normal crying, more like convulsing. She rocked forwards and backwards for a while, then she just sat still, crying, and looking down at the table. All the anger had gone now. It had all been shouted out, spent, boiled away to this: the salty sight of her tears. Then she went and sat in the chair by the window where I usually sat, and cried there. It hurt, not hugging her.

'I think you should go now,' she said.

Nothing more. We walked to the door. She had lip-balm on – I saw it shine – and I knew that little blue stick would be beside the clock on the cabinet by her bed. I thought: I don't know if I can live without you. Then I saw the clothes I'd seen a hundred times before – covering the body I'd seen a hundred times before – and I got a faint twinge of excitement. I'd forgotten what it was like to get off with someone new and now I would be able to again.

She said: 'You'll end up very lonely if you're not careful, Rob. Not everyone lives happily ever after, you know.'

'I don't want to hurt you,' I replied. Uselessly.

'Do you know, I was convinced I'd found the person I was going to spend the rest of my life with,' she said, opening the door. 'I thought this was it. That night we met. I knew, I just knew you were the one. Wrong again.'

One of her flatmates was coming in as I left, and she waved.

For a second, I thought she was going to call me Ace. I'd have given anything in the world, right then, for her to do so. One last time. *Wrong again, Ace.*

But she didn't.

The traffic was heavy between her flat and mine, and for once that was good. I had an hour when I had to concentrate on driving. I made myself focus on it. Hands at ten to two. Checking the mirror. Listening to the engine and changing gear at precisely the right point. Two years she'd invested in me. And for what? For what? What would she do now? What would I do now? I didn't know what I hated more, her having to make a new life for

12

herself or me not knowing where and how she was doing it. My Emma.

Then I remembered how she'd said 'Wrong again' about me being the one, and a little part of me balked. How many times exactly *had* she been convinced she'd met the one?

What's weird, I thought, is that I *might* have settled down with her. Only a little while before, it had occurred to me how lucky I was to have her. But now look at us. I knew the way I was going I'd never do anything; it was as if I'd hit twenty-nine then stopped, as if I'd gone into suspended animation. What if one day I woke up and did want all that thirty-something stuff? It can't have been all bad. Most of my mates raved about it. But, settling down? Something so final about that. It's like saying: This is as good as it ever can get.

I drove faster, dreading the sight of my road, my flat. When I got back I'd have to not ring her. When Simon or Helen asked how I was, I wouldn't know what to say. I wouldn't know whether to leave my mobile on or off tonight.

I wondered if she'd sleep. Wondered how she'd be tomorrow. How strange, I thought, that her memory of tonight – what was said and how – will be different to mine. Like two separate events: one happening to her, one to me. Different people.

Even as I drove, our time together was unravelling. Soon, she'd start calling me her ex and I'd do the same. Something inconsequential about that. Trite. Past. Ex.

I drove on, back to Wimbledon.

When I reached the flat, *EastEnders* was on and I tried watching it but every time Pat appeared, I could hear Emma shout, 'Nice earrings!' and I went to my room and pulled the curtains and remembered how Emma always complained it was like a dungeon in there and turned on the stereo and it was the Fatboy Slim CD she'd given me for my birthday. I lay on the bed and could smell her perfume and I knew how difficult everything – absolutely everything – would be from now on.

Chapter Three

I went straight to Merryfield Road and stood outside Number 65.

The old place looked the same, except no lights were on and they always were when we lived there. I wondered if it was still a student house.

It was 104 paces to the Sun from here: 104 there and anything between 150 and 200 home depending on how straight a line you could walk in. Two hundred and twenty, if you went for chips.

Matt reckoned he could do it in under ninety. Or, as he said that morning he arrived back at the house after spending the night with that girl from the other side of the city: 'Ninety paces there, but a five-mile round trip.'

I always promised myself I'd buy this house one day. Buy it even if I wasn't living here, buy it and use it for weekends or holidays. I'd been convinced I was going to earn a fortune when we graduated. 'That's the great thing about a geography degree,' our tutor always told us, 'it opens so many doors.' But not many had opened for me. No way did I earn enough to pay my rent in London *and* buy somewhere in Newcastle. Plus, work was so boring. I ought to go and find the old git – Physical Phil, we called him, because he taught Physical Geography – and put him straight. Tell him that devising questions to ask people about breakfast cereals wasn't exactly my idea of fun. Not that it was entirely his fault I went into market research. The careers officer recommended it as well, and then at my interview my firm went on about all the opportunities I'd get. Well, I'd been there seven years now – seven years and four months – and hadn't seen many opportunities (other than for fabricating expense claims). I'd been so excited when I got the job, too; I loved telling people I was going into market research. It sounded exciting and glamorous: a sort of cross between consultancy and

PR, business but with lots of socialising. A cross between IT and accountancy, more like.

I sat down on the wall. The tube rattled past. The Metro. I remembered that party when everyone spilled out into the road. Our get-togethers in the greasy spoon on the corner. My old Escort loaded up and down on the springs when I left for the last time.

I wondered if that little school where I'd done a few days' voluntary work after we'd graduated was still round the corner. I only really did it because I couldn't get a job, and wanted something for my CV; but I'd never enjoyed anything so much. I'd seen straight away why Dad had loved teaching.

A man looked out at me from behind the curtains in 63 – Edie must have died – so I started walking. This had all seemed so strange at first: the rows of red-brick houses, the concrete yards, the grey slate roofs and cobbled alleys. Like my worst stereotypical image of the North. Cold, too, like everyone said it would be. It *is* grim up North, I'd thought in those first couple of days as I'd hidden away in my room in Halls, petrified by it all. I'd got used to it, though. Got so I loved it. When I moved back south, I used to watch *Coronation Street* because it reminded me of here. People used to laugh at how I'd started saying 'aye' instead of 'yes'. Waitrose seemed strange then, not Morrisons.

And to think, I so nearly didn't come here. If it had been down to me, I'd have gone somewhere more local – London or Reading or possibly Guildford which was right on my doorstep – or more likely just got a job, but Mum was insistent I went to uni and she suggested Newcastle. She didn't know anything about the place, she later confessed, but had heard it was a good place to study. I was surprised she wanted me to go so far away. 'It's an opportunity to see somewhere completely new, Robert,' she'd said. 'Besides, I don't want you back here every weekend with your washing.' And I'll always remember that because it was the first time I'd heard her laugh – really laugh – since Dad died.

I walked to the hotel. It was called the Hotel Seaview, but on his e-mail Stevie had written 'The Hotel Where We Spew'. God knows how it got its name; it was miles from the coast. The carpet in the foyer must have been bright red one day, but it was faded and worn now. There were a few 'Welcome to the North-East' leaflets pinned to the wall, and a thin old man in a grey suit on the check-in with a cigarette.

15

'All right, son,' he said, broad Geordie.

'Hi. There's a room booked in my name. Rob Purcell.'

'You must be with Steve Jones's party?'

He wrote something in the book. Stevie, I could just imagine him, would have rung from that swanky office of his. He'd have put the phone down and told his colleagues – the partners, the secretaries, his clients, everyone loves listening to Stevie – about this stag weekend he was organising and they'd have wondered what he'd get up to and think what a laugh he was, a laugh but great at his job, and then he'd have gone back to one of his big design projects – offices, or whatever it is he does nowadays. He was working late tonight but he'd probably still manage to go out. Knowing Stevie, he probably had a date.

'Two of you due tonight and two tomorrow,' the old boy said, handling me a keyring. I got a stab of panic; it was too big to fit in my pocket and I knew I couldn't leave it on reception because I probably wouldn't be able to speak, let alone remember my room number, when I came in.

'Room seven. Lucky for some. Upstairs, turn right.'

I lay on the bed. It smelt funny, probably of whoever was in here before. A couple were talking quietly in the room next door.

Emma would be finishing work about now. Going for a drink with the girls from the office, then walking home over Kew Bridge. When we were in her flat last Thursday, when it was all going tits up, it had been a help knowing I was going to Newcastle. It had helped knowing I'd be in a place I lived before I met her, with people I knew before I met her. I'd hoped coming back might make me see there would be stuff after her, as there had been before. But now it just seemed a shame she wasn't with me. I always said I'd show her the city's sights. She loved weekends away. We went to York, where she was at uni, but never here. Never Newcastle.

Outside, gulls shrieked. I remembered the gulls we'd fed on holiday in Devon barely a month before. Her, running excitedly into that bakery to buy a loaf, then taking a big bite out of it herself. Her white trainers, covered in mud outside the door of the cottage. Her, standing in a towel beside the bed, dripping water and shivering. And it struck me that I'd made the biggest mistake of my life, letting her go.

A girl was laughing in the car park and I wanted to be out there right now – out there with her or people like her or my friends or anyone, anyone, just as long as there was noise. Noise and company.

Then it occurred to me: the Sun's not far from here. I could sit at our table, the table behind the glass partition: the one we sat at for my twenty-first, the one James danced on the night we got chucked out, the one Stevie nearly set fire to once. Five o'clock. It will be warm and quiet in there at this time of day. It's all wood, yes, a dark, rich wood and there are those big armchairs, the huge leather ones you can sink into, and the lighting's low and soft on your eyes. It's split into two; we'd always go in the busy side on Fridays and Saturdays and the snug the rest of the week where it was quiet and you could chat or read the papers or relax or, if you got there early and were waiting for the others, sleep. And there's that long, smooth dark bar you can lean on, with the little rail you can rest your feet on and those soft, port-red carpets with the swirly patterns which feel all cosy if you're barefoot. And outside there's the sign that says The Rising Sun, all in yellow, that shines in the sunlight, that brittle sunshine I've never seen anywhere quite the same as in the North-East, and the bricks are that lovely red – a Mediterranean red, Stevie always reckoned – and I remembered how we always used to joke about buying that place, too, buying it between us and keeping it as our sort of local, wherever we all ended up living.

Always time for a quick one before Matt arrives.

Chapter Four

We were seeing Emma's parents tomorrow, so I reckoned I deserved a drink.

I was stressed, despite having met them twice before. Plus, there was a load of shit flying around at work about stuff not getting done properly and of course it was *me* who got the blame. I needed to get away from it all for a few hours. I did suggest to Emma she came but she didn't fancy it. I'd asked, at least.

'But you've already had a couple on the way home from work,' she'd said.

We obviously had different ideas of what a couple meant. To her, it *meant* literally a couple – as in two. A couple, as far as I was concerned, meant four. But there again, one, to me, meant three; a few meant five; and some beers, well, some beers meant anything from five upwards. And, like I say, I'd had a couple and you always want another one after a couple.

'Let's spend tonight together,' Emma said. 'Please.'

And that – the emotional blackmail – was the final straw.

Soon I was standing at my favourite spot in the Star at Wimbledon, and by the time I'd had a second swig almost half my pint was gone. Already, the tightness – the tightness like indigestion – which had been in me all day was easing.

I loved this place. You could prop up the bar and watch the world go by; no one made you talk or expected anything of you. You couldn't hear any one conversation, not in detail, but two, five, ten – all melted together, indistinguishable, and every now and then laughter breaking out like when you suddenly notice part of a song coming out of one particular speaker in your car. And every song that came on the juke box – every single song – was one that I would have chosen. And a girl came and stood at the bar next to me, a girl

18

on her own; she could have stood anywhere but she chose to wait next to me. She had dark hair up in pigtails, and was wearing a long skirt and boots. I waited until she was about to order a drink and finished mine and after neither of us had been served for a few seconds, I said: 'A man could die of thirst in here.'

She laughed. Definitely a laugh, not a sneer. 'Try playing with the taps,' she said.

I wished I'd shaved; I'd stopped shaving every day at some point after I'd started going out with Emma.

I told her it was probably because the bar staff were new, they were always changing in here, and how the place used to have a bad reputation, but had cleaned up and how it was, if you believed the notice, one of the oldest pubs in London. 'Mind you, it also says Good Food,' I said. She laughed again.

The barman, some Aussie, came round and I caught his eye – bar presence never was my forte but it worked this time – and he said, 'How are you tonight, mate?' like he knew me and when he asked what I wanted I gestured to this girl and said, 'After you,' and she ordered a half and I had another Stella and told her it would have to be a quick one because I was going on somewhere to meet some people which, of course, I wasn't. I was here now for the evening; then I'd head back apologetically to Emma's and tomorrow I'd sit in her mum and dad's living room and sip tea and nip to the toilet every now and then to throw up.

She went to make a phone call and I ordered a vodka – just a single – and finished it in two swigs and slid the glass up the bar so she wouldn't realise it was mine. I didn't want her thinking I was wasted. I liked sliding the glass up the bar. I grabbed it after it came to a halt, and did it again. Then I did it a third time and it fell over. Some bloke looked round at me, then looked away. The feeling of invincibility washed over me.

This girl came back and I offered to get her a drink. She declined – her friend would be along any second – but she did light a cigarette and offer me one. It was a Regal, a lollypop lady fag, but it tasted OK. I didn't smoke when I was with Emma any more, she'd helped me stop, so I made the most of it when she wasn't around.

'I'm going clubbing later,' she told me.

'What, seals?' I asked, but she didn't get it.

We smoked and I thought: Maybe I'm in here after all. And I wondered how I'd feel if anything did happen. I knew Emma would

19

chuck me on the spot if she found out and she would find out, she was bound to, I was crap at keeping secrets. I knew, too, how bad I'd feel. Hence why I'd decided when we met a year ago I wasn't going to mess her around. I hadn't, either.

Shame she couldn't exactly say the same.

It was just exciting, this. Being with someone new. Anything could happen with this girl. When you think you've blown it, then they offer to buy *you* a drink or give you *the look* or tell you the person they're waiting to meet is another girl, not their boyfriend. That's magic. That's worth all the hangovers in the world.

I'd come out alone, fed up, and here I was a few minutes later, feeling like this. Something always happens when you're drinking.

I decided I might, if she hung around, suggest we find a table to sit at.

She left.

I stayed.

Chapter Five

'What the hell have they done to this place?' Matt said, walking into the Sun, holding his arms out, palms up.

'I know. Shocking, isn't it.'

We shook hands and turned to our right, towards the spot where we always used to sit. It was a set of stairs that led up to a balcony bar. At least, I think that would have been where we used to sit.

'Got you a drink lined up,' I said. 'Thought you'd need it. They don't do Timothy Taylor's any more – it's Boddie's.'

We found a table and sat down. Bar staff were milling around in colour-coordinated uniforms and name badges.

'No sign of Den, I suppose?' he said.

We used to call the landlord Den because he was the spitting image of Den Watts. After we left Newcastle, he got a big pair of milk-bottle glasses and the students started calling him Frank Butcher, apparently.

Matt looked around again, puzzled. 'They can't have refurbished this place. There must be a law against this sort of thing.'

It was open-plan, with lots of bright lights, plastic furniture and mirrors. Mirrors! Where did the leather armchairs go? The table lamps? The fruit machine? They can't have done this to me. I shut my eyes, held them tight shut for a few seconds, but when I opened them it was the same. It had really happened. It was like going home and finding your mum's had a crew-cut.

'It's like Denise Van Outen having breast-reduction surgery,' Matt said.

I was glad he was here; I knew I wouldn't feel miserable all the time he was around. He pulled the same e-mail out of his pocket that I'd got from Stevie. Matt had scribbled stuff all over it; I recognised his handwriting from the messages he used to write on the inside of

21

my files in lectures. *What time are we going out tonight? Did you buy bread? How's your hangover?*

'The only bit that's the same is the bogs,' I said. 'It's a breath of fresh air going in there.'

'That's something,' he said, touching his Boddie's.

'Someone should have stopped this. The National Trust or someone. We could have started a campaign if we'd known. Got a petition up. Hands Off Our Pub. HOP.'

'HOOP,' he said.

'What?'

'It would be HOOP, not HOP. Hands Off Our Pub.'

It occurred to me it was little more than a week since I'd split up with Emma, a week until he got married to Katie – and here we were talking about this stuff. It was why I loved the bloke.

'You should have told me what the hotel was like,' Matt said, 'I'd have brought a groundsheet.'

Matt took his jacket off and carefully hung it over the back of the chair. It was a blue pinstripe; expensive-looking. I'd long since stopped asking him how much he earned; last time I'd enquired, two or three years ago, he was on twice what I was. He tugged off his tie and, open-necked, looked a little more like himself.

'Get a few of these inside you,' I said, nodding at my pint, my fourth, 'and you won't even notice. Besides, it was nothing to do with me. Blame Stevie. So how are you feeling then? Nervous? Excited?'

'Broke.'

'A week tomorrow and it'll all be over. The wedding – and life as you know it.'

'The whole thing's out of control, Rob. Sometimes I feel I'm no more than a guest myself.'

'Well you best make the most of *this* weekend – it'll be your last one away for a while. Katie's softening you up, if you ask me. You've had a few trips away recently, haven't you; she's lulling you into a false sense of security. But the second you've said "I do", the drawbridge will be pulled up and that's the last you'll see of the outside world.'

'She's fine about me having weekends away. If I want one, I have one.'

'Yes, course you do. Like the Amsterdam trip you couldn't make because of Katie's auntie's silver wedding. So when did Katie head off for her hen night?'

'This afternoon.'

'How many are going?'

'Eleven. Eleven girls.'

'Eleven girls,' I repeated.

'Yes, and before you get excited, most of them are married. That means they've got husbands. That means out of bounds next weekend.' Matt smiled, sipped his beer. Nothing had changed.

'You never know, one of them might be sufficiently disillusioned to want to sleep with me,' I said, not really knowing why. It wasn't as if I really wanted to sleep with anyone at the wedding – other, perhaps, than Emma. And she obviously wouldn't be going now.

'None are that disillusioned.'

'They can't all be blissfully happy. Just going on the statistics, at least four are heading for the divorce courts.'

'Yes, and?'

'Well, the cracks could already be appearing. They might need a shoulder to cry on. You know, a sympathetic ear.'

'Sympathetic ear. Sympathetic tongue more like! Most of the girls you meet need a shoulder to cry on *afterwards*!'

'Who are the bridesmaids?'

'Leave it. You've no chance with any of them. You made a pass at one of them at our engagement party, not that you'll remember that. She certainly remembers you though.'

I got a sudden sense of Emma. A sudden feeling of her, filling me, all over me. Like how it is when someone leaves the pub door open and you get that rush of cold air. 'Bet Katie's quite looking forward to it?'

'What?'

Matt's mind had wandered; he was looking around. It was a different crowd to the old days – younger, but fewer students. Today's students would be somewhere else, they'd have their own pub.

'The wedding, of course.'

'Yes, but my bank manager isn't.'

'Well, it was about time you got married, about time you did the decent thing and gave us a stag night.'

'Remember James's?'

'Not really,' I answered.

'Bet you remember the strippogram? That whipped cream cost me a fortune.'

'It didn't cost you a penny, she brought it with her.'

'Yes but she probably factored it into the price. It was a *hidden* cost.'

We laughed. We'd both done A-level economics.

'She had it hidden pretty soon,' I said. 'You made a pretty good job of licking it off though. James was supposed to do that.'

'Yes, well, I was best man,' Matt said.

'I'm surprised you weren't still covered in the stuff when you got home. Katie·could have made a trifle out of what she found stuck to you.'

Poor old James. He complained that the strippogram neglected him. And Stevie, well, Stevie got a bit of, as he put it, 'afters' out the back, by all accounts. 'Complimentary,' he reckoned.

It occurred to me I'd only seen Matt twice since then, and that was a couple of years ago – not long after he'd met Katie. 'We don't go out often enough these days,' I said.

A woman wearing leather boots walked by and – and I would have put money on this happening – caught Matt's eye.

'We ought to get the old double act going again,' I went on although I knew he wouldn't, not now he had Katie. And it was never much of a double act anyway. Matt always pulled and I tagged along and sometimes got off with the girl who was tagging along with whoever he got off with. 'My wing man', was what he always called me. 'No harm window-shopping – as long as that's all it is,' he said, smiling, watching the girl with the boots. He smoothed his hair behind his ears, and I remembered how he'd had his hair long at college for a while and then how he'd shaved it all off for a bit in the second year. Now it was normal length; respectable. But I suppose he didn't have any choice: management consultants didn't tend to have ponytails or skinheads.

'Doesn't look like *you'll* be helping us out with a stag night now, does it,' he said. 'We had such high hopes this time. The girls were all buying hats. I was looking forward to getting my own back on you and chucking up at your engagement party.'

'Yes, sorry about that.'

We laughed again, swigged our drinks.

'So what was the score with you and Emma then? What did you do to this one?'

His words jarred on me. *What did I do to this one?* It made her seem somehow dispensable. And she didn't feel dispensable. Besides, I wasn't sure I *did* anything.

I wanted to talk it through with him, hear what he had to say, but I didn't know where to begin and I didn't know *how* to begin. I thought of Emma, possibly sitting in a pub right now with a friend having an identical conversation to this, and felt suddenly tired. I wanted to be with her, things like they were, say, a year ago: that weekend we had in the Lakes, that open-top bus trip we took round London, the first night I took her to the Star.

I moved uncomfortably on the stool; it was like sitting in a McDonald's. The place had big windows now, so the people outside could all see in as they walked past, and for the first time I could see out – not that there was much of a view, just houses. Before, the windows had been small and covered with those tobacco-yellow net curtains but at least they stopped it getting too hot in the summer or too cold in the winter and it meant those table lamps were always kept on so it was never too light or too dark. It was always the same. You could never see out, but what did that matter? You never got any time to look out and, besides, why would anyone want to?

It struck me that this was the wrong way round: that usually I only ever talked to Matt about girls *when* I was seeing them; it was Claire I talked to about them *after* we'd split up.

'So?' he asked.

And all I could say was: 'One of those things, I guess.'

Chapter Six

I saw it as a trial run.

I knew Emma was going to dump me sooner or later. She'd started complaining more and more about how much time I spent in the pub. I'd lost count of the number of times she'd said as much recently.

Still, water off a duck's back to me.

Even so, I figured I ought to try a dinner party solo, just to get a bit of practice. A sort of dry run.

'I'll have a quiet night then,' Emma had said, pretending to look hurt.

I could have said: 'Forgive me, baby'.

Instead I told her it was just a small gathering, college people, no partners, which wasn't the case, but I couldn't exactly tell her the truth, could I. And one bloke I knew from college was going, so it wasn't exactly a lie.

'Enjoy yourself then,' she said, hamming up the hurt.

I still spent the whole evening thinking about her – wondering if she would have liked the punch, the music, whether she would have joined in the water fight. Wondering if she'd have liked these people. My friends. She hadn't met a lot of them, which wasn't an accident. I knew that when we split up, I'd need places to crawl back to that weren't loaded with reminders.

We'd been going out for nearly two years and did virtually everything together as it was. I tried telling her that having our own space was good for her; that she could do the French night school she'd never had time for, that cookery course, that she could go to the gym more, even start looking at flats. If she was busy, I figured, I could get to the Star more often.

And it wasn't as if we were joined at the hip or anything.

'I hear you're in market research – how is it?' the girl sitting next to me asked over starters.

'Fine,' I said, but couldn't for the life of me think what to say next. It would have sounded silly to continue: I'd resign tomorrow if I could and become a teacher, that's what I've really always wanted to do. I was itching to tell her, as well, how Emma was taking me to an old school friend's wedding the next weekend and how we'd be staying in this fantastic hotel. It was really expensive, this place, but Emma had got a discount because her firm had set up its website or done something with computers for it. But I couldn't be bothered; I didn't have the energy.

'Are you a golfer?' she asked, and it struck me how difficult this was, compared to talking to Emma. Me and Emma didn't have to feel our way into a conversation, we didn't have to put any thought into it; so much was already understood. We always knew where to start.

'No,' I said, 'although I'm thinking about taking it up.'

I'd been thinking about taking up golf, or getting a hobby of any description, for years. Trouble was, after going out – and work – there was never any time left.

'This food is delicious,' she said, looking past me.

This, I knew, was what it would be like after I split up with Emma: getting sat next to the one other single person at dinner parties, ringing 1471 if I'd been out the flat for two minutes to see if the latest girl I'd given my number to *had* rung, wondering about every girl I met whether *she* might be my next girlfriend.

It would be awful.

It would be brilliant.

I fought the urge to ring Emma up to check how she was, tell her I was having a great time and ask if we could spend tomorrow together.

I thought about her, Emma, as the booze flowed and later we all danced in the lounge and the girl who'd been next to me at the table flirted with me – although she was flirting with everyone – and I thought about Emma alone in that room in that flat she hated, probably hoping it was just a bit more space I needed, since we did see each other three or four nights a week, and I felt ashamed. Later, though, I forgot about it.

I crashed out on the floor in the spare room about four and sometime later I woke up and felt it: the headache, yes, the hangover, but more than that. Something lower down, in my body. It was fear. Fear of being alone.

Or maybe it was just all the margaritas.

I wondered *how* she'd finish it. Whether she'd send me an e-mail or do it over the phone or write me a nice long letter, as Rach had done. Some bloke at work had been dumped by text. Imagine that. *Don't want 2 c u any more. Sori.* Knowing Emma, she'd probably do it face-to-face: she never was one for burying her head in the sand.

Thing is, she didn't seem to *want* to finish it.

Once, when I asked her for some books back, she stared, just stared at me, and I said, 'Don't worry, baby, I'm not clearing the decks,' and she put her face so close to mine it made me dizzy. Her eyes were this amazing brown, almost as brown as the wood pan-elling in the Star, and they filled with tears as she hugged me, hugged me round the neck, and said: 'I don't want you to clear the decks, Ace.'

I smelt her.

I felt the fear in those arms.

I never wanted to hurt her.

Maybe *I* should finish it? Save her a job. I wondered what that would be like. Sitting her down opposite me, starting talking – her assuming it was just me setting off on some silly story – and then me saying it, spitting it out: that I felt more for her than I had for anyone else, ever, but we wanted different things, we were too dif-ferent, we'd only end up making each other miserable and I liked her, respected her, loved her too much for that.

But I didn't want to finish it. The only thing I wanted to be dif-ferent was for her not to give me so much grief about letting my hair down once in a while.

I loved being with her.

What I hated was the way that before we went out she'd some-times started saying: 'Take it easy this evening, yes?' or 'You're not going to go mad, are you?' or even once or twice, bizarrely, 'You're more fun when you're sober.'

Even worse though, was the way everyone around us was chang-ing and it felt like everything I knew – everything I was good at – was slipping into the past; like sand through my fingers.

If I chucked her, she'd feel stupid because she had been so hon-est about me. About me being *the one*. She'd introduced me to her family, her friends, all the people at work. Even said once on a girls' night out – and I heard this from a friend of hers who cornered me one night when she was hammered: 'Yes, he *is* special.' He, as in me. She had as good as said to them: I've found the man I'm going to marry. For all I knew she may even have said those exact words. And that made me a bit scared, a bit angry that she'd presumed so much.

Anyway, I couldn't end it, not just yet. Matt's wedding wasn't far away and she was looking forward to that, we both were. And Christmas wasn't far away either; we'd talked about going away for a few days then and afterwards it was New Year's Eve, so we were going to buy tickets for a big Millennium party. And not long after that it was her birthday – I had a brilliant surprise lined up for her. If we were still going out then, I planned to take her to Paris to see the Mona Lisa. It's something she'd wanted to do ever since she was a kid. 'Ever since I was a mini,' she'd once said.

I'd told Claire about it, how I felt. 'Talk to her, Rob,' she'd said. 'Talk it through with her, that's all you've got to do.'

Thing is, I didn't need to. I knew what she'd say. She'd tell me that I preferred sitting in the pub to spending time with her. Which wasn't true: some of the afternoons we'd spent in the pub *together* were among my favourite days ever.

Something moved in my stomach as I lay on the floor in that spare room. I knew I'd be sick in the morning.

I needed her, and I knew if we split up I'd need her more than ever.

I showed up at her place about lunchtime and she was still in bed. A couple of her friends had dropped in the night before and they'd gone out for a pizza, which had turned into a pub crawl, and then they'd gone on to a club. They didn't get to bed until about four. I wondered if she'd been chatted up. 'I wish you could have been there,' she said. 'You would have enjoyed it – and you'd have loved my friends.'

29

Chapter Seven

'Have you exchanged on this house yet then, Matt?' I asked, not exactly sure what exchanged meant, other than that it was a fairly final bit.

'It's a nightmare. Don't ever buy a house, mate. There's a problem three up the chain.'

'That's terrible,' I said, but all I could see was a chain. Literally.

'You can't imagine the hassle I've had with estate agents.'

I tried to imagine, but couldn't, so changed the subject. 'Remember our cards table?'

Matt pointed. 'Over there.'

It used to be a little round wooden table under the juke box. A wall had replaced it now, with a hatch connecting it to the kitchen. Food was getting passed through: plate after plate of it.

'What about that girl we met at that table over there,' I said, nodding at where a fruit machine now stood. 'Do you remember her, the cross-eyed one? What was her name?'

'Gemma. Gemma-with-a-G.'

'Gemma-with-a-G-spot,' we laughed together. Remembering.

'Me and Gem were in bed within three hours of meeting,' Matt said. 'Three hours! It was surreal. I came here for a pint and a break from a climate change essay, and three hours later, I was having sex.'

Matt smiled. I did too. We both sipped our Boddie's. We were both, I knew, thinking the same thing, the same line. Waiting to see who said it first. As it turned out, it was Matt. 'I kept asking her why she wouldn't look at me when we were having sex. But she was adamant she *was*. I was convinced she was staring at my desk.'

It was the desk we'd sat at revising. Us two, and sometimes one or two of the others perched on the bed or that big green beanbag of his. Those little two-by-three-inch cards that Matt swore by, plastered all over the walls. Yellow highlighter all over them.

I still felt as if I knew Gemma, we'd talked about her so much. She'd have died if she'd known.

'Wasn't quite the record, though, was it – pub to bed in three hours,' he said. 'Stevie still holds that.'

Stevie's record was an hour and ten. Anyone else and you wouldn't have believed it, but with Stevie it was probably true.

'Wonder what happened to Gemma-with-a-G-spot?' I said.

'Dunno. And Ros, remember Ros?'

Matt got off with Ros and I had a bit of a thing with her best mate. We went out a couple of times as a foursome. Then me and whatever-her-name-was split up and Matt and Ros split up and we all bumped into each other in here a couple of months later and she was flirting with me, Ros was, and I thought I'd end up sleeping with her that night but she went off with these other blokes who were doing Biology. I never mentioned the flirting to Matt. She was probably just doing it to get back at him.

'When was that?' I said. 'Was that the second or the third year?'

'It must have been the second year because I was supposed to be doing a Geomorph assignment the night I met her.'

Matt always seemed to have a girlfriend when we were at college. When I was sharing the flat in Merryfield Road with him in the second and third year, I'd see them sometimes in the morning, making toast or walking back to his bedroom through the lounge with two cups of tea. Within a few weeks it was always the same though: him deciding she wasn't quite right and calling it a day. Then me and him, sitting in here and having one of our 'statutory debriefs'. He'd joke about there being plenty more fish in the sea, about lancing the boil, about getting back on the horse, but occasionally – just occasionally – he'd be really upset. Once – I can't remember who it was over – I'm sure he'd been on the brink of tears. But he always said he'd know when he met the right woman, and that there was no point carrying on seeing someone if they weren't. 'Jump or dump,' as he sometimes put it.

We used to bump into his exes round college from time to time; it never particularly fazed him.

I wondered if Matt could remember them all now; I certainly couldn't.

I never could work out why the women went for him so much. It wasn't as if they thought he was drop-dead gorgeous the way they did Stevie, but he obviously had something. I only went out with a few girls all the time we were here; and Rach was the only sort of serious one, not that she lasted long. I suppose at least I had more girlfriends than James, not that that was difficult. 'Nul points,' was what we always used to say to him if he as much as expressed an opinion on women. But he'd never been into short-term relationships; Sarah was only the second person he'd been out with.

'It always amazed me you didn't get their names muddled up,' I said.

'That's easy. Have the same pet name for them all. Call the new one whatever you called the last one. Sweetheart or darling or whatever. The new one will love it, and the old one won't know.'

It was a good idea, you couldn't deny that.

Him and Stevie used to sit round devising excuses to get out of seeing girlfriends. Assignments to finish, Football Club practice, Hockey Club dinner, doctor's appointments, family emergencies, funerals. You name it, they did it. Matt had one woman believing he worked in the video shop every night, when it was only Mondays and Tuesdays.

He can't have spent that much time with any of them; he was always with us.

Talk about a changed man.

But I suppose he always had said he wanted to settle down one day, that he was playing the field when he was at uni because it was the right time *to* play the field, and that it never really hurt anyone – it never had any consequences, he maintained, not like how it would if he was doing it when he was, say, thirty.

'Come on, then,' I said, 'seeing as you're about to get married and I'm Mr Single again, you can share a few of your and Stevie's old secrets. What do you recommend I should use as an excuse if I want a night on my own?'

'It's not something you really need to know now, is it. But, hypothetically, just in case you ever do get back on the horse, then you're a busy man, you've got commitments. You've got work to do, you've got family – ill grandparents, nephews and nieces that need baby sitting. There's a million and one reasons *not* to see a girl.'

'My grandparents are all dead. And I haven't got any brothers or sisters, so how can I have nephews and nieces?'

'The women aren't to know that. Or, better still, have your grand-

32

parents die. That gives you four separate excuses. And a huge sympathy card to play. Bereavement, your sympathy joker!'

I thought about my grandparents, what little I had known of them. They had all died when I was in primary school. It would feel weird telling a girl I was going to one of their funerals. How was I supposed to sound? And what if she started crying?

'Grandparents with cancer, parents in plaster, cousins in car crashes, you could have a very big and very accident-prone family,' Matt said.

I thought about my dad, how – when he died – I hadn't been able to talk about it, literally unable to form the words. Still couldn't, nearly fifteen years later.

That's horrible, I thought. Telling people that sort of stuff. But Matt was kidding. And he was with Katie now, he adored her – anyone could see that – and messing her around just wasn't on the agenda. It was me who was still upsetting girls.

It was Emma who was in tears last weekend, not Katie.

Emma who banged her fist on the table and shouted: 'I feel so let down!'

It didn't matter that I never intended her to feel like that. She did.

Matt jokes about there being a million and one reasons *not* to see a girl, but after he met Katie he once told me that he couldn't see enough of her.

'They were good times, Matt,' I said.

His phone rang and he answered it all serious – 'Hello, Matt Collins' – and went outside. I watched him pacing to and fro in the doorway, moving his hand that wasn't holding the phone in a sort of chopping motion, obviously emphasising a point. I remembered that night in the third year he bundled in here waving round that assignment he'd got 95 per cent for, when all he'd done was copy it word-for-word from his brother who'd been at Newcastle four years before. Course, that was a different door he'd come through then; one that didn't exist now.

The call turned out to be about some trip he had to take to America. Some takeover he was working on, something involving a factory and a bank.

I said: 'I'm better on takeaways than takeovers.'

'How's *your* work going?' he asked.

'It's going. I'm still not planning to be there for ever, you know. I still really fancy becoming a teacher.'

'You've *always* said that, Rob.'

'I know I have, but I mean it this time. It can't be any worse than what I'm doing.'

I'd got as far as checking out a few websites recently; a lot of people, apparently, did go into teaching from other careers. There was a case study of this woman who did a PGCE in her late twenties; she reckoned working with children gave her a sense of purpose she'd never had before. A sense of fulfilment. Trouble is, I wasn't sure if I could cope with academic work again. And what if I ran out of money? And what if I did all that, and ultimately wasn't any good at it?

I felt that familiar sense of fear, filling me like water from within.

But Dad always said I'd be suited to it.

And I could still remember, although it must have been over twenty years before, exactly how Mrs Martin, one of my teachers, made me feel. It didn't matter what subject we were doing – whatever it was, she made me believe I could do it. For the whole of that year it was as if she was standing there, in front of the whole class, saying all those things, just for me. She made me feel as if anything was possible. I'd thought at the time: One day I'd like to do that.

Besides, things couldn't go on as they were. Only a few weeks before I'd got in trouble for turning up at a meeting a bit the worse for wear. It was my own fault; I should have just cancelled. The boss called me into his office the next day, all embarrassed, and told me he'd just had a rather difficult phone call from a client who didn't want to deal with me any more. He blew the steam off his cappuccino and said that I needed more focus, that I could still turn things around and that he didn't want – no, he *wouldn't* have – another conversation with me like this. It was a lucky escape as far as I was concerned. I dragged a load of the others down the pub again that evening to celebrate getting away with it and, though I didn't remember much about that night, I vaguely recalled toasting the boss in his absence. 'The fool,' I'd said.

'Maybe I'll be able to concentrate on work a bit more now things have come to a head with Emma,' I said.

If she'd have been here I knew exactly what she'd have said about the teaching: Go for it.

Maybe I should have got another girlfriend lined up before she dumped me? Maybe then all this would easier now? Someone else to say 'Go for it'. Someone else to fill the hole, like Radio 4. But I didn't want another girlfriend.

Funny, that's how you're supposed to feel when you've met the one, isn't it. That you don't want anyone else. It's what happened to Matt: he met Katie and that was it, all the sleeping around, bang, finito, he switched it off like he was switching off a light or shutting a door. He'd fallen for her – as he put it once only a few weeks after meeting her – fallen head over heels. And I thought people only said that in films. And now, he never looked back, never was anything other than glad: glad he'd met her, glad she'd moved in with him, glad they were getting married, glad they were going to spend the rest of their lives together.

Me, I felt less sure about everything than I had when I was at college.

I *always* felt girls were the one when I first met them; but they never were. Soon, that feeling of uncertainty was eating away at me again. That fog. Soon, they'd be saying the same sorts of things to me that Emma had.

'How is she, Katie?'

It occurred to me I'd only met the woman who was going to become my best friend's wife *once*. That had been at James's wedding. 'Pull yourself together, woman,' Matt had said, when she started crying. 'Anyone would think we were at a funeral.'

A week's time, and they'd be married. That would make her, as well as Matt, different. I didn't know what to say about her, how much I *could* say. The goalposts had moved. I could say what I liked about any of his exes, it was always open season on them. But Katie was different; she was here for keeps. 'Bet Katie's excited about the wedding?'

'She's like me: stressed. Like me and Stevie. I'm going to forget about it this weekend, though. I'm going to forget about it all.'

He had begun to sound a little pissed and I liked it; when pissed, he was always more keen to talk about the old days. He got up and went for beers; his shirt was hanging out at the back. He always used to wear his Morrissey T-shirt like that.

I remembered how we'd both stayed on in Merryfield Road for a few months after we graduated – I was working in a factory, just a summer job to pay off the debts, and Matt was working as a runner for some consultancy firm – then he moved to Manchester for a new job. I'd stayed on here for a few months longer, but it wasn't the same. Hardly anyone I knew was still around. I used to go running sometimes – Jesus, back then I used to actually go *running* – and it seemed very quiet without the students around. For the first time in my life I had some cash, and work was certainly more of a doss than revising for finals had been, but it all seemed like a big anticlimax after our graduation ceremony. One evening when I'd been running round the park, it suddenly struck me: What do I do now?

Matt would turn up on the doorstep every now and then. He'd tell me about his latest girlfriend, and we'd wander round here and have a few beers and a statutory debrief.

'I'm glad you chose to have your stag night here,' I said.

'I didn't, Stevie did. But I wouldn't have let him have it anywhere else. I knew we'd come here. I don't mean a few weeks ago or when I decided to get engaged or when we were all first discussing it, I mean I knew years ago, I always have done. Even when we were students. I just knew I'd come back here with you guys one weekend for my stag night.'

Then, looking around again, he said: 'I still can't believe they've renovated this place.'

Chapter Eight

I had it all worked out. My speech. I had it all planned. My lines honed, my timing perfected. I'd start working on it the day Matt told me he was engaged. You can't put too much time and effort into your best-man speech, can you.

I was going to say that when Matt asked me to be the best man, I'd written down all the embarrassing things I knew about him and, as I spoke, I was going to unroll this long scroll of paper. But bearing in mind that a wedding is a family occasion, a religious occasion, I'd have gone on, I decided to exclude any sex- or drink-related incidents so here is my amended list. At this point I'd pick up one of those tiny yellow Post-it stickers.

I was going to do loads more like that: stories and anecdotes about all the stuff we'd done together. About how we'd stay out of Number 65 for the evening if the other one wanted to entertain a girl there. How I'd spent a whole night at the hospital that time he ended up on a stomach pump after having all that tequila. How we'd spent the whole week at his mum and dad's after his twenty-first. Him, coming back to college in the second year determined to turn over a new leaf, going straight out and buying all those books. Then, nearer to exams, being skint and flogging the lot so we could have a night out on my birthday.

And then, joking aside for a second, I'd say – looking at the groom then the guests – Matt is the best mate you could hope to have. And it's fitting then that he's marrying Katie (as I said this I'd look at the bride) because you couldn't hope to meet a nicer person than Katie.

I would have said how Matt changed after he met her. How he became happier, more content. Got a spring in his step. And in the two years since then, I'd have said as we've also got to know her a bit better (and 'Oh yes?' one of the guests would probably have shouted suggestively) we'd seen exactly *why* Matt thinks the world of her.

I see them together, I was going to say, and it fills me with hope and you only have to look at them to realise they won't need an ounce of luck, but we'll wish it them anyway – we'll wish them all the luck and good fortune they deserve, all the luck and good fortune in the world.

Will you please join me, I'd say, raising my voice, in toasting: the bride and groom.

And everyone would stand up, on my cue, warm and happy, and raise their glasses and repeat: the bride and groom.

Half of it, of course, was bollocks. All that stuff about them filling me with hope. No couple could do that. But it's what you say at a wedding. I'd been to enough to know.

Then one Tuesday Matt said almost in passing: 'I've asked Stevie to be my best man.' Like he was telling me something about work or his mortgage.

'Right,' I said. 'Right.' And I felt like I'd just been told something important had been cancelled.

It wasn't the first time I'd felt like this. Every time anyone I even vaguely knew got married, I'd convince myself that they were going to ask me to be best man.

It was just that Stevie had already been a best man three times. *Three* times.

And, more to the point, girls always fancy the best man.

Enough people fancied Stevie as it was.

When it came to getting back on the horse, I needed all the help I could get.

38

Chapter Nine

We walked back to 'The Hotel Where We Spew'. We didn't talk much walking back; there didn't seem any need. We were quiet and easy with each other, comfortable to be here. I must have had at least eight pints during the course of the day.

Outside my room, Matt shook my hand, which seemed odd. Nice, but odd. 'See you tomorrow,' he said. 'It's going to be a big weekend.'

I lay on the bed listening to the people outside. There was lots of good-natured shouting, the sound of cars – taxis, I guess, stopping and starting – and the faint hum of music. A bottle rolling along the road. It never used to be like this round here – all these bars, restaurants and cafés. There was even a deli. Newcastle was different.

Back at Kew, I knew Emma would be . . . no, I didn't know what she'd be doing, I didn't have the faintest idea. She might be out somewhere or she might be at home. It seemed a little unreal, bizarre, that I didn't know. I wondered about ringing her, but didn't. I wanted to be with her but even now I knew, too, I'd be feeling, as I had for so long now: as if we couldn't go on the way we were, yet at the same time unable to do anything about it.

I went to the window, drew the curtains and looked out. A light rain had started falling and people were huddling in doorways, bundling in cabs, walking off, away, in all directions. Blokes in T-shirts; girls in miniskirts. At least that was still the same.

Next time I came here, that new bridge on the Tyne would probably be open, Gateshead's Millennium Eye. That new gallery in the Baltic Flour Mill would be, too. This place had changed and yet it hadn't. The instant I'd got off the train and seen the clock hanging from the roof in the station (I'd met Rach under that clock on our first proper date) I knew it was the same. I'd gone to the tube – the

Metro – and the little yellow tickets, the colour of the seats, even the voice that made the announcements, were deeply familiar.

It still felt like mine, this city.

I opened the window and the noise hit me. Music and people and cars. Friday night. Some of these people were finishing their night out, heading home with each other, heading home for sex. And I wondered about the couple in the room next door, where and who they were. Right now, they could be sleeping a few inches from me. Together. I shivered. Other people out there were heading on out for more of this. Finding another bar or another club just to keep it going, keep it alive, keep it still Friday, and not have to go home – at least for a couple more hours. Friday always was my favourite night. All the weekend still to come. By the time you get to Saturday, it's as good as over.

They'd be off to bars in the city centre now: down the Quayside and the Bigg Market and that huge floating nightclub moored by the bridge. The Tuxedo Royale. Or, as everyone called it, the Boat. The Boooaaat.

I remembered our last night out when we where all still living here, the night of the ten-pub, ten-pint pub crawl down to the bridge (we let Claire have a half in each, so it was five pints for her). We started in the Sun and walked down to the city centre, stopping in our ten pre-planned pubs on the way. It was a mad night. Messy. We drank like lunatics, drank like there was no tomorrow, and the footie had been on that afternoon and usually we kept out of the way of the fans – or certainly didn't let them hear our accents – but this time we did-n't, we went and talked to them, about Newcastle being on the brink of something really big, and they'd won that afternoon if I remem-ber rightly and it really felt that night like they were *my* team. We played pool, badly, and chased girls, unsuccessfully, and somehow even managed to get lost a couple of times between pubs – 'down-time' – and we'd laughed about what it would be like when we got older, if we got older, and 'One out, all out' we cried as we left each one of those pubs on the way to the city's heart. And we got there, we made it: reached the Bridge Hotel, as luck would have it, at ten to eleven, just a few seconds before the bell rang for last orders, and we spent the last of the kitty and shook each other's hands as we fin-ished that last round, our tenth, and called 'One out, all out' as we fell outside, laughing, and watched the ships on the Tyne sailing away.

The sound of voices next door. Giggling.

I knew I wouldn't sleep. I had a nip from the bottle in my bag.

Matt was right: it was going to be a big weekend.

SATURDAY

Chapter Ten

What had sold Stevie on this place, apparently, was the bloke who answered the phone. 'Just lads, is it?' he'd asked. 'We're not the Ritz, but we don't charge Ritz prices.'

I was glad we were staying here. Sure, we could have afforded somewhere better, but something about these rooms – the dirty cream-coloured walls, the small desk in the corner, the Gideon Bible on the little shelf beside the bed – reminded me of Halls.

'You ought to bring Katie here for your honeymoon,' I suggested to Matt. 'Good chance to save some money.'

'Bong,' Stevie shouted, putting his hand out. He'd had this idea that anyone who mentioned girlfriends or wives got fined a quid for the drinks kitty. 'It's a stag night, we're not supposed to spend the whole evening talking about our partners,' he said. I thought it was a stupid idea – I mean, I was hardly going to bang on about Emma. Although I suppose that worked in my favour: I was less likely to have to pay up. 'Doesn't matter if it's your own partner or anyone else's – either way it's a quid,' Stevie said.

I handed over a pound.

'Glad I don't have to sleep in this room tonight,' I said to Stevie, looking out of his window. There was a fan outside making a right racket.

'Yes, well, I probably won't be,' he said, 'I'm feeling lucky. I didn't pull last night, so the law of averages suggests that I will tonight.' He smirked.

Anyone else had said that, and we'd have cracked up – but for Stevie the law of averages *did* suggest that. 'I can't help it if I've got the magic touch,' was what he always said. He'd been at another stag do last night for some mate from home, and it had obviously been a late one. His eyes were bloodshot; unusually for Stevie, he

43

looked slightly pale. Probably wouldn't stop him though. He'd grown his hair since I'd last seen him so that it was shoulder-length again, as it had been at college. That's what the girls always noticed about him, I remembered. The hair. Those big, black curls. Gypsy blood, people often suggested. 'Yorkshire's finest,' he always told them.

Matt was on the bed, flicking with the remote between some black-and-white war film, a programme about sharks and *Grandstand*. 'I won't get to see any sport next weekend,' he said. 'I know a wedding's a special day but it seems a shame to miss Football Focus.'

James came in and the little room, suddenly full, reminded me again of C12, my room in Halls.

'Dukie!' Stevie said, springing up and shaking his hand. 'How you doing, Dukester?'

James started getting called the Duke after his parents bought him a house in the third year. For them, it was a chance to invest some money; it gave James somewhere to live rent-free and, of course, having bought it in 1990 after the crash they probably made a packet on it when they sold it. We did suggest living there with him in the third year, but his old man wouldn't have any of it – he said that was the last thing you needed: friends as tenants and, besides, he fully intended to screw whoever did move in on the rent. (Stevie, it turned out, screwed one of them regardless of the rent.)

The telly changed channel. War, sharks, sport. War, sharks, sport.

'Make the most of the remote,' James said. 'That'll be one of the first things you'll lose control of when you're married.'

'I only flick when I'm nervous,' Matt said.

'Don't be nervous,' James said, 'be afraid. Be very afraid.'

Poor old James had been stripped and carried round Dublin naked on his stag night. He was billing tonight as 'payback time'.

'Come on then, best man, what's the plan?' Matt asked. We all looked at Stevie.

'Thought we'd go grab a couple of sharpeners in the Sun then head into town. And after that, it's simple. All you've got to do,' he said, putting a hand on Matt's shoulder, 'is make a fool of yourself.'

'No doubt you'll keep me company in that respect, Rob,' Matt said.

They all sniggered. Very bloody funny.

'At least we're not abroad.' Matt said, looking nervous. 'You won't do anything *too* bad to me, will you? Katie's really worried.'

44

Don't worry, I thought, we'll look after you. 'You can only get so lost in Newcastle,' I said. 'Besides, you ought to count yourself lucky – you only narrowly escaped Amsterdam.'

'Amsterdam or Newcastle? No competition, is it.' Matt stood up. 'Come on, let's get going.' He tried to turn the telly off but the remote had packed up. He turned to Stevie, did that thing with one of his eyebrows: raising it, waiting. I'd forgotten that.

'What did you expect for thirty-five pounds a night? Come on everyone, sup up,' Stevie said. His accent hadn't changed.

'Sup up thy beer,' I said, doing a bad imitation Yorkshire.

'Right boys,' Matt said, raising his can. 'I'm all yours. Here's to a good weekend. You only have one stag night, after all.'

As we went through reception, Stevie said: 'That's him, that's the bloke I spoke to. He's priceless.'

It was the man who'd checked me in the day before. There was a radio playing behind the counter and he was humming along, singing a word or two. I noticed, in the daylight, how purple his face was. The others sorted the arrangements out with him; I dropped a pound in the fruit machine, hit the button three times, then joined them.

'Off out then, lads?' the old boy asked.

'Certainly am,' Stevie said. 'Why, fancy joining us?'

'I'd love to,' he said. 'But I'm stuck in here. Don't get off 'til eleven.'

I could smell the booze and felt sorry for him. He wouldn't be able to get away until eleven and it was ages until then. That was last orders.

'What are you celebrating?' he asked.

'This man's stag night,' I said, putting my arm around Matt. He'd put on weight.

'Let me give you a bit of advice, laddie,' he said. 'Don't ever use the word "No" and you'll be fine.' Then he laughed, a deep fitful laugh, and the laugh became a cough and then that stopped. One by one we handed him our keys and, one by one, he said the room number and hung the key on the wall.

'Not that I'm best placed to tell you about women,' he said. 'Mine left me years ago.'

No one knew what to say. Not even Stevie. There was a can on the floor next to him, which he had knocked over, and you could see the wet patch where all the drink had spilled. He started humming

45

again, loudly, and erratically, wheezing for breath. 'You won't remember this song, you lads, you're too young.'

He was right, we didn't, although it did sound familiar. He reeled off the names of a few pubs we should try. I wanted to tell him that I knew them all and that I had lived here once, that it had been my home. But he annoyed me a bit; this wasn't how I remembered the people here.

'Get yourself down the Bigg Market or the Quayside, that's where the youngsters go.'

Youngsters. Youngsters! The four of us had a collective age of over 120.

'Enjoy yourselves, lads,' he said, standing up and doing a little flourish with his feet. It was a right spectacle. Three o'clock and he was off his face. It wasn't even dark or anything.

'Go on, son,' Stevie said, 'go for it.'

Another guest came down the stairs and went past, out, laughing.

'Enjoy yourself, lads,' he said again as we left.

'Onwards, upwards,' Stevie called, leading the way.

Chapter Eleven

We walked through town.

'Toon Army, Toon Army,' the fans yelled.

Newcastle were at home and everyone was wearing black and white; the whole city, it seemed, had gone black and white. We had wondered about trying to get tickets but, unlike when we lived here, Newcastle was a massive club now. Shearer had come back and, more recently, Bobby Robson had too. They were real heroes in this part of the world. Two of the city's favourite sons.

'I bleed black and white,' Bobby Robson once said in an interview when he was asked how much Newcastle meant to him.

And I thought now – as I had at the time – how wonderful that must be, to feel that strongly about a team, about somewhere. To feel somewhere is *so* much home. Guildford just wasn't in the same league.

'Toon Army, Toon Army,' the fans yelled as we walked up Grey Street.

The wind was cold but the beer was doing its job. Already, after just one, the sharp edges had gone. Things seemed smoother, softer. That could happen sometimes now. So much for your tolerance building up if you drink more. And yet, other times, I could have loads and still feel stone-cold sober. We'd had a pint in the Sun, then got the Metro into town. James was still shocked by what they'd done to the place, even though we'd warned him. 'But but they can't have,' he'd protested. Stevie seemed more bothered about getting the drinks in. 'I'll get the first round,' was all he said.

People laden with bags walked purposefully past. Heading home, I supposed. We paused at the Monument and the statue of Charles, Earl Grey. For the first time, I read the inscription. A great Reformist, apparently. PM, too, according to Stevie. Trust him to know that. Something to do with the tea, as well, although none of us knew what. It was here, I remembered, that Matt had broken his arm trying to skate on the ice. 'Playing squash,' was what he told Physical Phil.

I did my coat up, put my hands in my pocket – I was cold, but knew I wouldn't be soon. I knew, too, that all these people would shortly be gone and others would have replaced them: young people who wanted booze and music and each other. People like me.

I always felt like this on Fridays and Saturdays: this energy. And right now, having the whole evening ahead of me. The girls. You should have seen the girls. That random anonymous lust was something I had always felt guilty about when I was with Emma, but now I let myself stare. I caught a girl's eye and stayed staring at her and she, I swear, looked back at me for a instant or two longer than she needed to. See you tonight, I thought.

Then it occurred to me. Yes, that's what it is, that's why things didn't work out with Emma. It wasn't only that she could be a bit of a killjoy at times, it was that I haven't slept with enough women yet. It was obvious. I needed to go out with a few more people, then I'd settle down. Simple. Emma might have met someone by then, too. She'd be happy. We'd both be happy.

'What's that pub up there on the left?' Matt said. It was a Yates's Wine Lodge. A new place. Huge. We went inside and Van Morrison's 'Brown-Eyed Girl' started playing. It was as if someone pressed play as we went through the door. We all sang the first line together.

Just stay like this, please, just stay like this today and tomorrow and the day after, and I can get over Emma, I thought. I can survive this.

The place was beginning to fill up. My friends were leaning into each other, looking at each other, singing.

Soon, I'd be drunk. I shivered with pleasure.

Stuff like Emma happened. We were only together for two years; I had known these people for over ten. That meant more. Every day it was getting better. Soon I would have known them for fifteen, twenty, twenty-five years. I'd still be in touch with all three of them. We'd look back to tonight. This. Standing here, singing the chorus.

I felt glad – almost glad – I was me.

And besides, what was wrong with spending all my money on going out? What was wrong with getting pissed? I was only twenty-nine. Stevie handed out more drinks, Vodka Red Bulls – bit early for that, still, never mind. Yes, what was wrong with doing this? I didn't want to run marathons and get excited by wardrobes in Ikea. I wanted to be like I was, and tonight I was going to get drunk and it was good having that certainty. If it all went hideously wrong later so be it. All the time I knew what I was doing, I'd be feeling good and after that, well, after that I wouldn't know what was happening or what I was feeling so it wouldn't matter. Besides, these guys wouldn't hold it against me. They were my friends. They'd seen it all before.

We all sang together again.

I smiled. Sometimes, something just clicked. Sometimes, things were all right. I went for a piss; I couldn't get it over with quick enough – the prospect of being back with my friends was compelling, almost intoxicating. I came out the bogs and 'Sit Down' was playing, a real third-year song. It was going to be a good night. I saw the lads over the other side of the bar and the prospect of being back among them thrilled me. I bundled past people – arms and legs and torsos – who were similar to but not the same as my friends. I went to them, excited, familiar, curious, nervous. Cut through the busy pub. The slant of Matt's shoulders, just him; the blackness of Stevie's hair; how James was a couple of inches taller than every-one around him: seeing them, my friends, the people that knew me, standing together in a pub made me want to cry. I felt such a part of this.

I stood by them, listened.

'And we didn't see you at all for the first few days of college,' Stevie said to me. 'We thought your room was empty.'

'I was out partying all the time.'

'No you weren't,' he said. 'You were locked in your room on your own, that's what you told us.'

I was, too. I couldn't face anyone in those first couple of days. I felt so intimidated by it all. I sat in my room and knew that was the time to make friends and it got worse and it got harder and I so nearly went home, so nearly chucked it all in. It was only home-sickness, I later realised, but at the time it was suffocating.

'I was only doing it to avoid having to meet you lot.'

I looked around. I wanted to reach out and take hold of it, what-ever it was. Pull it close. I looked around again, more slowly, taking everything in. Groups of friends. Girls. The barman laughing. The sunlight streaming through the big glass window at the front. It made all the wood look a nice shade of yellow. The place looked clean. Even the white froth around the top of the nearly empty glass was nice. Watching my friends, almost like they were in slow motion: animated, laughing, real, close.

Don't ever forget how lucky you are with them, I told myself.

Chapter Twelve

I had to get out. It was the Thursday of Freshers' Week and I couldn't stay in that room one more minute. I'd decided to walk in to town to buy some books. As I came out into the corridor the bloke opposite was doing the same. I heard him behind me as I locked the door and froze.

'You walking to college?' he asked. A northerner. He had curly black hair and this beat-up black leather jacket on.

'Yes.'

'Mind if I walk with you?' It sounded formal and didn't go with the way he looked. I was expecting cool, aloof.

'Didn't think I'd make it this morning,' he said as we walked. 'Bit of a late one last night.'

It was the voice I'd heard late the night before and on the previous three nights. A load of them had been hitting a ball around the corridor and every time it hit the wall it made a dull thud. They were shouting and cheering and I had cursed them. Later, it had gone quiet – just talking and occasionally a can being opened.

'What did you do last night?' he asked.

'Nothing. Early night.'

'I'm Stevie.' He put the apple he was eating in his mouth and held out his hand.

It took me by surprise. I wasn't used to shaking people's hands. 'Rob,' I answered.

We walked down the big stone staircase and across the foyer. There was a queue for the phones. 'Halls of residence? Prisoner-of-war camp, more like,' this bloke – Stevie – laughed.

It was a bright clear day. I'd been to the canteen the evening before but, other than that, apart from some aimless, solitary wanderings on Tuesday night, the only times I'd been out of my room

51

since I'd arrived on Sunday were to sneak out, once a night in the middle of the night, for a shit. I'd been pissing in the basin. A girl wearing a baseball cap cycled past, wobbling uncertainly as she picked up speed. 'Morning Stevie,' she called. 'How you feeling?'

'Fine,' he said. 'Don't forget tonight, Claire – seven o'clock.' His accent struck me again. He winked at me and then he laughed, and it was the laugh I had heard outside my room except then it was slightly muffled, and now it was closer, louder. 'See her over there,' he said, nodding towards another girl struggling with an armful of books. 'You know what we call her? She's Madonna.'

We walked towards the campus. I felt a breeze on my face. It turned out we were on the same course: Geography.

'Where you from?' I asked.

'Sheffield. You?'

'Guildford. Well, just outside Guildford. You been going out much?' I asked.

'We've been going to the Onion mostly, it's cheaper.'

'The Onion?'

'The *Union*,' he said. 'Where have you been?'

There was no malice there. He just wondered: where *had* I been. I told him I was skint, that I hadn't been going out much.

'Don't worry about that,' he said. 'You're not here to save money. Why don't you come out with us tonight? We'll give you a knock just before seven.'

And then he burped and, I swear to God, it was the loudest burp I'd ever heard. 'There's a girl doing English who can say "Noel Edmonds" as a burp. I'll get her to do it for you tonight if we see her.'

'Have you done any work yet?' I asked.

'What, college work? No chance. Haven't done anything but this,' he said, miming a drinking action with his hand. 'Not going to for at least the first two years either.'

That night we walked down to the Union at seven, Stevie and me, and he introduced me to all the people he was hanging around with. That girl who we'd seen on the bike was there, Claire. When he introduced me to Matt and James, it was like they were already old friends. They shook my hand. No one asked where I had been; they must have just assumed I'd been going out to a different set of bars with a different set of people. Newcastle was a big campus, after all.

We were intending to have a couple in the Union – the Onion –

and then go on, but the atmosphere was fantastic so we stayed there all night. I felt then, for the first time, that, yes, this is what college is *supposed* to be like. Stevie put his arm round me at one point, clinked his glass against mine and said: 'Cheers then, Robbo, it's good to meet you. Here's to the next three years.'

I laughed at his accent and he laughed at mine. I tried to explain what Surrey was like, but gave up. Someone told us about this boat down by the Tyne Bridge that was a huge nightclub and we arranged to go there the next night, the five of us: Stevie, Matt, James, Claire and me.

Late that night we went back to Stevie's room and had coffee and threw a football around. I thought, as I threw it, I'm throwing this ball around the corridor with these people. Me. I imagined myself in my room, lying there, listening – but I wasn't lying in there listening any more, I was out here doing it. College started for me that night.

Chapter Thirteen

'Sorry to hear about you and Emma,' James said. 'You don't mind me mentioning it, do you?'

'No, course I don't mind. I should have told you. I wasn't *not* telling you.'

The other two were in the corner, engrossed in the 'Who Wants To Be A Millionaire' game. The pub was pretty empty, just a few shoppers and a group of lads at another table.

'There just hasn't seemed the right moment. It's not the sort of thing you yell across a crowded pub, is it?'

'I suppose not,' James said.

I was tired of telling people. It felt like I'd done nothing but tell people all week. I wouldn't have mentioned it at all if I could have got away with it, but what else could you say when people asked after her? 'We split up last week,' I told James.

'What happened? Matt reckons you got dumped, but I guess there's more to it than that.'

'Mutual consent, James. Mutual consent.'

'So you *did* get dumped.'

'Let's just say there was a conflict of interests.'

When he didn't reply, I added: 'Emma hoped I might change. I guess I was probably hoping the same.'

'What, that you'd change?'

'No, that she would. I should have known what was coming, though, James. It's not as if it's the first time this has happened, is it?'

'Any chance you'll get back together?'

'I suppose we could. It's not as if either of us went off with someone else, but it's never the same, is it. Knowing that you've split up once sort of eats away at you.'

Emma once said that the mistake people make is that they decide to call it a day and then don't stick with it. 'If you split up, you've got to be strong,' she'd insisted, then added: 'But we don't need to think about that, do we.'

I remembered what else she'd once said, too. She'd said, laughing: 'I'm never going to let you dump me.'

I wanted to ring her again.

Emma.

'Still, her loss,' James said.

'Thanks, Dukie. You know what I want. All I want is to meet someone and know it's right straight away.'

James looked at me as if to say: Are you all right? All right as in Holding It Together and all right as in Not Too Pissed? 'Yes, and I just want to win the lottery and spend the night with Mariella Frostrup.'

He didn't though. He liked what he had too much. I'd never known anyone as content as James. And not just about Sarah. He was one of the cleverest blokes I knew, one of those people who could do anything, but he'd worked as a fundraiser for one charity ever since we left college. I hated his contentedness; I loved it.

'I go out with a girl and there's always something wrong,' I said. 'Something wrong with me or something wrong with her or we're living too far apart or too close together or don't get on with each other's friends or there's one of our exes still on the scene. I want to be certain from day one. To just *know*.'

Why couldn't Emma have drunk more, I suddenly thought. That would have solved everything.

'All you've got to do, then, is decide you *are* certain. That's what's important. In some ways, it's irrelevant who it is.'

This complicated things. I'd always half believed I'd eventually meet the right person and it would be great from day one. Now, James seemed to be saying that meeting someone would be just the start of the hard work. Years before, he'd once said that a willingness to compromise was a sign of maturity. I hadn't known at the time whether to agree or not – still didn't. Something in me railed at his remarks, though. Then, and now. I'd lost Emma. Something better had to come out of this. It just had to.

'You'll be telling me next that the reason so many people get divorced nowadays is because it's so easy. And don't tell me, Granddad, people don't put enough effort into marriage either.'

'They don't. A marriage *is* hard work. Worth every bit of it though.'

'Not everyone's *capable* of spending the rest of their life with the same person. This is a lifetime together we're talking about. Think how much you've changed in the last ten years. Think how much Sarah's changed. You could be married for thirty or forty years. What are the chances you go on changing together?'

'That's the point though. You have to work at it so that you *do* change together. It makes you stronger, individually and as a couple. That's what makes it so worthwhile. That's what makes it so, well, so beautiful.'

'I'll tell you what is beautiful – that woman over there,' I said, pointing at a girl at the bar. She had a white top on and her skin was a lovely honey colour; she had freckles like confetti or snowflakes, but the colour of sand. '*She's* my perfect woman,' I said. 'She's stunning.'

James lit a cigarette. 'Want one?'

'Better not. I tell you, it's weird, but not smoking has been one of the worst parts of splitting up. Everyone else feels guilty about smoking, I feel guilty about *not* smoking because it was Emma who helped me stop. Quitting was always something she gave me, a part of our relationship. Now we're no longer an item, I feel as if I'm using her help when I shouldn't be. I've been getting really bad cravings and every time I resist, I know it's Emma I've got to thank. Look, sorry I'm banging on about all this. What I'm trying to say is: Thanks but no thanks.'

I had the same feeling about smoking that I did about drinking when we'd been watching *Grandstand* earlier. I'd said no to a drink then, once, but I knew I wouldn't be able to say no again. Sooner or later someone would offer me a cigarette and I'd take it.

'Sarah would kill me if she knew I was smoking.'

'Emma once cried when I lit up in front of her. Said she couldn't bear seeing me kill myself.'

James looked at me, surprised. 'I know people always say it, but things usually do come right.'

Usually. Usually wasn't good enough.

'Thanks.'

'You'll meet someone,' he said.

'Sometimes I think I'm destined to be single. Always the best man, never the groom.'

56

'Maybe you and Emma calling it a day was for the best in the long run.'

Up to now, everyone had wanted to know why we went our separate ways or how it had happened or how I was coping. 'Maybe it was for the best' didn't require an answer. It suggested some good could come out of all this, too. So James, to say that.

'Maybe,' James went on, 'it's just because you haven't found your life partner yet.'

Yet. I savoured the word.

I watched the girl with freckles swigging her drink. Now, as a few seconds earlier, I got that pinch of restlessness, almost hunger, from seeing her. Something familiar in her, too. Who was it she reminded me of? We made brief eye contact.

Maybe it was true: maybe I had just been unlucky so far.

'It's horrible though, isn't it?' he said. 'When I split up with Anna I got these massive mood swings. One minute I'd be ecstatic and feel like it was the best thing that ever happened to me, like a weight had been lifted off my shoulders, and the next I'd be bawling my eyes out.'

'I remember that time,' I said. It was in the first year, but I hadn't realised he'd been so upset. I should have known. Why didn't we talk more?

'I just feel like I've messed up, James – that maybe I've missed my chance. I don't think I'll ever meet anyone like Emma again. I don't know what to do, mate.'

The desire to call her snatched at me again. I still knew her number. It was still in my phone, too. Would her voice – the way she answered the phone – have changed since we split up? Because we split up? I always used to laugh at the way she answered her mobile. 'Hel-lo,' she'd say, as if she didn't expect anyone to be on the other end, like how you call into a house when you arrive and find the door open.

But I knew she was better off shot of me. That was the fact of the matter. I might have been a good mate, but I was a crap boyfriend.

We fell silent. This, I thought, is why we don't talk more.

I noticed how noisy the rest of the pub was. The hen party we'd seen in an arcade earlier was on its way out. The bride-to-be staggered past, off her face. All her friends were following with a load of blokes in tow. Has she found her life partner, I wondered.

'Emma was nice,' James said. 'I didn't get a chance to have a proper chat with her at our wedding, but she seemed really nice.'

Why are you telling me this now, I thought. I don't want to hear it.

'Sarah took to her as well.'

'You say that about everyone, James.'

'She did though.'

'Well thanks for telling me at the time, Dukie!'

'I did, I'm sure I did. We went outside for a quick smoke, remember, and I'm sure I told you then. My last cigarette ever, incidentally. Well, until tonight.'

'Don't worry, stag nights don't count,' I said.

Anna was married now. Maybe me and Emma would both be one day? But James and Anna had been a lot younger than us when they split up.

'You can't make something right if it's not,' he said. 'If it wasn't going to work out then it's better than this happens now than in a year's time.'

That was what Emma had said.

That, and: 'I'm tired of coming second to the pub.'

Chapter Fourteen

I wasn't happy.

Too much downtime already.

First, James had wanted to go shopping – shopping – then Matt insisted on having a walk around the University. Not the bar, either, but the campus. We even ended up in one of the libraries at one point.

It was gone six and we'd only had four pints and that one Vodka Red Bull. I was getting stuck into the fifth. We were in an All Bar One. 'All Bra None', as Stevie called them.

'Does she look like Demi Moore or what?' I said to Matt, nodding in the direction of a girl at a nearby table.

'Don't even think about it,' he said.

'Why not?'

'Because she's out of your league.'

'No, not necessarily.'

'Yes, necessarily. She's Newcastle United and you're Sunderland or Middlesbrough.'

I watched her when she went to the ladies', and when she came back I tried to catch her eye.

'She's probably going out with someone. Someone nice,' Matt said.

'I can do nice.'

'Yes, given plenty of notice. She's probably going out with someone who knows about interior decorating, someone who', and he reached out and rubbed my shirt, 'knows how to use an iron.'

'So I'll iron. I'll compromise. Successful relationships are built on compromise.'

'Just *look* at her, Rob. She's not you.'

She was sitting with two other girls. They both had wedding rings on – either engagement or wedding rings, I never knew the difference – but Demi didn't have either. The three of them were taking it in turns talking. Demi was smoking a cigarette from a box of Marlboro Lights on the table and, every time she took a drag, she tilted her head back and blew the smoke up, away from her friends. Again, I got that sudden urge to light up. She pulled her bag up onto the table, rummaged around, brought out a phone and put it to her ear. She smiled and her mouth started moving. Then she motioned to her friends that she was nipping outside. A few minutes later I watched her come back in. She had to walk past where we were standing. It could be my only chance.

'That wasn't for me was it, that call?' I said.

James laughed. Or maybe he was wincing.

'I'm sorry?' she said.

I didn't know whether she couldn't hear – or could hear but didn't know what the hell I was going on about.

'Your phone just rang. I couldn't help noticing. Only I thought it might be for me, that call.'

'Why would you think that?' she said. She didn't sound local; she could have been from anywhere.

'I can't really talk about it, it's a bit hush-hush, military stuff, you know, but I can't carry a phone so I've been using your number.'

It was a line I'd seen Stevie use once. Come on, he'd say to us, pick a girl and give me a line – any line – and I'll use it as my opener. James came up with the one about military intelligence and, whatever Stevie's story was, it was obviously good because it worked. It occurred to me I probably just sounded ridiculous. Military stuff!

'Excuse me,' she said and walked off. I took a big swig of the lager; whoever bought the round had got Stella.

'Maybe I should have booked that double room tonight, after all,' I said to Matt. I looked at her again – she was the spitting image of Demi Moore – and she was lighting another cigarette and Matt smiled, and it didn't matter that I'd just been blanked, I'd never see her again after tonight. I'd try again in a few minutes and if I got blown out once more it would be something we'd joke about, me and Matt. I could have another shot with the line about the phone and maybe she'd think me amusing. It happened. If we ended up in bed, we'd laugh about it in the morning. The worst chat-up line ever, she'd say. More drinks came, more Stella, and I noticed Demi had gone to the bar, which was more crowded now; I saw how silky her hair was as I approached. The music had come back on, louder than before. I nestled in behind her, beside her, then said: 'You'll die of thirst before you get served round here.'

She looked at me, then straight ahead again. She tried to catch the barman's eye. He had a crew-cut and wore a T-shirt. Both suited him. I watched her watch him.

'I see you've given up with the phone. Not ideal in here now, is it.'

'Sorry?'

'A phone call – you were on the phone earlier. I was just saying how impossible it is to hear anything. I don't know how these people work here.'

I pointed behind the bar and she looked in that direction and at the T-shirted barman. His arms completely filled the arm holes.

'Ask for three glasses of dry white wine and you'll end up with two Cokes, a Harvey Wallbanger and a chicken Kiev.'

She smiled and half-turned to me, then turned away again, obviously not wanting to miss getting served. She ordered three small glasses of dry white wine.

'How are your eardrums?' I asked.

'They're fine.'

She collected her change. 'Excuse me,' she said, squeezing past. I went back to my friends.

'What's her name?' Matt asked. 'It's not Lizzie, is it?'

We laughed. We had both gone out with a Lizzie – the same Lizzie, Lizzie Sheppard (Busy Lizzie, we called her) – in the first year and the gap between us could be anything between a month and minus three days depending on when you counted going out as having started and ended. Matt saw her for a couple of months and then I did the same. It felt a bit odd at the time, but the fact that it was a bit awkward then made it even funnier now.

'Didn't get as far as discovering names. We were just establishing sleeping arrangements. I'll find her name out later – tomorrow morning probably.'

I thought about Emma and realised it was the first time for a while – an hour at least. I made eye contact with Demi but couldn't tell if it was deliberate on her part. The boys were midway down their drinks and talking about moving on. There was a spare chair on Demi's table and all three of them were halfway down their glasses. I went and sat with them.

'Hello again,' I said. They stopped talking and looked at me. Each probably wondered if one of the others knew me. I leant in to Demi; the other two – relieved it wasn't them – watched her for her reaction. 'I'm bored,' I said. 'I was hoping you could amuse me.'

'Sorry, but have we met?' she said, flashing a glance at the other two. It was that 'No, I don't know this guy either' look. But it didn't faze me.

'You were saying something at the bra – I mean the bar – about not being able to hear anything in here. Well, I couldn't hear a word of what you were saying and was hoping you might repeat it now we're in a quieter spot.'

She answered and I pretended not to hear. 'What was that?' I said, tugging my ear. 'You want two Cokes, a Harvey Wallbanger and a chicken Kiev?'

I caught a whiff of her; she smelt great. One of the other girls lit a cigarette; the third one screwed up her serviette, put it on the table and began rearranging the plates. This one had blonde hair, a deep tan and lots of jewellery. Expensive-looking jewellery. If they went, so would Demi. Had to keep all three of them. 'What was the food like?' I asked the one with jewellery.

'Fine. Absolutely fine.' She looked over my shoulder, away. Then she turned to Demi. 'So what's she doing about work?' And they started talking again, all three of them in turns; Demi puffed on her cigarette occasionally and tilted her head back to blow out the smoke.

This wasn't supposed to have happened. I could have got ignored in the All Bar One at Wimbledon or Clapham or Fulham. I could have been blown out in any of those places. This was identical to all of them: the furniture, the decoration, even the people: the girls in a slim-enough-to-look-good-in-a-skirt sort of way; the blokes in a broad-chested, confident sort of way. Sometimes I wondered why I came to places like this. The girls were so out of reach. Well, not tonight, I thought. Not tonight. I sat there.

'Look, can we help you?' Demi asked.

I wondered whether to ask for a blow job, just as a joke. Now that would have been funny.

'Sorry,' I said, 'you must think it really rude of me just coming up like this. Unannounced. I'm not some weirdo.' I left a suitably long pause, then added, 'Honestly.'

She didn't laugh, nor did the other two.

Why did I always have to start the conversation? Once, just once, couldn't it be me who gets talked *to*? If it'd been Stevie, she'd have been a bit more interested. They started talking among themselves again, so I looked at Demi more intently.

'So, can we help you?' she said curtly.

It was as much about saving face now as anything. The lads were probably watching.

'It's just that I recognise you from London. You get on a train at Wimbledon in the mornings, don't you?'

Bad line. Even if she did fancy me – which she quite obviously didn't – I would have blown it with that. I'd heard Stevie use a similar one once, but now I come to think of it he *did* see the woman concerned on the station every morning.

'No,' she said.

'Yes you do. I never forget a face. You get on a train at platform six. You get a cup of tea and a croissant from the little shop. Every morning, eight fifteen. Except Friday when you get the eight thirty-six. Obviously Thursdays are a late night.'

'I work in Newcastle City Centre,' she said, looking towards the other two. Jewellery snickered.

'You must have a long commute then.'

'Listen, you're thinking of someone else. Now it would be really, really good if you just went back to your chums and left us to ourselves.'

Chums, who says chums!

'No, seriously, you must have a double. And while you're at it, get me one. A vodka and Coke please.' It occurred to me I was becoming Benny Hill. A bad Benny Hill. 'Either that, then, or a twin,' I added. 'That's it, you've got a twin. Not a Siamese one, I hope. Burmese perhaps. Your Burmese twin isn't as slim as you of course. Or as pretty.'

Demi turned to her two friends. 'Shall we go?'

Jewellery scooped up her keys and put them in her bag; the other one began to stand up. The phone on the table rang. Demi put it to her ear and we all sat there, watching, waiting. 'That'll probably be for me,' I said.

'*Charlie*,' she said loudly. She swivelled round on her chair, turning away from everyone, put her spare hand over the other ear and leant down slightly. Her shirt stretched across her back and I noticed her bra straps. Sometimes, when I used to sit with my arm round

Emma, I'd stroke the bit of her shoulder where the bra strap was. I liked the familiarity of it, the calm intimacy. It always made me feel really horny, too. I had a big swig of Stella, finished it.

'I'll have a pint of lager if your asking then, girls.' They both looked at me briefly: it was mainly distaste although there could have been a bit of pity in there, too. 'We're on a stag night,' I said. 'What are you celebrating? You certainly look as if you're having a wild time.'

'We're not celebrating anything, actually,' Jewellery said. 'We came out for a quiet drink. At least, we came out with the intention of having a quiet drink.'

I turned round and James was throwing peanuts up in the air and trying to catch them in his mouth. They kept falling on the floor. He never could do that.

Demi finished on the phone. 'That was Charlie. The boys are going to be in the restaurant at nine. I said we'd meet them there.'

I thought how wonderful it would be having sex with her. That moment of connection, of expectation, just before we actually did it.

'How is he?' Jewellery asked.

'He's got to keep the plaster on for another month.'

'Poor Charlie. He'll be wanting you to wait on him hand and foot.'

I imagined Charlie – he'd have a floppy fringe and drink a lot and be a bit bawdy at times. Probably worked in finance. Wore polonecks. Had big thighs. Quite sensitive, no doubt, underneath it all.

'Yes, poor old Charlie,' I said. It occurred to me that I must be a ludicrous sight, perched on their table, interrupting their conversation. But I didn't care and maybe, if I kept going, they'd eventually think I was funny? Maybe they'd see what I was really like. I went to have some more beer, but it was all gone. I wanted Demi to look at me, laugh at my jokes, sit facing me and, as the evening unwound, move in towards me. I'd take her over and introduce her to my friends. She'd think it sweet: us, old mates on a stag night.

The barman, the one with the arms that filled the holes in the T-shirt, came round collecting ashtrays. Demi looked at him. I bet Charlie doesn't know you look at barmen like that, I thought. 'I saw that,' I said.

'Saw what?' She stood up.

'It's been a pleasure meeting you.'

'You too.'

I noticed they hadn't even finished their wine.

I went back to my friends. 'See you at Wimbledon,' I called as they went past, towards the door.

No answer.

Chapter Fifteen

'Want to come inside?' she asked. 'Pretty girls inside.'

We stared at each other, long and hard. Why don't I get eye contact like this anywhere else? She smiled at me. There were pink walls behind her and a big mirror with a picture of a woman's legs on it. Beside her, I could see a door.

I made it past her, into the market. It was busy and no one would have noticed if I'd stopped back there. No one would have noticed if I'd have said simply in return: 'How much?' People were buying vegetables at market stalls.

Here vegetables; back there, sex.

This is how I'd spent the day: walking around Soho, drinking and flirting with the girls on the doors of the strip joints. I'd come up here to meet a mate, but he'd cried off – something about a hangover – so I'd hung around and had somehow ended up staying. It was a Saturday, so it wasn't as if I had anything else to do.

I started walking my circuit. It took about ten minutes to complete and, as soon as I started round the second time, the girls began recognising me. They didn't look away however long I stared.

'Live strip show, sir?' they said. 'Fancy coming inside darling?' They knew.

I walked up through Chinatown and smelt the sweet cooked food and saw ducks and chickens hanging in the windows, glazed and golden. If I'd had someone to eat with, I'd have eaten. I kept walking and I didn't feel hungry – it was the smell I liked. I got to the end of Chinatown and made it past one pub, then a second, and killed five minutes in the arcade even though my favourite games were broken but those girls, those girls ...

I wanted something and, whatever it was, I certainly hadn't got it from going out on Friday or Saturday nights or from friends or at dinner parties or at work. I had tried all that, had done for years. I was tired of it. But I was here now and sex – or whatever it was that happened in these places – would have been better than nothing.

The girls stood or sat in those doorways, with short skirts on, and I thought: *This is so easy, why have I even been trying to meet people any other way?*

'Want a bit, darling?' a woman on the street said to me. She knew.

I kept walking. I was like a boxer, now, pacing before the fight starts: three, four, five times I went round, each time getting nearer something. Working myself up while the beer was still in me. Nervous as hell. I started speaking: 'What's the score in here then?' or 'What's the deal?' or simply: 'How much?'

'Just ten pounds here. Full strip,' they answered. 'Lovely girls. Black girls, white girls, Oriental girls.'

I kept walking.

'What sort of girl do you want, sir?'

Most of all, I wanted a girl who I could sit with in the pub. Who'd find it funny and endearing when I got drunk. And then who'd have sex with me.

Soon I'd have to do something. I couldn't just keep going round in circles. The lager was dying out of me, too; it wouldn't be any fun when that was gone.

When the walking wore me out, I went in the Prince. It was how it always was at this time on a Saturday. Nice and quiet. A few lads going over the night before, trying to fill in the gaps, then moving on to football; one or two old boys at the bar, sipping dark pints, their noses blotched red, their hands shaking when they wiped the ash off their sleeves, remembering. I wondered again what it would be like inside those strip joints; whether it would just be the two of us? Whether it would be through a screen? Whether they did anything more? 'Any extras, sir?' as the old joke goes. I imagined a woman – a couple of women – dancing naked, dancing naked for me, and sitting there, leaning against the bar, with the barman emptying the ashtrays and wiping the wet off the wood, I got a hard-on.

I checked the money in my pocket: nearly seventy pounds.

I decided to walk my circuit again and see what happened. I went out, my heart racing. The light had changed. Neon. Like New York, Las Vegas. Yes, I could be in Las Vegas. This is exciting. Butterflies, like you wouldn't believe. Butterflies like before finals or a job interview. It was as if things had been taken out of my hands now. I walked, the butterflies fighting with the booze, and I looked up and there she was: standing on the doorway, where she always was, smiling at me.

'Are you coming in or not?' she asked.

'How much?'

'Ten pounds to get in, ten pounds for a live strip show.'

'Yes, and what else?'

'That's it. Ten pounds to get in and ten pounds for a live strip show. Come on, darling, you'll love it.'

She had a lot of make-up on and reminded me of someone, but then I realised it was just because I'd seen her four or five times already this afternoon.

'OK, lead the way,' I said.

She turned and I followed, wondering if it would be her. She couldn't have been much older than eighteen. 'What's your name?' she asked, not turning round.

'Rob.'

We went down some stairs and she took money – twenty pounds, like she said – which she gave to another girl. This other girl smiled at me.

'So that's ten for the door, yes, and ten for the strip?'

'That's right.'

She pulled back a curtain and there was a little room with a red sofa, a tiny table with a lamp on it and a chair.

'Sit down, Rob,' she said, pointing to the sofa.

I sat down.

'I'll go and make sure your girl's getting ready for you,' she said, disappearing through the curtain. Another girl appeared. This one was older. Pretty, but older. She had black curly hair and was wearing a leather jacket and a short red skirt; she sat on the chair next to the sofa. When she crossed her legs, they were level with my face. Strong legs. I wondered if it would happen here. If I could touch her. Or would that be extra?

'Right, Rob, it is Rob, isn't it?' she said. 'Your girl's getting ready for you next door. I'm just here to keep you company until she's ready. Can I get you a drink while we're waiting?'

'How much?'

'Ten pounds.'

I thought: I'll give her ten pounds and she'll give me a drink.

There can't be a catch there. I've got nearly fifty left. And I could do with a drink.

'OK, ten pounds.' I got a tenner out of my pocket, passed it to her.

That leaves me forty, I thought.

'Do you want to buy me one? You don't have to but it'll be nice if you do. Means I can have a drink with you while we're waiting for your girl. Your girl's really pretty, she's one of the prettiest.'

I gave her another tenner.

Thirty pounds.

She disappeared behind the curtain. The room was so small, smaller even than my room in the flat. She was gone for a long time and I noticed how dusty everything was. I imagined myself ejaculating, here, on the frayed red sofa, and it wasn't a nice thought. I felt suddenly sober, then drunk again. Got to go through with it now. And this *will* become a good story for the lads. I repositioned myself on the sofa, tried to get higher up. Ruffled my hair, stretched my arms out along the top. Waited.

She came back with the drinks. 'Cheers,' she said, holding her glass up.

'Cheers.'

She clinked her glass against mine. 'OK, Rob, just to let you know what we do here. Like I say, your girl will be ready for you soon, she'll ... have you been here before?'

'Yes,' I said, figuring it might be useful for her to think that.

She looked at me with disbelief. 'In this place, yes?'

'Yes. A while ago.'

'Well, you probably know how things work then. But we've got all sorts of rooms here depending on what you want.'

'Let me just have the strip and see how it goes. That's what I've paid for.'

'You're the boss. So what are you doing in London tonight?'

'I live here,' I said. 'It's a mate of mine's birthday party,' I added, lying, thinking she'd be less likely to stitch me up if a big group of blokes could turn up at any minute.

'So where are your friends then?'

'They're finishing their drinks in a boozer round the corner.' I said 'boozer' deliberately, too; it's the sort of word people might use in this situation.

'So you're the scouting party?'

'You could say that.'

She took another sip from her drink. I did the same. Surely something will happen soon?

'So what do you do for a living then, Rob?'

I certainly wasn't going to tell her I worked in market research; she'd probably think I was loaded and try to rip me off. But I could hardly say I was a dustman or something, I didn't look like one. It occurred to me to tell her I was a teacher; I'd like that, and I wondered what she'd say if I did. Instead I said: 'I'm a mechanic.'

She looked at my hands disbelievingly and I took a swig of drink; not much vodka in this orange juice. I didn't like her. I felt scared.

'That's nice,' she said.

I didn't come here for careers advice, I thought. Just give me the strip and I'll go. Let me see someone take off their clothes and I'll go.

'All this talk about me, tell me a little bit about you,' I said. 'What's your name?'

'I'm called Nadalina.'

'Nadalina, that's a nice name.' So what if it's a cliché! She's hardly gonna care! 'Is that a Spanish name?'

'Half Spanish. My mother's Spanish, my father's Irish.'

She crossed her legs the other way. I wanted to see the strip and get out. Right then, though, I'd have settled for just leaving. Write off the money I'd spent – was it thirty pounds I'd spent leaving me forty or forty I'd spent leaving me thirty – and get out, but she was sitting in front of the door, blocking the only exit.

'Do you live round here?' I asked.

'I live in East London.'

'How is it?'

'Great,' she said, laughing. 'Excuse me.'

She disappeared back behind the curtain. Who else has been in here? I wondered. I looked at the faded red of the sofa covers and wondered if anyone else had come on it. How many people? The light from the lamp in the corner was bright, leaving much of the room shadowed. I tried to remember the arrangement of doorways and steps on the other side, but I couldn't. The steps must be just the other side of that curtain, on the right, the steps that led up and out into the street. I could be there in six or seven strides if I ran. Back, anonymous in Soho. No one asking me stuff. But the door at the top might be closed. She reappeared, pulled back the curtain behind her and sat down.

'Your girl's ready for you now, Rob. What I want to do before you go through is remind you of our charges.'

She leant across to the table and picked up a laminated piece of plastic. The writing on it was small. I tried to read it but the letters swam.

'The strip's ten pounds' she says, 'and—

'Which I've paid for.'

'Yes, you've paid for that and the drinks but the other thing is company – i.e. me – which as you can see here there's a charge for.'

She leant towards me, pointing at this bit of plastic. It was the closest I'd got to her. I looked at where she was pointing. Surely that can't be right? Surely it can't say that? I stood up. The room was spinning. *Company £180.*

'That's not what was agreed,' I said. 'You said ten pounds to get in and ten pounds for the strip. That's twenty ... which I gave you. Plus two drinks, which I gave you the twenty for too.'

She pointed again to where it said 'Company £180'. Next to it, it said 'minimam'. I got the urge to tell her it was spelt wrong. I moved towards the door. She did the same, cutting me off. 'Sit down,' she said. 'Sit down or I'll have to call security.'

I felt sick, sick and sober.

'Look, I asked what it would cost and you said ten pounds to get in and ten pounds for the strip. You must remember?'

She looked at me and there was nothing in her face. Nothing. I remembered reading somewhere about how prostitutes feel about their customers. How they pity them at best, hate them at worst. This one was a hater.

'It says it here quite clearly,' she said, pointing to the piece of plastic. 'A hundred and eighty pounds. Besides, if you've been here before, you should know that.'

Clever. Yes, a hater.

'I can't pay a hundred and eighty. I haven't got it.'

'Better sit down then, darling,' she said. I stayed standing. 'Tyson,' she called and some bloke appeared. Square head, square shoulders, square body. He stood in the square doorway, filling it. Stories came to mind of tourists getting marched to cashpoints and having thousands of pounds taken off them. Getting baseball-batted. The police. How did I get here? Me!

'Maybe we can come to some sort of arrangement,' she said. 'You can't pay a hundred and eighty, OK, fine, so how much can you pay?'

71

Tyson crossed his arms.

'I'm sorry,' I said, 'I should have known – I wouldn't have come in here if I'd known – I'm sorry for wasting your time ... just let me go? Please.'

'I said *how much money have you got on you?*'

Give her something, keep her happy. I went into my side pocket and pulled out a load of change. There was about ten quid and I gave her that.

'What about the other pockets?'

I went into the other side pocket, brought out some more change – maybe another fiver – and handed it over.

'And?'

I put my hands into my back pockets, felt the money in there, a pen, keys, a scrap of paper. I took out the piece of paper and unravelled it; it was the number of that girl I'd met at the party in Wandsworth the night before. 'Emma', it said in wonky handwriting under a smudged number. I tried to look like I was disappointed it was all I'd found and put it back. 'That's it, I'm afraid.'

'Do them again,' she said.

I pulled the same stuff out. The pen, the piece of paper. Unravelled it, showed her the same number, the same name.

Emma.

Nothing.

Where did she learn to be like this?

Tyson shifted from foot to foot. I felt my gut falling. I just wanted to go home.

'Listen, darling, I'm getting sick and tired of seeing that piece of paper. What other money have you got?'

She was calling me darling as she robbed me. Five minutes before she had said cheers, chinked glasses, asked about my job. I felt helpless. Jesus, what have I done. No drunkenness, just help-lessness. Helplessness and, already, regret.

'What's in his back pockets, Tyson?' she said, going behind me. And for some reason I remembered that line from *The Hobbit* when Gollum says about Bilbo: 'What's he got in his pocketses' and I remembered how Mum always used to read it to me when I couldn't sleep; I wondered what she would think if she could see me now, here. I felt Nadalina's hands in my pockets.

'I think this is what you were looking for, darling,' she said, clutching the last of my cash.

I let her take my money.

She nodded to Tyson and he moved aside. I walked past him and climbed the steps. Then I turned and headed home.

I didn't feel drunk any more.

It was ten past five.

Chapter Sixteen

A warm feeling started inside me. I felt it tickling the inside of my stomach and I felt it on my face, around my mouth, making me want to smile. Maybe it was this place, Newcastle. Something about it.

'Last Saturday I was at Countdown – that's a big nightclub in Leicester Square, country boy – and yes I was pissed but there was all that noise and everyone was on such a high and it must have been about midnight and they were playing songs from *Grease* and I was dancing and they released thousands of bits of paper from the ceiling and I stood there with them all falling around me and I felt, I really felt, I could laugh off all this stuff with Emma.'

James listened. The other two were having a game of pool. It was winner stays on, so that meant Stevie would be on the table all night.

'It was only two days after we'd split up, but standing there with all the paper coming down, I was sort of happy.' What I'd also thought then, I now remembered, was: I can get away with this as often as I like now. I'd been completely blotto. 'You said earlier about how it felt like a weight had been lifted off your shoulders once you had actually split up with Anna. Well, last Saturday that was exactly how it felt. It's like a moment of amazing clarity. I knew it was the right thing to have happened.'

'So quite how pissed do you have to be before you get these moments of clarity?' James asked.

'Very, obviously. But it wasn't just because I was pissed – it was more than that. I was happy because I was ...' It struck me as funny, how often I was getting wrecked at the moment. I raised my glass, chinked it against James's and some spilled. 'Cheers,' I said.

I realised I sounded like one of those blokes who hugs his mates and tells them he loves them every time he gets slaughtered. But I did love this bloke. I did want to hug him.

'Sounds like you should patent whatever mix of drinks you necked that night. You'd make a fortune.'

'Maybe it was just because I've never been to Countdown with Emma. It didn't remind me of her.'

'That's a hard part, isn't it,' James said. 'But you'll deal with it.'

So many reminders, though.

Walking past the restaurants we'd been to. Wearing the green shirt she liked – the one I had on the night we met.

Someone mentioning Devon.

Abba on the radio.

Horseracing on the telly.

Everyday things.

Everything, it sometimes seemed.

God only knew how I'd cope with going back to the bars and clubs I used to frequent. All the pulling joints.

I'd even started listening to Classic FM, because the music was new. No memories. No baggage. But you couldn't avoid familiar songs all the time. Sometimes they just hit you. I'd been walking out of Embankment tube on Tuesday on my way to a meeting in Charing Cross Road and a busker started singing that Alanis Morissette song 'Ironic' and what was I supposed to do, what *could* I do; me and Emma had listened to that all the time on holiday. I loved it, that line about a bloke winning the lottery and dying the next day, that bit about a black fly in your chardonnay – and there were pubs all around, everywhere I looked, and I knew I couldn't get to the meeting without at least a quick one.

I never made it to the meeting. Rang up, apologetically, the next day and told them the tube was closed due to a bomb scare.

Reminders, everywhere. We'd only been going out for two years, yet it seemed every aspect of our lives was intertwined.

I remembered going into my room on Monday and seeing ACE written in the dust on my computer screen. It could have been there for weeks, months – Emma could have written it one night as she undressed for bed; she could have written it with the finger that a few seconds later she run across my chest or along my knob. I went and made my flatmates tea and sat watching telly. Every time one of them looked as if they might be about to go to bed, I sparked up another conversation, made more tea, flicked channel, hoping there'd be something they wanted to see. In the end *Stand By Me* came on and it kept them there; both times I'd watched it were before Emma, so I coped.

75

'How long were you guys seeing each other?' James asked.

'Two years. Well, two years and two months if you're counting.'

'So, you'll be back in Countdown every Friday and Saturday from now on then, will you?'

'Not after the state I was in last Saturday. What is it they say: Never revisit the scene of the crime. I tell you, I don't know how I got home but I woke up fully clothed in Helen's bed. She was away, I should add.'

It sounded funny now. But I'd been petrified all Sunday about what I might have done. The only time the dread went was when Helen had rung that night and mentioned she'd been away all weekend. I had a moment of massive relief, then immediately started worrying again about getting home from Countdown because I couldn't remember any of it and I rang the lads but they didn't know what had happened to me after we all got split up sometime after midnight. I had laid on the sofa all Sunday, wondering whether to ring Emma and knowing I'd never sleep with her again – never see that nightshirt she wore with the Dalmatian on it – and it seemed like I suddenly had a long time to face without her. Too long.

Everything had changed. Even boiling an egg was too much, crushingly pointless. Slicing the top off with a knife and seeing the yellow run down the side was unbearable. I'd sat there thinking: I can't be bothered to scoop it up. I'd sat there remembering how Emma always turned the egg upside down in the cup after she'd finished and pretended not to have eaten it. But there wasn't an Emma to do that any more. Not to me. I'd been sort of anticipating it for months, but it was only then – the previous twelve hours a blank, gone, dead – that it really occurred to me that we *had* split up. I had cried and worried, as I sobbed, that Helen would see the tear-stains on her pillow.

I leaned across and took one of James's cigarettes. My hand was shaking. I put it to my mouth, lit it, sat back in my chair, inhaled deeply and blew out a long trail of smoke. I felt dizzy, but that passed. There's something very noble, I thought, about having given up the struggle to not smoke. Something almost sexual. I held the cigarette between my second and third finger, as I always did, and took another deep puff. My chest felt full and, again, I felt dizzy, but again it passed. I blew the smoke out at the same angle as before, as I always did.

We both sat in silence for a few seconds, smoking. I wondered what Emma would say.

'I thought you'd given up,' James said.

'I have.'

And I had. Sort of. I might have been smoking, but I wasn't a smoker any more. I had Emma to thank for that.

'Stag nights don't count,' I said. 'Anyway, how are things with you? I'm boring everyone with my problems tonight. How are you, Dukie?'

'We're fine, thanks. We're really well.'

'Are you still going to call your kid Mike?'

We laughed.

It was funny enough that he shared a name with a racing driver, but the idea of calling his kid Mike – Mike Hunt – always cracked us up.

'Let's see the vicar say that at the christening,' he said. 'Sarah wants Jack for a boy, Daisy for a girl.'

'Well, it's academic because you're probably shooting blanks. You know why you've got a low sperm count? God's idea of damage limitation. Listen, I'm sorry about being a bit depressing tonight. I've usually pulled by this point in the evening. Law of averages and all that.'

We both cracked up.

'Not a problem,' James said. 'Listen, I was going to say something earlier – make a sort of announcement – but I didn't want to steal Matt's thunder. Thing is, seeing as we're on the subject, I might as well tell you now: Sarah's going to have a baby.'

'She's pregnant?'

'That's want usually happens before you have a baby.'

'That's great, that's great news.'

I leant forward and shook him by the hand. 'Seriously, congratulations. Have you found out who the father is?'

We laughed again.

'When's it due?'

'March. March the eighteenth.'

I tried to work back nine months from then to see when it was, to see if the weekend the baby was conceived was a special occasion – a wedding or something, maybe one I'd been at – but I couldn't, and gave it up. And then I remembered, of course, I hadn't seen James since he got married.

'So at least one of us has had sex recently,' I said. Actually, I'd had sex a lot with Emma before we split up. The more we argued,

77

the more it seemed like we were about to split up, the more we had sex. It wasn't any better, the sex, and it didn't make any difference, but we had it more all the same.

'It's one of the reasons I was looking forward to this weekend so much; trips away are going to be few and far between soon,' James said.

A baby. James's baby. It seemed unimaginable. He wouldn't want as much to do with me, that was for sure. If nothing else, he wouldn't have time. I wanted to wind back the conversation a few sentences, to before the bit where James said: Sarah's going to have a baby. Then wind it back further, to college.

'Who'd have thought it? You'll be a proper grown-up soon. It'll completely change your life. Getting married is no big deal, so people say, but have a kid and everything's different.'

'That's why we got on with it. We can have it grown-up and out while we're still young enough to enjoy ourselves. There's nothing worse than geriatric parents.'

'There's a lot to be said for being an older parent. You've got more money for starters.'

'A kid deserves young parents.'

'You're not exactly old, are you?'

'This kid's not going to be grown up until we're over fifty as it is, and we want to have two. That doesn't give us much left at the other end.'

'You make it sound like having it's the short straw. It's not compulsory. If you didn't want to have it, you didn't have to.'

'We wanted it all right. We *really* wanted this baby.'

I used to get paranoid that Emma would get pregnant. That would have been just my luck: millions of people trying unsuccessfully for a kid and us – on the way out – lumbered with one. That would have been so typical.

'So, you looking forward to it, then?'

'I can't wait. It's the best thing that's ever happened to me.'

'People have kids later nowadays,' I said, on autopilot now. 'You could have waited.'

'You'd be surprised – if this was our parents' generation, Sarah would be considered gynaecologically geriatric.'

He had a point; although my dad was well into his thirties before he had me.

'Do you know what it's going to be?'

'We're probably not going to find out, we'd rather not know.'

I wondered if James was telling the truth. He might well know – but it was his secret, his and Sarah's. Things were changing. Friendship was no longer the closest bond. Marriage was. Pregnancy was. Soon, parenthood would be.

'As long it supports City and doesn't come out ginger I won't complain.'

'Hopefully, if it's a girl, she'll grow up to look like her,' I said, nodding at the girl with freckles. She was with her friends, not far from us now, and I got the feeling again that things would be different if I was with her. We made eye contact again. It was like we were moving in concentric circles towards each other. 'If it's a girl, you'd better introduce me to her friends when she gets a bit older.'

James didn't answer.

A group of girls walked past, on their way out.

I imagined the spare room in James's house. I'd gone through a phase of visiting him a lot a few years ago, and that's where I'd always slept. There'd just been a mattress on the floor in there then. He'd redecorate it now, put new wallpaper up – pink for a girl, blue for a boy – hang a mobile from the ceiling, put the toys he and Sarah had as kids on the bed. It would be tidy, the sheets would smell of clean washing. That room was bigger than mine.

'How does it feel?' I asked. 'Knowing that you're going to become a father?'

'I don't feel any different. Maybe it hasn't sunk in.'

'It's like, not for a day or a week or even a month – but for ever. It's not like you're becoming a born-again Christian or teetotal or an accountant or something you can stop being after a while. You'll never not be a father now.'

'It feels great, Rob,' he said. 'Just great.'

Splitting up with Emma, I realised, didn't just mean I didn't have a girlfriend. It meant I might never get married. It meant I might never have kids. Not that I necessarily wanted them. But splitting up had consequences beyond simply being single again and being able to go out more, and that scared me. I'd fallen off the horse before I'd even got to the first hurdle.

I could see Stevie over James's shoulder, chatting to a load of guys at the bar. He was downing his pint – not quite in one, but nearly – and held the empty glass upside down on his head.

Don't stop, Stevie.

Don't do that once tonight, and then stop. Be like this all evening. *Please*. Carry on like this, like how it used to be. Us, shotgunning cans in the Onion the night we finished our first-year exams; happy hour in Dempsters; cocktail night in that pub we used to go to down the Quayside on a Monday.

Carry on, please, until we're all so drunk that I can't remember how long ago all that was, or forget it altogether.

I was tempted to ask Dukie how long he'd already known about the baby for, but didn't. 'I suppose you'll be going to all those classes with Sarah, those antenatal or prenatal classes or whatever it is they're called.'

'Too right, I'm a modern man. Besides, they're full of women,' he said.

'If you want anyone to come with you, you know where I am.'

'Call me old-fashioned, but I was planning on taking Sarah.'

I imagined James in that room, that redecorated room that smelt clean and of warm milk, feeding the baby then touching its cheek, ever so softly, before turning the lights out and leaving it to sleep. Then I remembered him at college, the night of his twenty-first. Him tied stark bollock naked to a lamp-post outside the Sun. All the cars blowing their horns, and the people shouting and whistling.

'Hope this kid has good parties when it gets a bit older. We can bring him to Newcastle for his twenty-first.'

Neither seemed a million miles away – James's twenty-first, or this kid's.

'Him or her,' James said.

I felt happy for James, really happy. But I felt angry at him too for, without realising, leaving me even further behind. Abandoning me. I felt the same urge I always had when I was younger and some-one mentioned Dad to say something silly, something shocking.

'I need to sleep with *her*,' I said, looking over his shoulder at the girl with freckles. I sat up to get a better view but I knew, even as I did, that she wouldn't go for me and in any event it was Emma I really wanted. I'd wake up tomorrow and I'd still want Emma, more sharply than ever behind the headache and the sick feeling – which, inevitably, would now come.

Matt appeared. He'd been beaten at pool by Stevie so had come to tell James it was his turn. Matt only ever had one thing to say about kids: '*Why*?' He was never going to have any. There again, he always said he would never get married.

I waited to see what James said, but he stayed silent. He obviously wasn't going to mention the baby, and I liked being in on the secret.

'What's this, then,' Matt said, 'happy corner? This is supposed to be a stag night, not a wake.'

Chapter Seventeen

She was saying things like 'budget' and 'communication' and once I'm sure she even used the expression 'throwing the baby out with the bath water'.

It's Saturday night, I thought. Loosen up.

Thing is, Matt had bet me a beer I wouldn't talk to them, so I couldn't chicken out. Then she said 'us accountants' and I realised what trouble we were in.

I went across and asked if either of them had a cigarette.

'We don't smoke,' she said.

Now there's a surprise!

Her friend – she had a big mole on her nose – didn't say anything. Then they went back to talking, just how Demi and her mates had done, and I went back to the boys and Stevie said: 'Another triumph there, Rob!'

I ignored him and carried on listening to the two women; I knew Matt wouldn't count asking for a cigarette as talking to them; we'd had that exact argument plenty of times before.

She was Scottish – quite anglicised, but definitely Scottish. I'd forgotten that, how Newcastle was full of Scots, just as London was full of Aussies. The locals didn't mind them; it was us southerners they hated. They always thought I was a Cockney; I soon gave up trying to explain that Surrey and London weren't one and the same.

She didn't look very happy, either, the one who was doing the talking. She looked like the sort of person, to be honest, who was just waiting for the chance to complain. You know the sort: a fleck of cork in the wine, a slightly burnt chip, the music being too loud. *Didn't she know: I was alone.*

Then she mentioned something about taking the kids somewhere, some museum or something. Does everyone in this pub have them?

I used to be able to spend a whole day sitting in a pub and no one, not a single person, would so much as mention kids. Now everyone was at it.

I butted in: 'Yes, that's a nice idea. The kids will enjoy that.'

It took a moment for her to register that I was back. Then they carried on the conversation as if I wasn't there and I began to wish I wasn't. As if I was interested that her eldest – 'He's six now, can you believe it' – had the physique of a runner, he timed himself racing up and down the hall, he was small and skinny, but he smiled so much, he would be a hit with the ladies when he grew older. As if anyone was interested that, given half a chance, the baby would eat baked beans for every meal, including breakfast! As if there weren't millions of other babies and it might not be baked beans, but sausages or crisps or chocolate biscuits; they'd be demanding something with their little fat fingers and their noisy wails and the shit in their nappies.

Emma's voice – muffled and slightly slurred now – reached me: 'But it would be horrible to *not* have children.'

Emma once said she wanted a big family, three or four; that being on your own when you're old must be terrible. She might still have that big family. I could still end up on my own.

These two weren't going to drive me off.

'You got morning sickness really badly, didn't you?' the one with the mole was saying.

Like that's ever going to be a concern of yours, I thought.

I butted back in. 'I get that every Saturday and Sunday.' Then: 'I'm going to have three. One of each.' Neither laughed, but I did, and this time they looked at me. 'Can I ask you something?' I said. 'I don't want to be rude, but I'm thinking of having kids myself – me and my wife are sort of deciding – and I'm keen to hear as many people's views as possible.'

The one who had said about throwing the baby out with the bathwater relaxed a little, obviously relieved to hear I was married. So, I'm married and she's married: we're all one big happily married family. She probably liked the expression: 'hear the views'. Maybe I was her sort of person, after all.

'My only concern,' I went on, 'is that we'll get the chance of a big promotion or to travel or to retrain after we become parents, me and my other half. Don't children close too many doors?'

Promotion, travel, retraining ... she fell for it hook, line and sinker, Mrs Married. But half of it was true, I suppose: I might not have another half, but I did want to retrain.

'That's a choice only you can make,' she said. 'In my experience, people tend to use the "closed doors" argument as an excuse.'

The closed doors argument. What is this, a political debate? It was supposed to be Saturday night, a stag night.

'Don't you ever regret having kids? There's got to be some drawbacks.'

'Are you still serious?'

It occurred to me she could be divorced. She might have driven her husband off. Boring people do get left. Not that I cared how boring she was; if anything happened between us, it was only going to be a one-night stand.

'Yes, I'm interested. Seriously.'

'There hasn't been a single day when I haven't been glad I've got the boys,' Mrs Married said.

We exchanged earnest glances. All you have to do is hit them on their wavelength. Dress like them or sound like them and, however half-heartedly you do it, they'll fall for it.

'I haven't ever regretted having mine,' Moley said.

She's got a kid! Even *she's* got a kid. Am I the only person in the world who hasn't?

Mrs Married went on: 'Sometimes it's nice to give them to someone else for a few hours – but that's what grandparents are for.' They both chuckled, like it was funniest line ever spoken. 'And they grow up so quickly. You don't want to miss anything.'

She's not about to say, 'You'll change your mind one day,' or 'It's different when they're yours.' Please, anything but that.

I said: 'So if you go out for one night you might miss one of them gorging himself on baked beans or timing himself running up and down the hall. It's hardly fucking unmissable, is it.'

There was a pause – she obviously wondered how I knew about that stuff. Either that, or she objected to me swearing. Like her kids wouldn't swear. Like her husband, whoever and wherever the dullard was, wouldn't. Yes, and where was he? Probably baby-sitting. Keep her talking, keep kidding her. I'll have the last laugh here.

'Sorry, I didn't mean it like that. What I mean is, you two wouldn't have seen each other if you'd stayed in tonight,' I said, looking at both of them in turn. Good-looking; mole. 'That's worth it, isn't it?'

Mrs Married looked at me like I was a human being again. She smiled and I thought: You *are* attractive. Give me half a chance and I'll show you what your Ikea bed's for.

'It's hard to explain,' she said.

'Well, to be honest I can't see it as anything other than a cop-out. It's like that bloke says in *Four Weddings and a Funeral*, you know, the gay one who dies. Two people run out of stuff to say so what do they do? They get married. It's the same with kids. You run out of things to do so you take the easy option and have kids.'

'I wouldn't call being a parent easy,' she said, again looking at Moley like they were in on something I wasn't. 'And besides, it *is* what I want.'

'No, OK, it's not easy, but that's my point. It's hard work but that's exactly the excuse you need to not do anything else. It's the best get-out clause in the world. No one else will expose it for the lie it is because they've done it themselves. It's a fucking conspiracy if you ask me.'

I caught her sneakily pointing at my glass as if to say, 'He's pissed.'

No, I'm not yet, but I will be soon.

I didn't care now. This *is* what I thought. Sort of. And to think, I was so near with Emma. A 'yes' instead of a 'don't know', and before long this would have been us: her in a pub, a night out with a friend, probably being hassled by some twat like me, and me at home sober looking after some God-awful kid.

'I *didn't* ask you,' she said.

I thought: Yes, well, I told you.

She started banging on about something or other, using the word 'aye' a lot; her accent drifting in and out. Bet she accentuates it when the rugby's on. Boils a haggis on Burns Night and talks about home: how beautiful the scenery is, how friendly the people are, how she wants to go back there – she never will, but she'll cart the kids back three times a year and lecture them about the importance of roots. Roots, that's a joke. You didn't catch me banging on to people in pubs about how great Surrey is.

The poor little sods. They'd go to university and probably be consumed with doubts about their ability and the abilities of the people around them and whether they were working hard enough or too hard and then, when they graduated, who would get the job with most prospects and earn most and get the best car and get sent on the best courses and get the best mortgage and come out to pubs like this and have one drink then go home, never having realised how pointless it all was and by then they'd have kids of their own anyway.

'A conspiracy theory,' I said. 'If that's all you're going to do before you die, then you might not as well have lived in the first place.'

'What?' she snapped. 'What's a conspiracy theory?'

'Having kids.'

'Probably just as well you haven't got any of your own if that's the way you feel.'

How does she know that I haven't? I might have.

'You're telling me. I've got my own life.'

'That's precisely what kids give you: a life of your own.' She paused. 'Why are you so negative about children?'

Who says I'm negative? Where did she get that idea from? What I'm negative about is the way I can't get away from people talking about them, even on a Saturday night. Even on a stag weekend.

There was a long silence.

I should tell her I want to become a teacher, that would shut her up.

'How old are you?' she asked.

I didn't answer; I was thinking of James, James and Sarah, sitting on their sofa having a takeaway, the sound of a baby crying, its little voice crackling through the intercom he'd put up in the spare room, the baby's room. A family.

'How old are you?' she repeated.

'Why?'

'Because you seem young. You obviously need to be the centre of attention. How old are you?'

'Nearly thirty.'

'You'll change.'

'Not if I can help it.'

'Maybe you'll start acting *nearly* thirty one day.'

'Yes, and I don't know how old you are, but I bet you've acted forty since you were born. Maybe one day – and this has always been the height of my ambition – maybe one day I'll become an accountant.'

She hesitated; I let her sweat.

'I don't think you'd get through the selection procedure,' she said.

I imagined people scribbling out the answers to psychometric tests, solving logic problems, sitting bolt upright in an interview with a grey suit on. Number-crunching pension-watchers. I didn't know any accountants, but everyone knew what they were like. It was one of the few jobs that was more boring than market research.

'I'll take that as a compliment,' I said. 'You're right, your life's a success. You're wonderful.'

I looked at her again, stared, I knew the eye contact wasn't going to work, not now, not in a million years. Her mascara had run slightly; little flecks of it had settled beneath her eyes. It occurred to me that, no matter how I acted, I *would* be forty in ten years' time. I could live in a shared flat with a load of people in their twenties, I could treat my job like it was a big joke, I could act as if I was still a student, but I would still be forty. Well, almost.

'What are you doing that's so wonderful, then?' she said.

I didn't answer.

'Come on, tell me.'

She was red, although I didn't know whether she was angry or embarrassed. I thought how nice it must be for her husband, wherever he was, to know she'd be going back to him tonight. That they'd end their evenings in bed, together. All I had to look forward to was the Hotel Where We Spew and that room that smelt funny and was like Halls, and probably having to listen to some couple shagging next door. I'd probably try to have a wank, but be too pissed to do that. And when I woke up I'd feel tired and sick and empty.

'I'll tell you what I do, yes, I spend all my time concentrating on not letting myself become you or anything like you or your mute friend here. That's what I'm doing.'

'What do you mean, *like me*? You don't know anything about me. Why don't you run along back to your friends now, little boy.'

'I know you're dull. I know it's Saturday night and you're sitting here talking about dull things like budgets.'

It occurred to me that I had to finish a budget off on Monday; it was over a week late already.

'Dull, dull, dull!'

She hesitated, then said: 'Why are you being so horrible to me?'

The 'horrible' sounded very Scottish.

I couldn't answer. All I knew was that in a very tiny way she was a part of why I felt the way I did. Both of them were. Everyone in this pub was. It was nothing personal. Just that the more people there were like her, the less there'd be like me.

'I'm not being horrible. All I want is for you to tell me one thing you've done that's not dull and I'll go. Come on, it's not a trick question – one thing.'

Moley shifted uncomfortably and looked at her friend. I didn't care about making either of them understand now. They were a lost cause. I felt like screaming although I didn't know what – something about James having a baby and Matt getting married and Stevie getting another promotion and how happy I was for all of them, what wonderful news it all was, but how scared it made me feel. That our lives, in many ways, were so different nowadays. So unconnected.

'I'd rather you just left us alone,' she said. 'I've no intention of sitting here and justifying myself to you.'

'No, come on, fair's fair, you tell me one thing, just one thing you've done that's not ordinary, not average, not ...' I tried to find a killer line that would sum up everything I was feeling and was trying to say, but couldn't. 'And I'll piss off.'

I waited. It struck me how I never could find the words I wanted. And I wondered – don't ask me why, it was the first time I'd ever considered it – what Emma's kids would look like.

If it was a boy, he'd be dark-haired and tall. If it was a girl she'd be pretty, and have the same brown eyes as her mother – that same brown as the wood panelling in the Star.

Imagine that, another human being looking like you. Incredible, really. I'd never thought about it before.

'I'm still waiting,' I said.

'So, let's get this straight – I tell you one thing I've done and then you go. No more questions, no more hanging around bothering us. I say one thing and you piss off.'

'Exactly.'

'OK, I've travelled. Now go.'

I was tempted to ask where, but instead put my hand to my mouth and pretended to yawn. 'Bong. Wrong answer. Travel! Boooring. And, don't tell me, it taught you – let me see – independence. Sorry. Try again.'

'Will you please just leave us. You're getting irritating. Go on, please, go.'

Moley piped up: 'I should just go if I were you.'

88

What's it got to do with you? What course did you get that assertiveness from? Bet you weren't always like this though, were you. Bet there was a long time when you hated yourself for having that mole on your face, before you found this confidence and friends like this one, who told you it didn't matter, it didn't make you ugly, you were beautiful and there was someone out there for you, there was for everyone.

I thought about going, but something stopped me.

Why don't you hate yourself, I wanted to say. Why don't you hate all this?

'Come on, one thing. You can't, can you. You've done nothing – and for what? Two kids. Whoopee. *What else have you brought to the party?* Nothing. You've reproduced and that's it. What is it exactly about you that you think's worth reproducing?'

She didn't speak.

'Don't tell me, you've worked on some really interesting projects as an accountant with some really interesting people. Actually, you're right, it might be dull but compared with the alternative of screaming brats and a dull husband who, don't tell me, is a fucking accountant too, who can blame you.'

She looked me square in the eyes. There was a line locked in her jaw.

'How dare you. How dare you.'

Her friend put her arm out and touched her hand. 'Come on, let's just go. He's not worth getting upset over.'

'No, it needs to be said, he needs to be told. You asked me what I was doing. Well, I'll tell you what I'm doing. I'm bringing up two kids on my own. I'm bringing up two kids who are going to be decent and happy and know that their father when he was alive was a decent man. And if they grow up not to be like you, then I for one will be happy.'

I shrank into myself as I heard those words. *When he was alive.* It was like watching myself hear them. I wanted to apologise – but it wouldn't have been enough. Nothing would now. It was too late. She was staring at me, and I couldn't tell whether it was hate or pity or simply puzzlement.

A vision of her in black, wearing a hat, came to mind. I wanted to be behind the pillar or the bar or the cigarette machine or tiny, and behind the glasses on the table. Anywhere but here. Anybody but me.

I said: 'You can't say you wouldn't want them to have hair like this,' pointing to my hair. It was untidy and needed a cut. 'Or a physique like this,' I said doing a Mr-Universe-type gesture knowing I'd look silly and skinny and for once I was glad. The sillier and skinnier, the better.

'We're going now,' she said, gathering up her stuff. I tried to look at her, get a good, straight look into her eyes as if she might remember that later and know it was the apology I didn't know how to make, but her eyes were moving too quickly, as were her head and her hands and all of her.

'Good luck with the kids,' I said. 'Seriously.'

'Happy now?' the one with the mole said as they walked away.

Matt, from across the other side of the bar, was giving me a big thumbs-up.

Chapter Eighteen

'The good thing about prostitutes,' I said, 'is that they don't expect you to live with them for forty years just because you have sex with them.'

'And the good thing about wives is that they don't give you some hideous disease and rob you,' Matt replied.

We always had this conversation about this point in the evening when we were out. I didn't believe what I said, but I'd got in the habit of saying it. The other two had nipped out to visit one of Stevie's old flats; we were sitting at the table next to the ladies' loos.

'Surely there's a lot to be said for paying for it? I'm not talking about spiritual fulfilment here. I'm talking about sex. You're a businessman, Matt, it's a commercial transaction.'

'That's what I like about you, you're such a romantic, Rob.'

I was tempted to tell him about the time soon after we'd met when Emma had flu and I drove halfway across London to take her a Lemsip and some flowers. It gave me an excuse to take an afternoon off work, admittedly, but she seemed to really appreciate it. Matt would have taken the piss, though.

'No, it's not romantic, but it's simple. Sex for money. No lying. No kidding each other. No emotional attachment. No splitting up.'

I was tempted to tell him, too, about how I'd surprised Emma with that night out at the theatre; her face lit up when I told her – she looked stunning, that happy. I'd made my mind up there and then to surprise her more often. Trouble was, we had a couple of hours to kill so we stopped off in the pub and I ended up having to squeeze past her about five times during the show to get to the gents' and completely lost the gist of the play, which was a real shame because it looked as if it could have been quite good. I kept laughing at all the wrong bits and then I really pissed Emma off because I yelled at one point: 'He's behind you!'

'What about, what about the other stuff – flirting and romance and ...'

'You can do all that with prostitutes,' I said. 'Flirt with them by asking to pay after, not up front. Be romantic by paying, then giving them chocolates. Besides, you're hardly Mr Romantic. You couldn't even spell the word.'

'R ... O ... M ... A ... er, can I phone a friend?'

'Seriously, when did you last make a romantic gesture towards Katie?'

'Thursday.'

'What did you do?'

'I sent her flowers at work.'

'Why?'

He hesitated, then said: 'Because I hadn't done it before.'

'Thing is, you're in a different position to me. You're about to be married.'

'I was aware of that.'

'What I mean is, it's all right for you, you've got sex pretty much on tap.'

He laughed. 'Don't you believe it.'

'Maybe not on tap then, but you've always got the *prospect* of sex. For all I know, I might never meet anyone ever again.' I looked around the place – we were in some swanky new bar just off Grey Street now; some of the people who had been here earlier had gone and new people had come in and filled their tables, but you wouldn't really notice the difference.

'It just seems a bit mechanical, the idea of going with a prostitute.'

'What about the one-night stands you had when we were at college? Are you trying to tell me they were anything more than just sex?'

'No,' Matt said, 'but the difference was they might have been. I didn't know for definite they *weren't*. We were both looking for sex, sure, but we might have been looking for something else too. With a prostitute, neither of you are. There isn't that possibility. There *can't* be.'

It's all right for you, I thought. You've got someone. 'I'm tired of it, Matt. It's too hard work. I don't know if I can face it again, meeting someone. Going through all that getting-to-know-you stuff. I'm too old for it.'

'But, a prostitute?'

'I never said that I would. Just that I couldn't rule it out. Never say never, and all that.'

'It's sad.'

As if this wasn't. Chasing women in bars. Getting rejected, and trying someone new. Then getting rejected again.

So much for getting straight back on the horse.

I felt suddenly lonely and empty. This is it now, I thought. This is what it would be like.

It was all right for Matt – he had Katie; I didn't have anyone.

Funny, he started going out with Katie almost exactly the same time as I started seeing Emma. Just afterwards, in fact. It didn't seem fair that I'd got dumped, simply because I wasn't prepared to stop doing this sort of stuff – going out, seeing these guys. Why did it have to be one or the other? Emma meant the world to me, but so did they.

'Tonight's great,' Matt said. 'I love seeing you lot.'

'Me, too, mate. Me too.'

'I'm not going to get that many opportunities for a while now.'

'Don't say that; course you will. You're a past master at coming up with excuses to wangle weekends away.'

'It's not that I need excuses. Rob, it's that I've got so much on for a while after the wedding.' I wondered where we'd be going next, which pub; not that I really cared, as long as it was somewhere.

'I'm sorry, mate. Banging on so much about Emma earlier. I've been boring James all evening with this stuff already. This is probably the last thing you want to hear on your stag night.'

'I don't mind.'

'You really like Katie, don't you?'

Matt smiled.

'The rest of them were just women, right? But you really care about Katie, don't you?'

He smiled again.

'What is it about her, mate?'

'What do you mean?'

'Why her, and not any of the others?'

He shrugged and looked away; I followed his glance. Dozens, dozens of people in here. It seemed so hard, so impossible, so pointless choosing one when there were so many.

'Something's different. I can't explain.'

'Go on, try,' I said, wanting to understand my friend. To know, as well, why Katie didn't make a fuss about how often he went out and got hammered – or how often he used to anyway.

'I've been with her all this time and I still want to make her laugh. I've always stopped worrying about that after a few months with other girls. We know so much about each other, too. It's like she sometimes knows me better than I know myself. She sort of tells me stuff about myself and it's always what I would eventually have come round to thinking, but she gets there first. Knowing that you're going to be with someone like that for the rest of your life, it's a great feeling.'

I was tempted to say: How do *you*, Matt, of all people, know that? You've never made a relationship last. You're worse than me. But he wasn't. And this one, I knew, *would* work. Katie would last. He was putting the same energy and enthusiasm into making it work that he had once put into sleeping around. That was Matt all over, he was an all-or-nothing sort of bloke. That energy and enthusiasm would, I knew, make him a great husband. Just as it would make him, in due course, a great father – whatever he might say now to the contrary.

I was pleased that he seemed so happy. Yet I couldn't help wondering where I would fit into this new life of his and why the same sorts of things weren't happening to me. Maybe I should have stuck it out with Emma? After all, she never mentioned not going out completely. Maybe things *wouldn't* have changed that much? But that's the way it starts. I'd seen it all before. First it's the tongue-in-cheek quips like 'Surely you're not taking me to that place again'; then the seemingly innocuous – but trick – lines like 'You can watch the football at my flat rather than in the pub if you want'; and then before long it's full-on emotional blackmail with stuff like 'Fine, if that's the way you feel, piss off out then'. She might not have meant it to, but she wouldn't have seen it happening. Like how sometimes you only *mean* to go out for a quick one and before you know it you've stayed out all night.

Matt went on: 'That intimacy is nice, too – knowing that you know so much about someone.'

I put my fingers into my mouth, as if I was making myself sick, but took them out because it did make me feel sick. He had a point

– that intimacy *is* nice – but I was hardly going to agree here, in the pub, on a stag weekend.

'You don't ever know what anyone's really like,' I said.

'Course you do.'

'How?'

'They tell you; you tell them.'

'That's assuming you're honest. What if you lie?'

'Why would you want to lie?'

Because, I thought, that's what happens.

'So you've told Katie everything have you, about all your exes?'

'Yes, course.'

'What, all of them?'

'Yes. They don't matter. They're irrelevant.'

Was that, I wondered, what Emma had become. Irrelevant.

'That's all very well,' I said, 'until they start telling you about theirs.'

'What's wrong with that? That's part of it, part of getting to know someone. I love the fact that Katie *did* want to tell me so much.'

'It always upsets me, hearing about exes.'

'Well, you're not going to find anyone at our age who hasn't had a whole string of boyfriends.'

At our age. That's what it had come down to. In your twenties, your age was just a number. Hit thirty, and it suddenly matters.

'You're not going to find a virgin – believe me, I've looked,' he said, laughing. 'Besides, you wouldn't want to anyway. No baggage is more baggage than loads of baggage. I was flattered that Katie chose to be as honest with me as she did.'

'It just depresses me. Say she went on holiday with her last boyfriend – I'd spent all *our* first holiday together worrying what they did and how it compares. Get to thirty and both you and her have done everything before with other people. Nothing's new any more.'

'You worry too much.'

'I do, I worry about stuff like if she'd been unfaithful before she met me or something.'

'But it's what she's like now that matters.'

Katie, I remembered, had said something similar when Matt and I were reminiscing about all the girls we (well, he) had got off with on our Newquay holiday at the end of the second year. I couldn't believe how she seemed to find it all so funny, those stories about him and other women. 'You must have been dead funny,' she said. Then, to me: 'You'll change, too, when you meet someone properly.' It had struck me as patronising at the time. *When you meet someone properly.* I mean, what was Emma? A one-night stand? I wouldn't have slept with anyone else when I was seeing her. At least, I don't think I would. Besides, it wasn't me who'd been unfaithful. It should be Emma Matt was talking to, not me.

'Surely the past is important? It's not unreasonable, is it, to know how your girlfriend's acted in previous relationships. If she's been, you know, unfaithful or stuff. You'd want to see the log book if you were buying a car. You wouldn't just look at it and say: "Looks reasonable enough, I'll take it."'

'People aren't cars, though. People change; cars don't.'

'But surely the way you *have* acted is a good indicator of the way you're going to act. Say it was a car that had had a recurring problem with the fan belt. If it went wrong once a year, then it wouldn't stop going wrong once a year just because you bought it.'

'But if that was the case then the fan belt would have been replaced long before you ever got the car. It might have broken down a few times then but now, if anything, it's better than the original. Even more reliable.'

'It also could mean a design fault,' I said. 'Something that can't be put right.'

'You can mend anything.'

'You can't.'

'Course you can. Think about it: bit by bit, you could replace every single part – until eventually you've got a new car.'

'But I don't want to have to do that. That's my point. I want someone that's right, straight away. I've broken down enough times as it is.'

What I really wanted, it occurred to me, was a girlfriend who liked drinking as much as I did.

'You're after perfection,' Matt said.

'Is that so awful?'

'No, it's not, but if you aim for perfection, you've got to be ready to take the consequences of not getting it and one of those is ending up with no one. If you're happy to do that, then fine. Are you?'

'I don't know,' I said. And I didn't.

'Anyway, look at yourself. You've had your share of mechanical problems. Your big end's shot from what I hear.'

Matt tore open a packet of crisps on the table, split the bag down the side and moved it midway between us. He put one in his mouth, ponderously. 'What about if you met a girl and everything's right? Great looks, great personality, great sense of humour – the works. You'd throw all that away just because when she was, say, seventeen she might have, I don't know, two-timed someone.'

'Yes, it would prey on my mind.'

'So she's perfect, and you'd throw that away because of something that happened long before she even knew you, something that happened when she was virtually a kid.'

I had one of his crisps. They were salt and vinegar; he always used to have cheese and onion. He continued. 'The guy she was going out with might have been shagging around or treating her like shit, she might have lain awake in bed every night for a month worrying herself sick about what to do then one night at a party, you know how it is, the booze flows and some bloke won't take no for an answer and one thing leads to another. Think about it – if she hadn't done that, she might still be with the first bloke and she wouldn't be going out with you at all. This perfect woman. She might still be in a crap relationship. Is that what you want?'

'No, no, that's not what I want.'

I felt like I'd been tricked. It was like I used to say to him, though: Just because you're better at arguing your point than me doesn't mean you're point's necessarily right. Recently it was a line I seemed to be using more and more. 'I just want someone who's right, Matt.'

'The way you're going, you'll never find anyone who's right.'

I nearly said: Exactly. Then I realised he didn't mean it nicely.

He said: 'As far as I'm concerned, your girlfriend's past is none of your business, but you certainly can't hold it against her if you're going to have any sort of meaningful relationship.'

I wished some music would come on so that it would be too loud to talk. I could complain them, as I always did, that I hated bars which were so loud you couldn't hear yourself think, but at least they meant I didn't get drawn into conversations like this.

Matt continued: 'You need a girlfriend to forgive enough stuff about you. Do the same. Forgiveness is what makes adults different to children: children just forget, adults forgive.'

I wondered how Matt knew this stuff, where he had learnt it. I had always relied on him to bear grudges as much as the next man

– more so, in fact. That was half the reason I liked him so much. But what he was saying changed all that. It was like when you go to a different school from your best mate and, the next time you see him – it might only be a few days later – he's completely changed.

'You'll never have a relationship if you can't forgive,' he said. 'If you can't do that, you'll never be happy. Because people fuck up. People fuck up every day. Emma has, you have, I have, Katie has. We all have. There's enough of the now stuff to deal with without getting worked up about irrelevant stuff from the past. The alternative's being single at forty, getting bitter about everything and everyone. Is that what you want?'

'No, course not,' I said, remembering that's what Emma had told me I'd become: bitter.

In a week's time, he'd be married and flying off somewhere hot on his honeymoon; I'd be sitting on my own somewhere in a bar with a load of sad cases. And only nine days ago we'd been in exactly the same position. If it could mean getting Emma back, right now I'd take going out less any day of the week.

He went on: 'Are you sure you're not just using all this as an excuse? Are you sure you haven't just latched onto it – this idea of past indiscretions – because it's the one thing everyone can be faulted over? It provides an easy excuse. The ideal get-out clause. You've always got a good reason to end a relationship.'

'Why would I want to do that?'

'You tell me. Because you're scared?'

'Scared?'

'Yes. Scared of commitment.'

I nearly laughed. I mean, Matt accusing anyone of being scared of commitment was like Claire accusing someone of spending a lot of time doing their hair. But he was about to tie the knot. I suppose he was qualified to talk about commitment now.

'Maybe,' he said, 'you're scared of moving on. Scared of letting the past go. Scared that going out there and grabbing a future for yourself might in some way spoil your past.'

Emma said a similar thing once – that I was afraid of change.

I felt tired. I was sick of playing the game, the one that always ended like this. It's no fun any more. A barmaid came round collecting glasses. 'This one dead?' she asked Matt for some reason, nodding at one of my empties.

'You know Emma was unfaithful to me,' I blurted out.

'You didn't tell me that.'

'Well, she was. So now you know. It was a couple of months after we met; she saw her ex. That's why it's a sore point, OK. That's why I bang on about it.'

'Shit,' he said. Then, almost as if he didn't believe me: 'What do you mean, *saw*?'

'They went out for a meal – she reckoned they were still friends – and she stayed over at his place. She said she didn't shag him but some stuff did happen. She didn't waste any time telling me; it was almost as if she was pleased it *had* happened. She told me she couldn't just couldn't switch off her feelings towards him, she wished she could, but she couldn't. Then she said she was sorry, really sorry, and it was a mistake and that she hoped it wouldn't be a big deal, almost as if she was telling me she'd be late getting to the pub or had forgotten to put the bin bags out.'

'And this was how long after you started seeing each other?'

'A couple of months.'

'And how long was she seeing him?'

'Nine years.'

'I don't want to be unsympathetic here, but it's not *that* big a deal, is it? She goes out with her ex for a meal, stayed over at his house and something may or may not have happened and you've been holding it against her for all this time?'

'Something did happen, she told me that.'

'She didn't sleep with him though.'

'No, but it could have been anything else.'

'And?'

'Don't do this to me, Matt. Don't do this Shit Happens stuff. This is the one thought that has kept me going for the last week. I've imagined them fucking each other and having a good laugh at my expense.'

'Rob, it wouldn't have been like that.'

'Yes, and you know that for sure, do you?'

'From what you're saying, it all happened ages ago. It was the past. Move on.'

'Yes, well, you could say that about anything. Something happened a year ago, it's the past. Something happened a month ago, it's the past. A week. A day. Everything becomes the past if you leave it long enough.'

'It's hardly a hanging offence. What's the worst that could have

99

happened: she spent one night with someone who she'd slept with hundreds of times before anyway.'

The idea of her having slept with someone else that many times gave me a smarting feeling behind my eyes. I felt stupid, and – finally – a bit pissed. I wanted to explain to Matt how I felt, but it didn't seem like I'd done a very good job. *I know*, I thought. 'So how would you feel if right now Katie was doing the same? You wouldn't like that, would you? Say she slept with someone tonight, then it wouldn't matter tomorrow because it would all be in the past.'

'That's not the same.'

'Course it is. What if Katie was having an affair?'

Matt shifted uncomfortably. He took his pint glass by the base and looked at that, not at me, as he turned it around on the table.

'Come on, what if Katie wasn't in Birmingham? What if, right now, she was in some seedy hotel having sex?' A little part of me wanted to hurt him – no, not hurt him – just see how he reacted. *I'm single*, I wanted to shout. 'She's showering down after shagging some bloke, rubbing his semen off the inside of her legs. Tingling inside.'

Matt blinked in his right eye, that mannerism you sometimes see in people – except Matt had never done it before.

I said: 'He's bending down and kissing her goodbye through her car window in the hotel car park, and saying: I'll call you. He's, he's—'

'What do you want me to say? I'd be gutted. Course I would. But Katie's not like that, you don't know her. But if she was,' and he paused, 'if she was shagging some bloke, then she'd be doing it because she loved him and not me and, no, I wouldn't like that but it would be my fault, that I'd let things get like that. But that's not how it is, Rob. We love each other.'

It was the first time I'd ever heard him say that about Katie, or anyone. It stopped me in my tracks.

'I miss her, Matt. I miss Emma.'

Saying it made me realise just quite how much I did miss her. However much me and him, or me and anyone else, talked about it, we couldn't go anywhere but round in circles, when all the time it boiled down to that one simple truth.

'I just miss her, Matt. I never knew how much there was to forget, can't you see that. I never knew how much there was to forgive. It hurt, even thinking about it.'

'You could always ask her, you could always *have* asked her.'

I thought about Emma, her hand on another bloke's cock, and it made me feel dizzy. I saw her going down on her knees, in front of him, and I wanted to shout, to stop all this. And then I thought about *him* – whoever her next boyfriend might be; I tried to give him a face, a body. It could be someone like me, or someone like one of my friends – if he was anything like me, he'd think about me from time to time, Emma's ex. I'd be there in some vague undefined way: someone occasionally mentioned by friends, a photo in an album under the bed, a name on a postcard on the fridge. He, too, would think of me and, if he was anything like me, not mention it. Soon, he'd be laughing about the same things I did: her cutting her toe-nails on the edge of the bed, that tiny streak of ginger in her hair you could only see in a certain light, the way she snuggled her head into the pillow when she got into bed.

Maybe she'd go back out with her ex, but she hadn't spoken to him after that one night. She knew it would only upset me. Maybe we'd go back out? But no, that wouldn't happen – she'd had enough of me. What was it she said, that night we ended? 'You're impossible.'

'Sometimes I'd go weeks – months, even – without really thinking about that business with her ex. Then we'd be sitting in a restaurant – on her birthday, say – and I'd watch her pick up a menu and something out of the blue would make me think: But you got off with him. Rodney. He even had a silly name, Matt. Rodney! A comedy name if ever I heard one! I guess I took it personally. I guess I couldn't make my mind up about whether it was a big deal or not.'

'But Emma's lovely.'

Was, Matt, *was*. Not is.

Right then, I wanted to tell Matt everything, everything that ever happened between me and Emma – about how we had to sleep on the lounge floor in that cottage in Devon because there was a leak in the bedroom ceiling; about that time after we'd been in the Star all day and we went in one of those toilet cubicles and she wanked me off; about how she once left me that Post-it in the fridge saying: I love you – not because I was ever really into statutory debriefs, just because if I was honest with him, completely honest, then what happened between me and Emma wouldn't seem so bad because it wouldn't be the most important thing. It would be the second most important thing, after Matt's and my friendship. We'd talk about it, and it wouldn't all have been for nothing.

I stared at all the empties on the table in front of me – ours and other people's – and said nothing.

Instead, I had a drink.

'Talk to her,' he said. 'You could have talked to her.'

Chapter Nineteen

Sometimes it was like I was invisible.

A few minutes ago, I'd been pouring my heart out to Matt, and before that to James, and I'd felt so close to them, such a part of all this.

Now, it was as if I wasn't here at all.

We were sitting with some local lads and the conversation was going to and fro: everyone except me was speaking. I sat there and heard it to my left and my right; my mates were asking each other questions and making points and discussing stuff and it went past me, they went past me, from each direction.

I had nothing to contribute. I played no part. I was on the edge.

Different.

Alone.

Everything around me, grey.

It was that same old feeling, back again.

I was in the middle of the group but I might as well have been a million miles away from these people.

We were in another new bar on Northumberland Street and at first I looked at whoever was speaking, but I gave that up after a while. It was too much effort and all I heard was words, echoes.

Sometimes I felt that if they stood up and crossed the room they could walk *through* me.

And someone – Stevie – was talking and I watched him look round the table as he made a point, looking at Matt, then James; he was coming towards me but he looked past me, back to Matt.

I forced myself to laugh at something someone was saying somewhere – didn't know what – and I looked around again at my friends and out of the window. It was dark with drizzly rain and the car headlights were all fuzzy and I wasn't in here or out there. It was as if I was in a picture, a flat canvas, and everything around me was flat, me painted on like everything else: no colour, nothing in front and nothing behind me, not even earlier today or tomorrow, nothing to look back on or forward to, just this moment.

I tried to snap myself clear of it, looked at who was talking – it was James now – and who was listening – it was Stevie now – and smiled but they were talking about things of which I had no experience, things on which I had no opinion and I thought: How did they become like this? It was like they'd lived longer than me.

There was a conversation, a conversation that didn't involve me, and beyond that the noise of other conversations from people I didn't know and I felt myself disappearing; it was like I was falling, sinking, being sucked under.

So much of the time I sat in pubs feeling like this nowadays. Emma's words, cracked and wobbly – U2 in the flat upstairs – came back to me in the distance: 'The only thing you really love is that pub.'

I tried watching and listening again, felt my head going right to left, left to right and felt my mouth laughing and my head nodding but I wasn't here. I could have been invisible.

That was part of the reason, do you see, I liked the idea of being best man. I mean, I'm the sort of person you forget to say goodbye to after a party, the sort you forget you've met in the first place. I wanted people just for one day of my life, to look at me, to *see* me.

Katie's friends would have seen me and whispered to each other, '*That's* the best man,' and wondered what I was like.

I looked around for that girl with freckles – her lot had come in the bar shortly after us – and couldn't see her. I felt completely – and permanently – on my own. There was nothing here: just people, dozens, hundreds of them. All loud and hot and big, alive, breathing and sweating and with each other and alone and oblivious to me. All these people here, and not just here: everywhere. The pub next door, all along Northumberland Street and across this whole city, in wine bars in Fenham and Heaton and Gosforth and Jesmond, bars I'd never been to and never would, bars I couldn't even imagine – and across the whole country and the whole world, too; and in the Sun, my Sun, people I'd never met would be there now. I couldn't handle it, couldn't cope. Right then all I wanted in the world was to hug a girl and be hugged and kiss her face and lips and tits and have sex with her, not because I wanted to, not really, but because at least I'd be doing something to make me feel all the good stuff wasn't escaping and the sudden brittle intensity of coming would at least be something I'd feel low down inside me even now.

This, I remembered, is how I often felt before I met Emma. I'd always try to get off with girls, even if all I really wanted to do was talk to them. Just so I felt *something*.

Everyone carried on as they were.

My friends carried on as they were.

Someone was using the phrase 'five a day'. What was that, five cigarettes? Five pints?

Portions of fruit, apparently!

I had a big swig, lit a cigarette. I wanted that feeling I got sometimes when I'd just started another pint and just sparked up a cigarette. That sudden click. The invisible feeling went then. Me, off the flat canvas. Everything became *more* than one-dimensional. The warm feeling, a whole pint, a whole cigarette – and the evening not yet over. That moment was the best feeling in the world.

In that moment, I felt differently to myself yet the essence of who I really was.

Like a perfect state of balance.

As if, somehow, there was more still to come – more of tonight and more of everything. As if, somehow, there was a point to it all.

I was even funny in that moment. Even in a group, if that feeling came, I'd be there: straight to the centre of it. Interesting. Funny. People responding.

So quick, though, and it was gone. And so soon after, it got foggy. Years ago, that feeling could last the whole evening. Now it sometimes lasted a few minutes, but usually not even that. And mostly it was precisely that long: me laughing out loud, knowing: *This* is the moment.

I drank quickly and smoked, striving for that moment. It used to be the fourth pint – when I lived here you could set your watch by it – but I'd had a lot more than that tonight and nowadays I never could tell when or whether I'd get it at all. Sometimes it could take six or eight pints and sometimes the booze might simply make me feel ill and nothing was funny – certainly not me. And all I could do then was keep drinking because I wouldn't want to stop, and besides, what else was there to do.

Chapter Twenty

That girl with freckles was standing near us with a couple of friends.

Forget Mrs Married.

Forget Demi.

Forget Emma.

This girl was gorgeous, and within a few feet of me now.

The back of her arms were white and a little plump; I could see a line where the whiteness stopped and the freckles started. Who was it she reminded me of? Someone. Her breasts bounced ever so slightly as she moved and I wanted to stand close in front of her and kiss her face, her neck, her arms. Then move down into those breasts, hear her moan, gasp. Our eyes met momentarily once again.

'I'm feeling lucky,' I said to Matt and laughed noisily so she could see me laughing. Then I looked back at her and she broke off for a second from talking to her friends and looked at me, I'm sure she did, and our eyes held contact. My heart started racing. *Yes.*

If only Claire was here. Girls were sometimes more willing to talk to you if you had a girl in your group. She used to complain like mad that we invited her out on lads' nights for that reason. 'You only want me as a decoy,' she always used to say.

Later, she was standing with us. This girl. Well, between us and her friends.

This is how it had been the night I'd met Emma. I'd been pissed off with work and gone out and there she was. We'd talked and I'd asked for her number and she'd given it to me.

It could happen again tonight. Then this girl was talking to James. Didn't know how, but she was. That was good, it'd be a way in for me, and he wouldn't be trying to get off with her. He once told me he could never be unfaithful to Sarah. 'Physically, I don't think I could,' he'd said. Which was dead sweet, and pathetic.

Mrs Married, the poor cow, would be in the restaurant now with her friends but soon she'd be home, alone again. Just the kids, asleep upstairs. And her sitting there, remembering her husband. What a shit I was, saying that stuff. But I wasn't a mind-reader: how was I supposed to know her husband had gone tits up. Besides, I couldn't do anything about it now. There was no point in letting it spoil all our evenings. Onwards, upwards.

I sidled across.

'You all right, Dukester?' I asked. Then, to her: 'Sorry, I don't mean to be rude, but we can't talk to you. We're on a stag night and there's no fraternising with the enemy.'

'Who's the groom?' she asked, smiling. We pointed at Matt – him and Stevie were with a group of blokes by the bar – and she gave him a long look but didn't say anything. I wanted James to leave us. I tried to will it. *Leave us, James. Leave*.

'And who's his best man?'

'That bloke with him,' I said.

Stevie had his arm round Matt and was laughing animatedly. She looked longer at him than she had at Matt.

'It's an important job,' she said. 'He's got to look after the stag.'

Stevie came to the end of whatever story it was he was holding court with, and ran his fingers through his hair. She kept looking at him.

'Yes, partners in crime,' James said.

I looked at Matt and Stevie. The groom and his best man. I know him better than you, I thought. If we were to talk about all the things we've done together, I'd have more stories. He's *my* friend.

'What's the best man got planned for the groom then?' she asked.

'Usual sort of thing,' I said, before James could get a word out. 'Get him horribly drunk, get the names of all his exes tattooed on his forehead then strip him and leave him tied to a lamp-post in the Bigg Market.'

She laughed. It sounded great. See, I could be funny. I know I'd cocked it up with that last girl, but that wasn't deliberate and this one was one laughing *with* me.

'Come along if you want,' I said, trying to sound casual. But I had no breath, I felt like how I had that night I met Emma and she'd joked about the wine being like paint-stripper. 'You can be our honorary bloke. It's easy to do. Just as long as you can drink lager, name a football player or two and burp occasionally.'

107

'That Beckham played a blinder,' she said, drinking from her pint.

I laughed and smiled at her. *Leave, James, please.*

Bet she's embarrassed about those freckles, I thought. She needn't have been: they were dead sexy. Her skin was mottled brown, like a polished egg; she had the lightest covering of hair on her arms – just down, really – and I wanted to blow on it gently. I gritted my teeth, felt my fists clench: it was all I could do to stop myself touching her.

A couple more of her friends came over; they were celebrating someone's twenty-fifth. We all shuffled around and, when we stood still again, she was standing next to me. Before, she had been a person away; now, she was next to me. Surely, that wasn't a coincidence? We'd had eye contact, I had asked her to join us for the evening and if she was smart that was enough. Her arms were a few inches away from mine. I rolled my sleeves up, that our skins might brush. I couldn't wait any longer.

'Seriously, why don't you and your friends come along?'

'The groom probably wouldn't approve, girls on a stag night.'

'He wouldn't mind.'

'What about the best man? Would it be OK with him? How would he feel about it?'

Fuck the best man, I thought.

'He'll be fine. Come on, come.'

'We don't know where we're going later anyway.'

I thought of her in a club, somewhere hot and sweaty. Her drunk with a bloke, someone I couldn't imagine. Then, later, the sex and, after that, the quiet gentleness. I wanted it to be me.

I wanted to touch her arms. They would be soft and warm, like a fresh bread roll. I wanted her to put her fingers in my hair, feel them on my scalp. Know that she was like this just with me.

Those freckles.

Her hair was slightly red. Stevie, I knew, would fancy her something rotten when he saw her.

And then I remembered who it was she reminded me of.

Abi.

Chapter Twenty-one

I first saw Abi the summer Dad died.

I was fourteen and had a holiday job in some stables which Mum had arranged – she said I needed to be kept busy – and we were taking hay to the big house behind the church. Abi went up there to ride the horses.

She was a year younger than me, apparently, but she looked two or three years older.

She had sandy hair in a bob and was wearing tight jeans and a tight top with some of the buttons undone. Underneath, there was something white. When she bent forward I could see cleavage. I stood where I would be able to see it. I knew from porno mags what came after the cleavage. She was red from the exertion and the freckles on her forehead and cheeks and arms were beaded with sweat. There were flecks of hay in her hair. It was a hot, still day without a breath of wind.

'I know what you want to do,' Jack, the farmer, said. 'You want to take her to that haystack in Cowslips, don't you?'

Cowslips was a field down in the valley and, yes, I did. I thought about it every night in bed. I often thought about it at other times but didn't let myself dwell on it then; I saved it until I was on my own, somewhere quiet and warm. I saved the deliciousness of it. I thought about me and Abi climbing into the haystack, building a nest. Us stripping. Me telling her about my Dad. I thought about us kissing a lot and I knew I would touch her: touch her titties and her fanny, but I didn't know exactly how I'd touch her there. Thinking about it made me feel strange, all empty and hungry. I'd try to think of how it would be, sex, and never could be quite sure. Often that summer I couldn't sleep.

'Yes, that's what you'd like to do, you dirty little bugger,' Jack had said; I enjoyed him saying that. I always exaggerated the way I stared at Abi when I knew he was watching me. I was fourteen now, after all.

The next time I saw her we were mucking out the horse boxes. She was standing just a few feet from me. I noticed quite how many freckles she had on her arms and how red they were from the sun, and I imagined myself rubbing cream on her later that night, her in suspenders. My nostrils flared. She looked at me; I looked away, and carried on working.

That summer I saw Abi a lot. I would be sitting on the back of the tractor and she would be riding a horse or walking away from the big house in her jodhpurs carrying a whip or a riding hat. I would see her and feel a strange sensation deep inside me, one I'd never felt before. It was about the time I started masturbating.

Everything else I wanted – the motorbike, the exam passes, catching more fish than anyone else – all of it just disappeared after I saw Abi. She was what I wanted now. I'd be good to her. I'd take her to pubs when we got a bit older and eventually nightclubs. We'd have sex in the field and she – lying on her back looking up at the sun – would scream, like that woman did in that film.

I used to think about her all the time that summer, then I'd feel guilty that I wasn't thinking about Dad more.

Then school started again and I stopped working at the stables. I used to go up there on my bike when I thought I might see her, but I never did. I figured she must have moved away. I started fancying a girl who worked in the post office and felt slightly guilty about it at first: I wanted lust to be something I had just for Abi. I thought of her sometimes when I wanked and sometimes I alternated it with the girl in the post office so I didn't feel like I was completely abandoning her. There was something very comforting about how I felt when I imagined her; there wasn't any embarrassment.

Then one of my mates sold me a German porno mag and I started thinking about the girls in that and, after a while, some of them and the girls from the post office and Abi all at the same time together.

We moved house.

I stayed on at school and passed my exams.

I never did get that motorbike.

Chapter Twenty-two

I was leaning on Matt, my arm round him. There had to be a woman here for me, had to be. That wasn't too much to ask, was it? Then through the bodies I saw her; she'd got her back to me but I'd recognise her anywhere. Wanted her to turn round so I could see those freckles. She hadn't gone, she was still here. Matt was talking to some bloke; I couldn't understand what he was saying. It wasn't supposed to be like this.

'She's still here,' I said, but he wasn't listening. I turned back to her and Stevie was with her. Stevie! I took my arm off Matt. 'You OK?' he asked. I walked nearer to where they were. So many people. Bumped into a few; no one cared.

Felt queasy. If I get off with her – start going out with her – maybe I wouldn't need to keep getting pissed? I'd have got hammered again tonight, but that was OK, I wouldn't have met her if I hadn't; but I wouldn't need to *keep* doing it. Not that going out with Emma stopped me.

She was looking at Stevie all doe-eyed. Staring up at him with the look she had given me, only now it was more intense. It was *the look* all right. Didn't know what they were saying but they were smiling at each other like a couple of teenagers.

You can't do this to me. Not with Stevie. What about a few minutes ago?

I moved nearer. Watched. She was doing all the talking and he was listening, appearing interested as he always did. She smiled, he smiled. Her head was tilted upwards slightly towards his. She was aware of nothing else.

Don't fall for it, I thought. He's like this with everyone. He once said to me: 'Most blokes just talk to women; I listen to them.'

The smart arse.

Any other girl and I'd have thought: Well played, Stevie, good effort. But not *her*. She was going to make me feel better. She reminded me of Abi. I didn't want her to be made to feel special by someone who didn't really think she was. I went and stood behind them, but they didn't even notice.

'So how many sisters *have* you got then?' he was asking. He asked about her family, her flat, her job. Always about her. And he always listened to what she said, almost as if he *was* interested.

Then it struck me what irritated me about him: he never gave anything away about himself, not really. Sure, he'd happily tell me about that time he got a blow-job on a roundabout or how painful his piles had been or how he'd virtually turned into a stalker when Vicki left him – but he was like that with everyone and you could never get behind that to what things really meant to him. I'd known him all this time yet he was still a stranger. When did we talk, really talk? Never.

They laughed a lot. Loads of eye contact. I might as well not have been there. He knew I was trying to get off with her earlier; he was doing this deliberately. Why couldn't it be my night just for once? It had to be about you, Stevie, didn't it.

'I'm going to be your honorary bloke for the rest of the night,' she was saying to him. 'I can drink pints. Look,' she went on, taking his pint and slurping from it. I wondered if she knew she was drinking from the same side he had been. When she finished, she wiped her mouth and went 'Aaargh', like an old man. Then she smiled at Stevie.

It was going to be *him* she slept with tonight. He will pull like he said he would. *He'll* be the one who feels her skin, who kisses those freckles. It wasn't fair. I'd never get the chance to sleep with her again after tonight. Now, as I had about Abi, I'd always feel as if I'd missed a chance. That fact would never *not* be there now, and it would eat away at me. I realised she hadn't even noticed me. Not earlier, not now, not at all. Tomorrow, she wouldn't remember me even if someone asked her about the blokes Stevie was with. Even if she didn't sleep with Stevie – which, let's face it, she would – she would remember *him*, not me. That was the way it always was. 'He was *niiice*,' she'd say to her friends, her eyes narrowing slightly. No one ever called me nice, not in that way.

When they called me 'nice' it was in a silly-but-probably-harmless sort of way. But no one had even said that for a while.

Chapter Twenty-three

I saw Abi once more. I was at a party – must have been when we were in the lower sixth – and when I went into the kitchen to get a drink there she was.

She was laughing and swigging a big bottle of Thunderbird. It's Abi, I thought. Her hair was just the same, although it didn't have the flecks of hay in it, and she was slightly chubbier. She looked four or five years older than me now. She carried on talking to her mates. 'All right,' I said, and went back into the living room. I stood, silent, tingling, knowing Abi was in the kitchen.

Later, she came out of the toilet when I was waiting outside. My stomach knotted. 'All right,' I said, hoping she would remember the horses, the farm, that summer. 'Hi,' she said, walking off. I smelt her perfume as she passed. The smell of her was in the bathroom, too, and I sat on the edge of the bath and wanked.

When I went downstairs she was sitting with a group of people on the floor listening to music.

'It's shit here,' one of my mates said to me. 'Let's go somewhere else.'

Somewhere else at that time of night invariably meant the service station to play on the amusements.

'This might liven up,' I said. 'Besides, what about the girls?'

I could see them in the kitchen. Abi looked pissed and was talking to some bloke I vaguely recognised as having been a couple of years above me at school.

'I wouldn't touch them with yours,' one of my friends said. 'They're slags. Dave Hendry's shagged all of them.'

I hated it, that Dave Hendry might have shagged Abi. He was a right wanker. But it was good news, too; if she went all the way, I might have more chance.

I looked at Abi and tried to get back the feeling of two summers before, but it seemed a long time ago. I felt a bit of a weirdo at having had a wank in some stranger's house.

And I realised, then, that sleeping with her would be something I'd never do – *ever* – which made me feel all hollow inside.

Then some gatecrashers arrived and there was a fight and we left and went to the service station to play on the amusements.

Chapter Twenty-four

'You're obviously not used to drinking pints,' Stevie said, touching her chin, 'you've got it round your mouth.'

I wanted to yell: Don't touch her. Then, because I didn't have anything else to do, I stared straight at her and kept staring; no harm now, she wasn't going to notice. There was just one thing on her mind: Stevie.

She shook her hair and memories of Abi flooded back to me. Things I'd forgotten. The redness in her hair. Brushing against her once, and feeling my teeth grind. Trying to work so hard I forgot about Dad, and failing. Getting sunburnt.

That was when it occurred to me to punch Stevie. I'd never been in a fight before, not even as a kid, but it must be good to know that I did at least have it in me. I was nearly thirty – this might be the last chance I'd get.

If you knew there was a chance I'd hit you, you wouldn't have done this, would you, Stevie. You started this. It's your fault.

Yes, imagine it: throwing a punch, kicking, feeling the wind go from me as another man's head rammed into my gut and we fell backwards across the tables. Us getting pulled apart and standing up and facing each other, held back, neither of us willing to back down. Falling backwards, locked with another man, hitting the ground wrestling and punching even as we fell. Feeling my fist connect, feeling the resistance, knowing the next day where that soreness in my knuckles came from. Yes, that would be something. Tasting blood on my lips. The only time I ever tasted it nowadays was when my gums bled in the mornings.

But I wouldn't know where to start or what to do. Would I punch or kick? In the stomach or in the face – and if it was in the face, where? On the side or straight on? I wouldn't want to hurt him too much – but it had to be a proper punch. He had to at least feel it, feel me, if there was to be any point in doing it. Otherwise, I'd know afterwards I hadn't done it properly and that would eat away at me: knowing that the one time I'd had a fight I'd gone into it half-heartedly and so it wasn't even a proper one.

This is so me, I thought. Thinking about stuff instead of doing it.

Thinking about how much I hated my job, but never changing it.

Thinking about moving out of the flat and getting somewhere of my own, but never quite getting round to it.

Thinking about drinking less, but never actually doing it.

No more.

I was tired of being walked over. I couldn't run this time. And if I stuck up for myself, I'd salvage something from tonight. Dignity, maybe, or pride or self-respect? A bit of respect from other blokes. People look at men with black eyes differently. It wouldn't matter if I lost the fight. I'd get over it. I'd live. It wasn't as if I was a stranger to a few aches and pains.

Stevie had leant in and was whispering in her ear.

Surely at least once in each man's life it was right to fight.

My once was now.

That anger, that restlessness, that feeling of being invisible, all those feelings I couldn't understand – this would be where I could put them. I'd do this and in a few minutes or even seconds it would be over and those feelings would be gone and I could relax and get on with the rest of my life.

If I didn't confront him now, I'd never forget it. What was Mum's expression? 'Sometimes you've just got to go with your heart, Robert.'

Well I am, Mum. I'm going with my heart. I won't be pushed around any more. When was the last time I did anything that made you proud?

This, I thought, is what it's really like to be a man. Sure and right and the rage rising in me: rage at Stevie and that girl and me, me, for not feeling this for the last thirty years. Not doing anything about how I felt all that time.

The pair of them were in hysterics now; he put his arm round her and she sank in towards him. Cocky bastard. I'd seen him do that so many times before. Working the magic. Some mate. All we ever did together was get pissed, and nowadays we didn't even do that very often. He'd upstaged me since the day we'd met. Not any more. Not any fucking more.

116

I went up to them. My heart was racing. Fuck knows what they were talking about – it was all quiet and close and I was out of it – but whatever it was they made no attempt to stop. I moved between them and stared at her until they actually managed to drag their gazes off each other and turn to me.

'How's it going?' I asked her.

She didn't say anything. I still might as well have not been there.

'All right,' Stevie said, then waited for me to go. That's what he was doing, I knew how he operated. But I wasn't going.

'So this man's looking after you, is he?' I said staring at her then him. 'You look after ladies well, don't you, Stevie.'

And then – this wasn't what I was planning but it just came out – I burped. A long loud sea lion burp. I started laughing.

Stevie didn't say anything – he certainly didn't laugh or pat me on the back or say, 'More tea, Vicar?' like he usually did. And this girl, she just said: 'Charming,' and looked away from both of us. I wobbled, put my legs apart.

'You'll have to excuse Rob,' Stevie said. 'He doesn't get out very often. He can't take his drink either.'

So what if I was pissed. It wasn't a crime. Like you've never had too much to drink. It wasn't that long ago you were pissed once for three days solid. 'Told you about his wife, has he?' I said.

Neither of them laughed. But I couldn't stop. I took a swig of beer and some of it dribbled out of my mouth onto my shirt.

'Wouldn't be so bad, but she's got leukaemia. Poor Stevie's gutted about it, aren't you, mate? Looks like he's bearing up though,' I said, putting my arm round him. He bristled and I felt the tension in his shoulders like a piece of wood.

I burped again, this time in Stevie's ear. She looked at me like I was pond scum, and then at Stevie. 'Nice meeting you,' she said. I didn't know if it was directed at him, or at me and she was being sarcastic because it always sounded like that when women said it on a Saturday night. But I saw her expression and I knew it was him, of course.

'Might see you a bit later then,' she said. Then she went.

'If she's stupid enough to believe that, you're better off shot of her, mate,' I said.

'She didn't believe you, she just thought you were a twat. And you are. What the fuck did you do that for? I was getting on well with her.'

'Just testing her reaction. I've got your interest at heart. They're like kestrels: set them free and if they come back, they love you. She doesn't look as if she's coming back though. Ah well, suppose you're stuck with us. Onwards, upwards.'

Better that she wouldn't sleep with either of us than not with me.

'Hardly surprising if she doesn't come back, is it? Why the hell did you tell her I was married? And that stuff about leukaemia – that's sick. You're sick.'

'No, I'm not, mate, not yet, but I will be after a couple more of these.' I held my pint up – a little spilt; I hated seeing it fall to the floor.

'You're a prick sometimes,' Stevie said. 'Piss off and sober up somewhere.'

He'd never talked to me like this before. I spread my legs again for balance and, deep down, got the feeling that this would be something I'd remember and regret in the morning. But Stevie couldn't just go round nicking other people's women. He needed to be told. I was angry and he should know. The anger might be about more than just him, but he was as good a place to start as any.

'You do realise I was going to get off with that girl, don't you?' I said.

'Yeah right, sure you were,' he sneered.

'I've been flirting with her all evening.'

'Well, you've obviously worked the Purcell magic there then.'
Cocky bastard.

'You couldn't bear it to be someone else who got off with the good-looking girl, could you? You had to take her off me, didn't you?'

'What do you mean "take her off you"? She wasn't interested in you. Women don't generally go for blokes who burp in their faces.'

'What, and she appreciated your lines? She'd have seen through them a mile off.'

'They weren't lines. We were having a conversation. You ought to try it sometime.'

The tosser. This was so Stevie, this certainty. He told me at college he wasn't going to do any work for the first two years – and didn't. Still got a 2:1. He walked into a good job and got promotion after promotion. He played football, went out with the lads, had a great social life and the women loved him, they fell at his feet like flies. He really was one of those people who had it easy, had it all.

I remembered how I struggled with the college work; how hard it was, how it didn't come naturally and how it had been the same, all of it, ever since. Work and women and mates and now Stevie was Matt's best man. You couldn't even give me that, could you. I felt angry that he'd never known, never would know, what it was like for the rest of us.

'Must be a bit of a comedown for you not to have pulled by now. You're running out of time, pretty boy.'

'Plenty of time for me and freckle-face,' he laughed knowingly. He said it coolly as if he knew there was – which there always was for Stevie. And don't call her freckle-face, I thought. She's got a name.

'Yes, well you're the good-looking one, you know all about pulling.' It occurred to me no one – certainly none of the lads – had ever actually told him he was good-looking. I grabbed his wrist and pulled his watch up to my face, close to my eyes. It was blurred, gradually taking shape – ten something. Not long to go.

'Ten, and the women aren't swooning round you Stevie. How are you coping? I mean, it's not like you to not be the centre of attention.' I remembered that girl – what was her name – the one who said the same to me earlier. 'And you have to be the centre of attention, don't you? You and your T-shirt and your big black belt and your oh-so-beautiful hair. Not working tonight, though, is it?'

I touched his hair, the black curls that I'd always wanted. I must have touched it inadvertently a thousand times before – playing football, play-fighting, falling onto and over each other in pubs; we even cut it once in the third year when we were drunk. But this time it was different.

He looked at me, a holding stare. Confused.

'Yes, you couldn't dream of coming out and not having the women swoon round you, could you, Stevie?'

It was all so easy for him; he had it so good. I wished I was him. But I wasn't, I was me. This.

'I'm glad that girl went. Abi.'

'Abi?'

'Yes, the one with freckles.'

'You mean Becky.'

He was enjoying this. *I know something that you don't know.*

'Whatever. Welcome to the real world. It's just funny that this didn't do the trick for you this time.' I said, touching his hair again,

119

snatching at it. He grabbed my hand, my wrist, and I felt his grip. We looked at each other, old friends. His eyes drilled into me, that brilliant green that the women always banged on about.

'Oh, you're so masterful, Stevie – is that what the women like?' I laughed, but he didn't say anything. And he didn't let go of my wrist. 'So are you going to let us into your secret tonight, then, us mere ...' The words wouldn't come – what it is, when you die, when you don't live forever? What is it? 'Us twats,' I said. 'We all can't wait to hear how you do it. You're so special. We're all so glad you're here. This group, see this group,' and I waved my arm round, hitting some people in the process, 'we would be nothing without you.'

I thought: I've been building up to this – whatever this is – for ten years.

'Let go of my hand,' I said.

He held it.

'Stevie, I mean it, I'm not joking, let go of my hand.'

He held it and I felt his strength. You only had to look at Stevie to know there was power behind those shoulders, though it still surprised me, feeling it. If we wrestled he'd soon be on top. Holding me down. The thought of him hitting me frightened me. You saw it in films, the stronger man on top, punching and punching and punching and the smaller one just lying there getting it.

'Yes, or what?' he said. 'What are you going to do, Rob, if I don't let go?'

And so we stood for a few seconds, neither of us knowing what to do or say or what happened next, where it went from here. Because neither of us had been in this situation before. At least, not with each other.

I tried to pull my hand away but he held it.

'What is it with you?' he said. 'Why are you being like this to me tonight? You've done nothing but snipe all day. Have you got a problem with me?'

It occurred to me that this could be the end now, a way out. I could say 'Sorry, I'm upset over Emma, sorry I'm being a dickhead,' and we'd go back to how we were and no more would probably ever be said of it. But something kept me going. You talking to that girl who looked like Abi, that's my problem, and I'm pissed again, all right, I'm pissed and you've got it easy and everything's perfect for you and I hate myself, Stevie, I hate myself. That's why.

'What are you talking about, sniping? I haven't sniped,' I said.

'You've never really liked me, have you?'

So typical of Stevie, he couldn't bear even one person not liking him!

'What? You're talking bollocks!'

'And you've got a chip on your shoulder about something, Rob, you always have had. You always seem to take it out on me. Doing this now, on Matt's stag weekend, it's pathetic. You're pathetic.'

How dare you? Make out you're the only one who wants Matt to have a good time. The only one who's worried about spoiling his weekend. As if I would do that. 'Matt's having a great time, for what it's worth,' I said. 'He told me a few minutes ago. Not that you'd have noticed, you've been too busy with that girl.'

'Pathetic,' Stevie repeated, shaking his head.

'Well, sorry for not being as perfect as you. If you're so perfect why do you think Vicki chucked you?'

I knew again that tomorrow I'd regret saying that and starting all of this, all of tonight.

Vicki was the one girl I'd seen him close to. She'd chucked him because he spent too much time with his friends – with us – and not enough with her. He was pretty cut up when it happened. Or so he said. But Stevie had never been cut up about anyone in all his life. He had another girlfriend within a month. Another stunner.

I felt his grip on my wrist tighten. He didn't say anything. It was like he'd lost the power of speech. Stevie: who was never short of something to say, usually something funny. Again, I could have left it there. I could have said sorry and it could have ended, but something drove me on. The thought of him next weekend at the top table in his morning suit, standing up and banging his spoon on the table, the thought of how freckle-face had looked at him. I had to stick up for myself. He had to be told. And she *was* flirting with me earlier.

'That's you all over,' I said. 'You think you can have any woman you want. You think the sun shines out of your arse, you always have. Well, I've got news for you – we don't all worship the ground you walk on. Some of us wouldn't give a shit if you weren't even here. We'd still enjoy it.'

I felt like telling him I'd got off with Vicki. Of course I hadn't – she was far too pretty to even look at me, but I felt like making it up, like I had with that stuff about him having a wife and her having leukaemia.

'Where's Vicki now, then? She's not here, is she? She's in

121

Australia with some bloke. Wonder if he's as good-looking as you?'

I felt stupid, keeping on mentioning his looks – like a kid in awe of an older boy. He tightened his grip on my wrist and it hurt. I went to snatch my wrist away, but we stumbled a step or two and his drink got knocked off the table. It smashed, sounding very loud, but nothing around us changed. Except Stevie was staring at me, and I didn't recognise the stare. I was frightened. His left hand grabbed my shirt and I felt myself pulled closer into him. And it occurred to me that he was left-handed. So you, Stevie, to be left-handed. I saw his face, angry, flushed and new.

He said: 'You're a wanker, you know that. A fucking wanker.'

I felt my heart pumping. No breath. Not pissed now, just wondering: How did this happen? How did it come to this?

'Take it easy,' I said. 'We're just talking.'

'Talking, yes?' He shook me like a doll.

I swayed and he held me. I wasn't sure whether he was holding me up, supporting me, as he had so many times before, or whether he was stopping me getting away. Either way, I knew if he let go, I'd fall.

'Come on then, let's talk,' he said and with the hand on my shirt he pushed me and I fell backwards. I stumbled, regained balance. He barely flicked his wrist and it knocked me back. He stayed staring at me. I wondered if this was a fight. Doing something back seemed wrong – what would I do? – and it might make this worse; I couldn't believe it, me fighting, me fighting with Stevie. The taste of lager, acid and tart. I smiled at him. But he didn't smile back, he just gazed at me, and he didn't look how he usually did; instead he appeared older. Older than me. He looked, and it was the first time I'd ever noticed, not like a student or someone in their twenties, but like a man. This must be what people saw when they met him. It struck me how big his curls were. His neck was thick and there was a vein pumping on the side of his forehead. I wanted this to stop now; it had gone far enough, too far. Wanted things to go back to how they were ten minutes ago, but it felt as if a lot would have to happen now before we could get back there. Like we'd have to go round something. Fear paralysed me. Then there was a slap on my face. Stevie had slapped my face. It sounded loud, though no one around us noticed. I wanted to cry. It came from nowhere, and it hurt, it hurt so much. An alarm clock waking me from sleep.

'Come on, then,' he said, rebalancing himself. 'You want to talk about Vicki, do you? Mention her again, go on, say her name again and see what happens.'

I had nothing to say; I wanted to be at home. The next few seconds would change everything: tonight and me and Stevie and the rest of us.

All that stuff before about pride and guts and self-respect disappeared, leaving one consuming thought: I'm scared. Just let me get away, let this pass without pain and I'll be different. I couldn't fight. Fear choked me.

Then Matt was with us. Between us. Thank God. He didn't have a clue what was going on. He put his arm round Stevie and Stevie relaxed, his shoulders went back to the shape they had been before, his face loosened, his neck got smaller. That vein in his forehead disappeared. Even so, he was still bigger than Matt – and Matt was bigger than me.

'We've run out of kitty money,' Matt said, smiling at Stevie. 'Call yourself a best man.'

'Sorry, I've been distracted.'

I thought: I would have done the kitty better than this.

I am pathetic. I am!

'I'll fill up the kitty, shall I,' Stevie said, walking off and, as he went, he sneered at me. Sneered.

Nothing more was said. No explanation. He just walked off.

I watched him go across to the bar and I felt stupid and sad and confused again, like this wasn't the end of whatever it was that had happened. I went to the toilet and half of the piss went over the floor, but I wasn't sure whether that was because I was shaking or just because I was rat-arsed. It wasn't as if it was unusual, missing the urinal. I went into a cubicle and sat on the bog and stared at the walls as they shone and span. The sober feeling of a little while before had long gone, and I found myself back to the drunk feeling. It felt horrible, but normal. The walls continued to shine and spin. And Stevie was out there, hating me. Someone I'd known for years might never talk to me. Maybe, right now, he'd be saying to Matt: It's either him or me.

And the walls shone and spun.

Stevie could literally kill me. That happened in fights. I'd never seen him in one but you could tell he could handle himself. He might be biding his time. Waiting. The minute I went back out or when we were walking to the next pub or later, last thing, when we'd come out of the club or wherever we ended up, he could go for me. Wait until I was out of it, pretend to the others he was taking me down an alley to help me be sick or have a slash – as he had done so many times – and beat me. Beat me in the dark and leave me on the floor with the bins and the chip wrappers and the blood and sick and piss – mine and other people's – and I'd wake up tomorrow there, in that gutter.

I felt like I'd fucked up: not in an ordinary, Saturday-night sort of way, but big-time. I blew my nose and spat and wondered if I was going to be sick but no, nothing came out when I hung my head over the bowl; it would be tomorrow morning, I should know that by now. I went back out, back into the noise and the people. Out there, it was like nothing had happened: the people were still drinking, still smiling, the same people and different ones, too, and I walked through them, the Saturday-night crowd, sweaty and close; somewhere that Travis song 'Driftwood' played; I moved nervously, still shaking, through the backs and the fronts and the faces and the tits and the arms and the wooden pillars and noise and fear and people all around until I got through and went to my group – Stevie centre-stage – where I stood on the edge and swayed. They didn't notice. Someone just asked: 'Whose round is it?'

Chapter Twenty-five

Oasis, one of the biggest bands in the world. Knebworth, 1996. A hundred thousand people. I looked around, and walked around, and there wasn't a single person there but me.

My friends had abandoned me. It was the first band we'd been to since we'd left college five years before, but they were somewhere in the middle of all these people dancing. I was standing at the side. I'd been so looking forward to seeing them; I wanted to spend every second with them, talking to them.

I was trying to have an evening without beer or cigarettes but they were all I could think about. I fought it and, for a while, won. Later, when I had a drink and stood on the side, smoking, it didn't feel any better. The cigarette burnt down and the beer went.

I stood there alone.

Couples dancing, couples holding hands, couples arm in arm, couples kissing.

I couldn't bear to look at them.

This isn't how it should feel at a concert. I should feel how I used to: that I was part of this, that we all were, that we'd all come to see this band together.

I tried going back to my friends, stood in those hundred thousand people. But I felt it again – loneliness, so complete that there was nothing else.

I bought another drink and went back to the edge. When I drank the loneliness fell back a bit.

Then Oasis sang 'Wonderwall' and wave after wave of it washed over me. It was always there, waiting, watching. I just had to let my guard down for a second, and there it was. It was like the boss once said, talking about the competition at work. 'They're always there, snapping at your heels.' He looked tired when he said it, and it was the first time I had ever seen him look tired. I wondered why he'd told me. I realised then that, for me, the loneliness would always be there, snapping at my heels. It wasn't like I could run away from it: that's how loneliness worked.

Sometimes, after I'd been drinking all day, I'd collapse on my bed in the early evening and I'd wake about three am when the loneliness would be back, hovering over me. I would go to the bathroom, just to get moving, turn on the tap and look in the mirror and my face would be red and blotched and the drunkenness would have gone out of me; all that was left was the empty feeling. I'd splash water from the cold tap over my face and not feel it, then turn the tap off and dry my face. I'd go back to my room and lie down and know there was a hangover coming, know that I hadn't eaten properly for days, that I'd be constipated, weak, sick. Sometimes I put my hand on my chest and felt my little heart beating fast and erratically, fast and erratically, like that of a startled rabbit and I knew, then, the way I was living was killing me.

Chapter Twenty-six

My head fell forwards. I reined it back. Felt it going forwards again. Reined it back. Wooah. Stood. Concentrated on standing. Feet apart. The music had got loud. Didn't know what the song was. Busy. Noisy. Pushing.

'I'm pissed, Matt,' I said, and the words were slow, slurred. Heard them coming back to me, a voice through water.

'You did right choosing Newcastle. For your stag weekend, for your stag weekend and eleven years ago because otherwise, otherwise, we wouldn't be here.'

'You up for a club?' he asked.

'Course,' I said, swaying. We weren't in the Cross Keys any more. We were somewhere else, busier. A bar in the Bigg Market – or had we been in there earlier and were on the Quayside now? Music pounding.

'You do realise you're running out of time, Rob,' Matt said, pointing towards a girl on a sofa. She can't have been much over eighteen. She was wearing a short skirt and had dyed blonde hair, though half of it had grown out. 'Why don't you go and work your magic on her? Go on, go and work the magic, Rob.'

'You taking the piss?'

'No, I mean it, go on.'

It would be funny. I ran my fingers through my hair. Wondered if I looked how Stevie did when he did it. She was with some thin girl who had dyed red hair. It had grown out too. The girl I liked was concentrating on what the thin one was saying. I imagined her doing the same to me. That would be nice.

The music changed, threw me off balance. I felt sick. I'd want to take her back to the hotel straight away. No more booze. I wanted to be in the bed. I lurched to one side and felt the drink wash round in my glass. It was like I was full of liquid and that too was wash-ing – sploshing – around in me. Nauseous. No more booze. Matt thrust another pint into my spare hand.

'Buy you another one too if you go and talk to her.'

I fished around in my coat pocket and found my glasses. I didn't need them, but had bought a trendy little pair a while before I met Emma as girls seemed to like them. 'Maybe a half,' I said, walking towards her, pushing through. Some of the people moved aside, some didn't. Squeezed past, the music pounding and the cleavages, close, so close to cleavages. Kept walking, walking towards this girl pretty and warm who looked at you and listened and had that cleav-age and legs under that skirt and knickers under that that I'd be on my knees in front of, and the boys would think it dead funny and no Emma, forget Emma, fuck her. I went round some big bloke, was-n't going to bump into him, that's for sure – and there she was. Our eyes met; I tried to hold it, tried to hold . . . I was there, on her. She stayed sitting. I stood. I was above her.

'Please can I have a fag please?' I bellowed.

She looked up, startled. Young. Her friend was walking off with some bloke.

'I've bought about four hundred packets but that lot have smoked them.' I pointed around, wanting her to know who my friends were. But they weren't there, or I couldn't see them. She offered me one. A good sign. She hadn't just pointed to the box, but picked it up and held it out towards me. 'Thanks,' I said. 'I'm giving up. Tomorrow. Always tomorrow, hey?' I stood up straight. Tried to puff my chest out. Swayed.

'I'm supposed to be giving up, too,' she said. 'I'm not doing very well.' She sounded like that bloke in the hotel. At last, a local girl.

She waited for me to speak but I didn't have anything to say. I hadn't expected a conversation. Just my luck. She lit up. She looked barely old enough to be smoking in the first place, let alone giving up.

'Stick with it, you're doing fine,' I said, lighting up – it tasted strong. I realised I must sound like her dad.

I felt sleepy. Knew there was something – tiredness or sickness or a hangover – behind this, waiting for me. Thought about leaving, giving this a miss. My hotel room, water by the bed, asleep, sleep. Could probably make it back on my own if I went now. If I left, I might remember something of tonight, come tomorrow. Asleep,

128

then sober. But hungover – no, no way. Get the feeling back. Keep it, need it, need more drink. I finished the vodka. Warmth and goodness streamed back into me. Look at me, boys, I thought. Matt, Matt, I've won the bet, I'm working the magic. We could drink here then go to a club and drink there and tomorrow's hangover would pass. I wanted to hear this girl's accent again; I loved it. I wondered what I looked like from where she was. I held my chest out and imagined her down there, sucking my cock, her head bobbing to and fro, her eyes occasionally looking up at me.

'I don't even know your name,' I said, putting out my hand. 'I'm Rob.'

She took it self-consciously. 'Nicki.'

'Is that Nicky or Nicki?'

'My name's Nicki,' she repeated.

'Yes, but Nicky-with-a-y or Nicki-with-an-i?'

She looked at me like she never really considered it before. 'An i.'

'Aye, an i.' Who said I wasn't funny! 'Will you help me, Nicki? Only we're not from round here and you've got to tell us where to go now. You know some good places, I bet. Clubs.'

'What sort of music do you like?' she asked.

Alanis Morissette, I thought. Alanis Morissette and Travis and U2. Anything by U2 other, perhaps, than 'The Sweetest Thing'. Anything as long as it's quieter than what they were playing here. 'This sort of stuff,' I said.

'What?'

'Anything. *Anyfing*,' I bellowed, emphasising the *fing*. They always used to think I was a Cockney up here – well, let them. And she might like it. When you're young, anything different is interesting.

'The Palace is all right,' she said. 'It's a bit expensive to get in though. Eight quid after eleven.'

She was moving. Moving from left to right, right to left. Swaying. My head wobbled forwards and backwards again. It felt like my turn to talk but there was nothing there. She said: 'You could try Ritzy's, they play loads of old stuff from the eighties there. Phoenix is cheap, but they get a lot of trouble.'

I couldn't find anything to say but it was as if she knew and was happy to do the work. She was so lovely. I took a swig from a glass on the table. I couldn't taste it, but I knew it would be doing something inside.

129

'I only ask you that stuff about the i because my friend Claire, she's got an i, and it drives her mad when I leave it out. That's why I stopped sending her birthday and Christmas cards!'

It occurred to me that I hadn't sent her either a birthday or a Christmas card for a few years. When was her birthday? Sometime in the summer, because we all went out for a picnic on the Town Moor one year. It seemed like I saw everyone less than I used to. Again, I felt as if I was falling, sinking, being sucked under.

'Are you with a bloke? Have you got a boyfriend?' No answer. 'You can tell me I'm a doctor.'

'Yes,' she said. 'Luke. But he's not here.'

'Where is he?'

'Out with the lads. To tell you the truth, I'm not sure if we're still seeing each other. He slept with someone else.'

This is all I need, some charity case. Suppose she might be distraught. Might need a shoulder to cry on. Sympathetic ear. Sympathetic tongue. What was Stevie's line? *Listen* to them. If I could only get her to drink a bit more.

'Yes? That's a choker. How are you coping?'

'All right. A bit upset, I keep crying.'

Don't cry now, please, don't cry now. It would be funny in one way, though, if she did. The lads would say me even talking to women could make them cry!

'It was his mates' fault,' she said. 'He wanted to look good in front of them, he's different when he's with them.'

I imagined burying my face in her breasts. I felt drunk, drunk and tired, and there would have been something new, new and fresh about them.

'We were on a hen night in there last weekend, had a right laugh.'

'Where?'

'Phoenix's.'

I felt sick. Steadied myself. Deep breaths. 'That's all that seems to happen round here.' I said, 'Stag and hen nights.'

'Yes, we hate the stag dos. They come here and get off their faces and wreck the place. At least they're not as bad as the students, though.'

'Bloody students,' I said. 'I suppose I shouldn't be telling you this, but you look like you can keep a secret. I'm on a stag night, we're on a stag night. We're stags.'

I looked again for my friends, but couldn't see them. Was Stevie still sulking over what happened earlier? So I mentioned Vicki. It wasn't that big a deal. And it wasn't as if they were married or anything. I was seeing Emma longer than he was seeing Vicki – and I don't recall getting too much sympathy from him about her. Not from him, or any of the others, come to think of it.

'Well, just as long as you don't wreck the place? You don't look the sort. You look all right.'

As if I would wreck the place!

But I might be the sort for all she knew.

'Neither do you,' I said.

'So, who's getting married?'

Time to move in for the kill.

'I am.' I wobbled, plonking myself down on the sofa next to her. She was bound to be on the rebound if she'd just come out of a relationship.

'No, only kidding. Matt, my best mate, the bloke over there. We've known each other for over ten years.'

'How old are you lot then?'

'Twenty-four.' I put her at eighteen. She'd think I was ancient if I told her I was nearly thirty. I looked older than twenty-four, but not much. Young people liked blokes who looked older than they were anyway. Might be pissed, but I could still play the game. 'You?'

'Nineteen.'

'Say that again,' I said.

'What?'

'Nineteen, say it again. Go on.'

'Why?'

'I like the way you say it.'

'Nineteen,' she said self-consciously.

Her accent reminded me of being here before. Of those three years I'd loved so much. And nineteen, Jesus, just imagine. God, I want you, I thought. I need to fuck you.

'I love your accent,' I said.

She smiled. It was a gorgeous smile. Baby.

'I do, I really love it.'

She smiled at me again, and I remembered Emma and thought: I'm over you, baby.

It's you now, Nicki.

Last orders any minute. Get her back to the hotel. Quick.

131

Whatever else had happened tonight – that stuff with Stevie and all the other stuff that tomorrow I wouldn't remember – wouldn't be so bad if I could have this girl. She would make everything better.

'I'm going to get a drink. What do you want?' I said.

Don't say no. Don't say no.

'I'm OK, ta very much.'

'Come on, let me get you something. I'm buying white wine, Harvey Wallbangers and a chicken Kiev.'

She looked confused.

'Where you from?' I asked.

'Here. Newcastle, of course.'

'I wish I was. It's a great place. You're lucky, I love the people here. Best city I've ever lived in Nicki – Nicki-with-an-i – and I've lived in loads.'

She smiled. Like taking sweets from a baby. This was so easy. I must have been unlucky earlier. Well, fuck those girls earlier. I was in here.

'You lived here?'

'Yes, I used to live here. I loved the place.'

'You're not from round here though, are you? You're from down south, aren't you?'

Well done, Sherlock, I thought.

'We're from London,' I yelled, throwing my arms in the air as if I was celebrating a goal. Beer went everywhere. She looked at me, then smiled. The beautiful, beautiful, beautiful girl smiled. I loved all this. It was magic. I could do this as often as I liked now I was single. I could do this every weekend. 'I live in London,' I said, sinking back in the sofa towards her.

'I'd love to live in London,' she said. 'What's it like?'

I almost laughed. Wait 'til I told the lads *this* one. *London, what's it like*, I'd say, putting on a Geordie accent, giggling and puffing out my cheeks. And they'd say: 'Oh Rob, you're so well travelled.'

'It's shit.'

'No, really?'

The way she said *really* reminded me of Ant and Dec.

'Honestly, it's shit. It's overpriced and all anyone thinks about is money. All they talk about is how much they're earning and how much their house is worth and how much they spend in posh restaurants and there's other things in life, Nicki, other *fings*.'

'It always looks great on the telly. I've never been myself.'

'You're joking?'

'No. I've got an auntie that lives in Milton Keynes I went to see when I was a bairn, but that was years ago.'

'You must have been to London.'

'What about that big wheel? What's it called, the Eye?'

'Eye, the Eye, Nicki-with-an-i,' I said, doing my best Geordie accent. It sounded Scottish but she laughed, so I went for eye contact again.

'Have you been on it?' she asked.

'It would have been a bit difficult, it doesn't open 'til New Year's Eve.' It occurred to me I'd have to face New Year's Eve without Emma. Millennium New Year's Eve on my own. The prospect gnawed at me somewhere deep down. Nicki looked round the bar. 'It's on the South Bank, down by the National Film Theatre,' I said.

She didn't have the foggiest what I was going on about.

'I'd love to visit London even for a day.'

Was that a come-on? Was she waiting for me to invite her down? Bit obvious, but to the point I suppose.

'It's hardly Timbuktu, it's three hours on the train. You can get there and back in a day. Where've you been all your life?'

'Here.'

'Well, you're not missing much. No one talks to you, I tell you. Go in a pub and everyone's so up their own arses, you can't chat with anyone. We wouldn't be doing this if we were in London. I couldn't have come and started chatting to you. You don't mind talking to me, do you, Nicki-with-an-i. It's nice, I like you, I really like you,' I said, wobbling, moving closer.

'No,' she said. 'I don't mind talking to you. We're just talking though, yeah? I'd still love to go one day.'

'Where?'

'London.'

'Well, steer clear of the people if you do. All Cockney wankers! Cockney Wanker, yes? The bloke in *Viz*?'

She didn't twig.

'Is that where you were born and stuff then, London?'

'No, I'm from Surrey.'

'Where's that?'

'Near London, and I hate it.'

'Why?'

'Because it's not here, is it. I might be from Surrey, but I bleed black and white, Nicki.'

'What about that Dome, have you been there? I saw it on the telly and it looked brilliant, just brilliant.'

'That's not open either. Going to be shit anyway. Seven hundred million they've spent on it and it's going to be shit.'

'Well, what about all the other places? Like the Houses of Parliament and Big Ben and all the galleries?'

What is this, tourist information?

I felt my head go towards her – just falling on its own, so I pulled it back up straight. A cigarette was burning my finger and I dropped it on the sofa. She didn't notice. I felt sick. Just hang on. Hold it together. I wanted it to be like it had been half an hour, an hour before. I had a stab of fear about what would happen next – for the rest of the evening – but that passed. All I knew was that the next thing I'd know would be tomorrow morning. I needed another drink to get through this.

'What about Tate Modern?' she said. 'Is that open yet?'

If I wanted this conversation I'd be talking to Emma; she was really into all that modern art stuff. Time was running out.

'Enough tourist information,' I said, 'let me get you a top-up. I'm going to have a large one this time because it's nearly closing. I'll get you one, too. Have whatever you want, I'm not worried how much it costs.'

'I'm all right.'

'Yes, I know that, but what do you want to drink?'

'No, really, I've had enough.'

'Don't worry about it, you're having one.'

I pushed my way to the bar. She was on the gin, I think; Emma liked gin. I liked gin; not as much as vodka, but I liked it. Please let me get served quick. Don't let her go.

'A double vodka and Coke and a gin and tonic – a double too, mate, yeah,' I shouted. Some bloke standing next to me turned round; he probably noticed my accent but I didn't give a shit. I went back and she was still there, still there on her own. It *was* going to happen. Again, the invincible feeling.

'Something to make you feel better,' I said, sitting down again, pushing the drink into her hand. It was the first time we'd touched and I wondered again how she'd feel, how she'd taste. I wanted her so much I could have screamed.

'I told you I didn't want another,' she said.

'I know what, let's go up to the Sun. The Rising Sun. You must know it, it's not far from here.'

'It'll be closed. It's nearly eleven now.'

'I don't care, come with me tomorrow instead. Let's have some beers there at lunchtime.'

'I'm busy tomorrow.'

'So what's the score about clubs now then?'

She named some places, Zoots or something, and then somewhere called Heaven and a couple of others but her attention was going, I could tell. She looked around – probably for her friends or for Luke. I swigged my drink, picked up hers from the table where she'd put it and pushed it towards her.

'Go on, it won't drink itself.'

'I don't want it,' she said.

She sounded like some kid now, some baby that wouldn't eat its tea. *Don't want it*.

'That cost me a fortune.'

She shrugged and looked around again.

Lukey-boy's not here, is he, I thought. You're stuck with me.

'Ah well, waste not want not,' I said, taking it back and downing it. 'Are you going clubbing then?' I lit another one of her fags, dropped the match on the sofa. 'Which club?'

'It's been nice meeting you,' she said, picking up her bag from the floor and edging forward on the sofa.

Don't leave me. Don't leave me.

'What's wrong, can't find your friends? Know the feeling. No sign of Luke either by the look of it. No sign of Luke, by the Luke of it. Get it? No point hanging around for him, Nicki-with-an-i, he won't be thinking about you. He'll have moved on, blokes are like that.'

She bit her lip as if she was about to cry. The bell for last orders went, the lights got brighter, the music went down and a sudden panic gripped me. Then the lights went down and the music went back up and it was OK again.

'You've just got to get on with your life. A pretty girl like you, a clever girl like you, if he's not going to treat you right then find someone who will. That's what I'm doing. Life's too short.' I put my hand on her knee; it felt small and slightly clammy.

She shrank backwards. I put it there again, rubbed slightly.

135

'What are you doing?' she said.

'Getting back on the horse, that's what I'm doing.'

'What?'

'Nothing.'

'It doesn't feel like nothing. Get your hand off me.' Her voice was loud, and a couple of people glanced over.

'Sorry,' I said. 'You're just so attractive. You stand out, do you know that?'

What was she going to do, slap me? That'd be funny. Stevie had done one side, might as well get the matching set. I picked up my glass again and went to drain it but it was just ice. I felt it hit my lips. Did the same with her glass but that was empty too.

'Come on, let's go somewhere. Let's go somewhere and get pissed.' I had my hand on her knee again, and she jerked back and stood up. She knocked a few glasses off the table next to her.

'What is it with you?' she screeched. 'You say you just want to talk and then you're all over me. You're like a fucking octopus.'

She looked down at me, hard, unyielding. It was odd, all that shouting and swearing coming from her face. I smiled at it, at her. I felt the sofa swaying like I was in a dinghy. I just made it to my feet. I wanted to quieten her, avoid a fuss. 'Look, I won't touch you again. I'm sorry. I just want to go somewhere with you.'

'I'm no going anywhere with you, you pervert.' The word pervert made a couple more people look. I rocked backwards and forwards. How did this happen? How did I get like this?

'Look, if it's the money, I'll pay. I'll pay the eight quid to get in if that's what you're worried about. Eight quid's not going to break the bank, is it.'

I picked up the cigarettes from the table – just to do something, really.

'What are you doing with my fags?' she shrieked. 'Give them back, you thief.'

The word thief made more people look.

'Sorry, I didn't know they were yours. Here, have them.'

Stop shouting at me, I thought. Stop shouting or this'll get out of hand.

'Come on, it's just a bit of fun. Putting my hand on your knee's hardly a crime. Calm down.'

'Don't tell me to calm down, you fucking pervert. You come over here and grope me and walk off with my fags and then

136

you tell me to calm down. Why don't you piss off back to London.'

Shut up, for Christ's sake. That's all I need: everyone in the bar knowing I'm a southerner. Something had snapped in her. Her straggly friend would probably show up soon, they always did at times like this.

Fear reached me, faint and lukewarm: the same feeling I'd had with Stevie earlier, but fainter, almost out of reach, telling me these girls weren't like the girls I knew. The blokes they knew weren't like the blokes I knew. Something bad was happening. Make her laugh. Make her laugh.

'We're on a stag night,' I said. 'We're stags.'

I put my hands to my head, pretending to be a stag, and wiggled my fingers like antlers. Put my head down and made a snorting noise like how a stag might. 'We're stags,' I said again. 'Stags.'

I started scuffing my feet. 'Stags.'

She had taken a few steps back and was staring at me.

Please laugh, I thought. *Please laugh at me.*

She didn't.

Do it again. Try it again.

I lurched backwards, ready to do the stag thing again, and met something solid. Resistance. Then I felt myself moving forwards, except I hadn't done it myself. There was something in my back, that was why I was moving. A sound like a bag of water exploding. Glasses smashing. Was that me? I tried to crane my head round. Some bloke was pushing me, following. Please make it someone I know. But his face was new, he had short hair. Then I stopped – we stopped – as I slammed into people and the bar. Pain throbbed in my forehead and all down my side.

'Sorry, sorry, sorry,' I said, scrabbling to right myself, pain almost pulling me over. This bloke had stopped pushing and was standing staring at me.

'What do you think you're doing, man?' he said, jabbing his finger at me. He sounded like she did. 'You stupid fucker.' He surged forwards again at me, but someone behind him had their arm round his neck and was holding him back. I could see the strength it took in that arm just to stop this bloke coming at me. Don't let him go, *please* don't let go. He was the same shape as Stevie, this bloke, but nasty-looking. He still had a pint glass in one hand and the other one was held out towards me, palm up. 'What am I gonna fucking do

137

with this?' he said, touching his shirt with the empty hand. It was covered in beer. The fruit machine flashed behind him. 'Well?'

People had gathered now. Hoping to see someone get their face kicked in. Me.

'I'm sorry,' I said, 'I'm really sorry.' There was nowhere to go: the crowd had closed back in around us. The drunk feeling had disappeared. His face was close to mine and his eyes were slanted and tired-looking, like he'd been rubbing them. Pasty, raw. The hand he was holding the drink in had slumped down to his side and more of it had spilled. I could see the glass, almost horizontal. I glanced away, but it was just more similar-looking blokes, watching. This bloke staggered slightly, then got his balance back. It occurred to me he was pissed, and knowing that made me feel even more sober. I don't know what you're capable of, I thought. God or whoever get me out of here in one piece and I'll never come back anywhere like this, I swear. Something dropped out of me. Speaking was a struggle – I had to force, stretch the words out like I was learning to speak. 'I'm sorry. I'm really sorry. I didn't see you there.'

'What d'you mean, you didn't see me? What are these fuckers for then,' he said, leaning forward and grabbing my glasses. I saw his wrist, all thick, the hair on his forearm, a tattoo under the rolled-up sleeve. A sort of snake round a dagger. It was green, pale green – like it had been there for a long time. He's going to stamp on my glasses, I thought. But he put them on, then laughed, probably imagining how they looked. The bloke holding him back laughed, too. I latched onto the laughter.

'Sorry,' I said to his friend. 'Let me get your mate another drink. What's he want? I'll get him anything, doesn't matter how much.'

'They've rung last orders,' the friend said, another local. 'I'd just leave if I were you.'

Then the bloke that had come for me threw my glasses on the floor, between me and him. 'Fucking students,' he said. 'Act as if you own the place.'

I bent down and picked them up from a pool of beer. Then I backed away, not knowing whether to look at him or not, knowing either was reason enough for him to lose it.

'Go on then, run along,' he said.

'I'm going, I'm sorry,' I said, walking backwards. My heart was pounding. I considered running. Will he think I'm a coward and come for me? Anything in this situation could make him go psycho.

'Go on, Student Grant, fuck off then.'

Whatever it was I'd felt earlier – the tiredness, the sickness, the hangover – came at me again in a wave. I found the others, who obviously hadn't seen what had happened.

'Come on, quick,' I said, 'we've got to go.'

But they didn't want to. I tried to get them out, pushing. I was staggering.

Matt said: 'This isn't like you, Rob.'

Stevie, looking at me all funny, said: '*Why?* We don't want to go.'

More glasses broke somewhere. We bumped into more people. It was crowded, a struggle. I could feel my shirt clinging to my chest, the sweat on my face. I tried to push Matt out, but he was moving slowly. The music was deep in my head and far away at the same time. My coat. My coat was in there somewhere. I squeezed out, past groups of girls, oblivious. Men, bigger than me, not having seen a thing or caring if they had. No sign of Nicki. Glad Emma wasn't here. We got to the door and outside the rush of cold air met us. I felt myself sway, leant against a railing. The Quayside.

'Right then,' someone said – was he with me? 'The Phoenix it is then.'

And we started walking towards the sea.

SUNDAY

Chapter Twenty-seven

Awake. In bed. The hotel room. Newcastle. Matt's stag weekend. My clothes still on. Stevie hit me – oh Jesus – Stevie hit me. A splitting pain deep in my head. That girl whose husband died. I'm sorry. Numb. Pain outside my head too. Not the usual pain, something different. When I touched my forehead – rough and wet – it hurt, so I stood up – everything inside me moved – and went to the bathroom mirror. There was a big graze on my forehead, red and caked with blood, the size of a tennis ball. How did that happen? *When?* What would they say at work? I dabbed it with toilet roll and some dirt and grit came away. What if it scarred? Please don't let it scar. I went back to the bed. Remembered putting money in a juke box. Where was that, was I with the others? What have I done? And Stevie slapping me: I couldn't see why, couldn't get to what happened immediately before; I just remembered his hand hitting me . . . Then later pissing in an alley, the stairs in the hotel, lights flashing, must have been some club. That Geordie lad pushing me in the pub.

I rolled over: seven twenty-eight. The others would be waking up soon and going for breakfast. How could I face them like this, not knowing what happened? How could I face Stevie? I could have done anything. I'd done it again. So alone. Emma, I need you.

I shut my eyes. There was a stale sweet smell – maybe the room always smelt like this or maybe it was me? Stale beer. Smoke. I smoked, shit, I smoked.

Emma, it is going to be OK, isn't it?

A blonde girl shouting at me, something about her cigarettes. Glasses on a table. I tried to remember whether I'd been sick, but couldn't. Tried to remember getting back to the hotel. Nothing. Me doing that stag impression, what was I playing at? And that bloke pushing me. Was that how my head happened? Gone. All gone. A brittle acid taste filled my mouth. Nothing to swallow. Dry.

If I'd have known this was going to happen, I wouldn't have drunk. Or certainly not as much.

What if I'd done something terrible? What if the others had finally lost patience, decided it wasn't funny any more, decided they weren't going to put up with me any more? I just wanted to be with them now: sitting in the same room listening to them would be enough because it would be like yesterday, yesterday afternoon, and that would mean things hadn't changed.

I went to the bathroom and opened my mouth; puke came out, loads of it, all watery and tart and as I was being sick I saw the mess: wet all over the floor – fuck knows if it was water or piss or beer – and bog rolls everywhere and stuff all knocked over, and turned my head back so it was facing straight down the bog and the puke kept coming.

Then, immediately afterwards, I experienced the clear feeling, like the badness had all gone. It was going to be OK.

I went back to bed and lay there and started feeling sick again. Too scared to touch my head. So quiet. Some woman telling me: 'My husband will be here soon, I'm sure he'll like to meet you,' and all her mates laughing. Talking with James about Sarah, I could talk then. Ordering Stella. Stella! Thinking the word almost made me heave. Why did the others buy me that? Didn't I learn! The rush of music as we walked down the stairs with the red carpet – was that what I fell on, how I did my head? I remembered red near my face at one point, red on my cheek. Hopefully it was the hotel carpet. Spitting beer at Matt. Trying to put cigarettes up his nostrils. Buying cigarettes, leaning against the machine, trying and failing to push the money in, pushing harder. Music. Stevie hitting me. Matt saying: 'You bring me to all the best places.' He was laughing as he said it so I can't have done anything too awful by that stage, not to Matt. Vodka Red Bulls on the table. I could taste it now, even after being sick. I had to see my friends, check we were still friends, but I couldn't face them, couldn't move. I was back at the hotel, that was something. Listening to 'Through the Barricades' – was that the slow dances? That would have meant we were still out at two. We can't have stayed out until then, surely; I was wasted by eleven. My hands out in front of me to break the fall, the slap of my body on the ground, being hauled up. Matt and James's faces. I couldn't remember if they were smiling but they were there. I might have offended them, but they would have stopped anything too awful happening. I could apologise to them, beg, they'd forgive me, surely. I needed to see them now and apologise and laugh and hear them say it's OK, it's OK, it's OK.

Emma would have said it was OK. 'Just a hangover,' she'd have assured me. The first thing she'd always tell me on a Sunday was: 'Don't worry, nothing bad happened.' Then she'd talk me through it, the night before, downplaying it, smiling occasionally, as if to say: These things happen.

At least, she would have done until a while ago. Recently, she'd been more likely to come out with: 'This isn't funny any more,' or 'This has got to stop,' or, for the last couple of months, 'This isn't fair on either of us.'

But she wasn't here today; I didn't know where she was and I was in a hotel room alone in Newcastle and anything could have happened, and she didn't know.

It was just me. Alone. Trying to do it on my own. I'd only had a week of it and look what a mess I'd made.

I cried.

I forced myself to think about what happened with Stevie; it felt like that was the first step in a direction I had to take, but there was nothing there except the slap and I felt as if there was too much to deal with beyond that anyway. If it wasn't Stevie it would be something else and always would be and maybe I could just sleep sleep sleep and forget.

But I wouldn't sleep again now.

I forced myself to try and remember what it was about, us falling out, but couldn't. There was just this vague feeling of anger. Anger, and jealousy. I tried to recall what I had been trying to say to him, but couldn't.

I forced myself to try and work out what I'd say when I saw him today, but couldn't do that either.

'Sorry' was pretty much all I could say, and I probably wouldn't even say that.

I was shaking, Jesus, I wasn't even trying to move and I was shaking.

Emma was right: this couldn't go on.

I sat up, forcing myself to check the sheets for blood. None.

That was something. There was some blood on the pillow from my head, but it was dry, so that must have stopped bleeding a while ago. I fingered the wound – it hurt, but there didn't seem to be any other cuts. I moved my toes, my feet, my legs, my arms. Soreness, but everything was there, everything seemed to work. It was too early for bruises, I knew; they'd only appear over the next two or three days, long-lasting tobacco-coloured reminders on my white skin of what I couldn't remember.

I ran my tongue round my mouth – all the teeth were intact. One day, I knew, I'd lose those.

I rolled onto my side and the pain in my head shifted round. I pulled the sheets back up to my neck. Somewhere beneath the beer and smoke there lingered the faint smell of cleanliness, of how sheets used to smell.

If only I could sleep, let time pass with the tiny tender knowledge that its passage might be making things less bad. In sleep, there'd be no worry about last night or today or tomorrow or Emma or Stevie or what I'd done last night or all those other weekends and this pain might go; I hated to think what I'd be like inside, my liver and guts and lungs.

Why was it always at times like this, hungover, that I missed Emma so much?

Pain, throbbing and beating like the music from last night, and me swaying, staggering, falling into people – 'Sorry mate, sorry, sorry' – that bloke pushing me into the bar, the sound of glasses breaking. 'You're a wanker, you're a fucking wanker,' his finger pointing at me.

The fruit machine flashing.

Matt holding me up.

Me saying to him: 'But I loved her.'

Pain in my head so sharp I could scream.

Seven thirty-six. The others wouldn't surface for a couple of hours yet.

Let time pass . . . If it passed, and if I could get through today, it might be better. By the time today was over, I would have talked to my friends and then I'd be on the train going home and I'd have got away with it again.

A siren started in the distance, then stopped. Not for me, that one.

I moved again and felt a pain in my armpit. The others had probably manhandled me into a cab, up the hotel stairs and into bed.

That would bruise. I remembered that bruise I got at James's wedding. I was sure that was cracked ribs. Waking up on the hotel floor, puke around me, and that pain all down my left side. I was too scared all that day to check it in the mirror. It was only the next morning showering that I caught myself in the mirror and saw that big swelling purple patch the size of a grapefruit on my side somewhere near my kidneys.

Jesus.

It felt like something was pressing down on me. A pillow over my face. Couldn't see. Couldn't breathe. I wondered how much was left of that little bottle of vodka in my bag. I didn't want to get pissed again, not like how I was last night, but I'd need a drink later if I was going to get through today. I leant out of the bed to reach my bag and retched but nothing came out.

This couldn't go on.

I wanted to ring Emma, tell her about last night, make a joke about it.

'Baby,' I'd say, 'I feel shit.'

'Don't worry, nothing bad happened,' she'd say. 'Just a hangover.'

But she wasn't my baby any more. She wasn't my baby and I wasn't hers. I never would be again.

And she wouldn't say that now, would she. She'd say: 'This has gone beyond a joke.' Or: 'You've *got* to drink less.'

What the hell have I done?

I felt dizzy and it struck me like a slap: the pointlessness of it all. Emma wasn't the first person I felt like this about. What about all the girls before her? I'd tried so hard at times – but it always ended up the same. Splitting up. Feeling empty and scared and hungover. *This*.

All of it, turned to nothing now. Less than nothing.

I tried to remember Emma's number but couldn't, and what was the point in ever having known it if I'd forgotten it within a week?

It was all so fucking pointless.

It was all right for the others, they were different. They'd found people; or, if they hadn't, they would. But this was me, this was always me – in a hotel room, alone, everything smashed and feeling sick and not knowing what happened the night before.

I didn't know if I could stay on top of this.

Another police siren wailed in the distance. Lots of people must have been more pissed than me last night though. They were all big drinkers in this part of the world. I wouldn't have got back to the hotel if anything really terrible had happened. One of Stevie's mates woke up once in a police station after a stag night. Stevie always said it was because he was tight and was trying to avoid the hotel bill. I met the bloke last year. He was married now, had a kid.

I pulled myself up in bed, made myself look for my stuff. My wallet – a present from Emma – was on the table, a load of coins scattered around it. My cash card was there, too. I saw my shoes on the floor. At least I'd got them off. Someone had, anyway. I lay down again.

If I go on like this, something terrible will happen.

Say I got in my car one night when I was pissed and killed someone? Bang. That would be it. Over. I'd never driven pissed, but that didn't mean I never *would*. It might be the morning after a sesh, not even pissed, just technically over the limit, and someone steps out. Not even my fault, but I could still go to prison. Prison!

Say I got a tattoo? Got really hammered and woke up with a tattoo. Not something on my arse like Matt, but on my neck or my forehead. It could happen. Teachers always used to say I was easily led. Something that takes only an instant for a cog to move in your brain, snap and say yes – and everything's changed.

Say I reached out and touched a girl at the supermarket checkout one day? I'd be tired of being lonely, tired of being tired, and there she would be – all beautiful and within reach – and I wouldn't think, it would just happen.

Say I fell down a flight of stairs? I'd fallen down enough times, God only knows, but somehow never really hurt myself. But what if I crippled myself? I must have been lucky so far – either that or like Mum said when I was a kid, made of rubber – but say I broke my leg or back or neck? Things like that happen.

I thought of Mum for some reason, thought of how she spends her Sundays gardening and drinking coffee with her friends and circling in red the things she wants to watch on the telly. And she didn't know I was like this, she couldn't; she knew I'd got lots of friends and went out a lot but she didn't know *this* was what it meant.

I could hear her voice, breaking but resolute, saying: 'Be strong, son, be strong.' Her voice, faintly but firmly saying: 'Hang in there, Robert, hang in there, Robert.' Except she wasn't talking about the hangovers, of course; they were the words she used sitting on the edge of my bed holding my hand the day Dad died.

Chapter Twenty-eight

I started walking on the Tuesday night. I didn't know where to go; I just had to get out.

Walking: hours of it, miles of it. Putting one foot in front of the other, and keeping on putting one foot in front of the other until I was so tired that when I went back to that room in Halls I'd feel numb.

I walked randomly and later, when I began to feel tired, made myself do a circular route until I was exhausted.

If I could make myself walk for one, two, three hours then I could get through tonight and maybe I could get through Freshers' Week and then it wouldn't be all that long until Christmas.

I walked round the campus and looked into other rooms: a girl drying her hair, a Cure poster, books under an anglepoise lamp.

I walked out onto the Town Moor and watched the traffic, trying to work out which way was south.

I walked down onto the Tyne Bridge, and stared over the edge at the black, oily water.

It wasn't supposed to be like this, college. They said these were the best years of your life.

It was dark and cold. Everyone had told me it would be cold in Newcastle. I wondered what the place would look like with snow on the ground. Three winters.

A group of lads were throwing a rugby ball to each other. The ball made a deep thudding every time someone caught it. One of them smiled at me, said hi. I walked on, their voices faded, and the sound of the ball quietened. What would I have done if I had stayed back there? Caught it, perhaps, then thrown it on? Then what? They would have talked about what they were going to do that night – things I wouldn't do – and what they'd done the night before – things I hadn't done – and I'd have smiled and wanted to get away, knowing all I had to get away to was that room. I'd spent two days solid in there: terrified, doing nothing. Not meeting anyone.

There had been a few knocks at the door on the first day, but I ignored them and they stopped.

So much for Freshers' Week.

The huge grey radiator spewed out a dry heat and the sun shone in, pale and yellow. The desk someone had written their initials on. A Gideon Bible. A dirty, chipped basin which I'd drunk water from and pissed in.

Maybe I should be working? There was always that. Take up one of the books I'd brought and read, make notes, read, make notes. Physical Geography. Applied Physical Geography. Research methods in Human Geography.

Maybe if I unpacked it might help? But what was the point if I wasn't staying? I didn't want my clothes in that wardrobe, where all those other people's pants and knickers had been.

Home's still there, I told myself continuously, sometimes out loud, as I lay there listening to people hitting a hockey ball along the corridor. And I wondered how Mum would react if I went home. She'd be fine, I knew, but knowing that only made it worse. I would walk up to the door, hear the telly playing, and ring the doorbell because I'd be loaded down with bags. It would sound familiar. Then I'd see her coming through the hall, smiling instinctively when she saw me, probably wondering: What's Robert doing here? She would open the door and kiss me softly on the cheek, squeeze my arm and smile; and she wouldn't say anything, not at first, she'd take me in, tell me to put the bag down in the corner and take some food out of the fridge and after I'd eaten maybe say: 'You decided to pack it in, then?' or 'So it didn't work out?' or 'At least you gave it a go, Robert.' She wouldn't expect an answer. And I'd climb to my room and lie there not sleeping, hearing the familiar theme tunes from the telly downstairs, and know that back in Newcastle, back on C corridor in Halls, they'd be throwing a rugby ball on the grass or hitting a hockey ball along a corridor.

Later, she might ask why I'd left – but what could I say? That when I saw the Blu-tack marks on the wardrobe from where everyone else's posters had been, I felt inexplicably sad. That when I looked at the pillow, all yellow and stained, I just couldn't bring myself to put my pillowcase on it. That when I saw people queuing for phones in the foyer I wanted to cry.

Wednesday, I made myself eat. Made myself go to tea. Supper, as I'd heard a couple of people in the corridor call it. In the canteen, I sat opposite some girl and the silence was so crushing I could barely breathe. I asked her what her name was; when she said 'Margaret' I could have cried again. Margaret. The way she said it made it sound old-fashioned and plain. She had long straight brown hair and spots worse than mine and I didn't know whether I felt sorry for her or for me for being reduced to this.

The girls I was used to seeing at home were girls with peroxide good looks, nightclub girls, and I remembered how uncomfortable those nightclubs made me feel, how I only went *there* because everyone else did and how I knew *that* wasn't me but now I *was* somewhere completely different and *this* wasn't either.

It was more of the same: feeling sick and tired, that everything was pointless, like I was permanently about to cry.

Margaret opposite me, chewing.

There was nothing inside me. I'm here, I thought, I'm here – I've left home and gone to college – but what now? I hated the way I felt and myself for feeling it. All the people I was letting down. Mum, Dad. My grandparents who hadn't been to college. It was all leading to me, to this. And knowing that those people wouldn't want me to feel like this just made it worse.

My throat was dry and, every time I swallowed, I nearly retched. Someone was talking about the food, how it was overcooked. It all is here, they said. I wanted to tell them that it just didn't matter. Other people passed jugs of water confidently. Chatting. Laughing. How could they?

A guy on my table talked about cooking chicken in an orange sauce. 'Absolutely *superb*,' he said. I'd never heard anyone my age talk about recipes, nor use the word 'superb'.

After tea, I walked past the Porter's Lodge and all the notices were up for Club meetings. Badminton Club. Clay Pigeon Shooting Club. Running. Chess. Conversational French. I wondered about going to the Sailing Club meeting – I'd loved it when Dad had taken me as a kid – but I knew I'd turn up and stand a few feet away from the rest of them like I was waiting for something else. They wouldn't notice me or would think I wasn't with them if they did; and I'd go and read a sign on a wall, just to get away, out of sight, and then I'd go back through the quads and past the science labs and out onto the Moor and back to the Halls and through the stone entrance and past the people on the phones and to that room and that bed and that unpacked suitcase in the wardrobe.

At the bottom of a notice for the Sailing Club someone had written: REMEMBER, WHAT YOU GET OUT DEPENDS ON WHAT YOU PUT IN.

I scribbled FUCK OFF in big letters over it.

Then, paranoid about being chucked out for defacing the notice, I walked on.

The buildings each had different names. What was the point in that? They were written in plaques on the walls and the plaques had got all dirty. No one had cleaned them. That didn't seem right.

I felt tired, so very tired. I could feel nothing. Precisely nothing. There, all the time: an emptiness, a hollowness. Once or twice, the word 'suicide' sprang to mind. It came from nowhere, like a dog barking in a dream, and I never got any further than mouthing the word. I was too numb, too tired, to do anything more with it. But it was strangely comforting, knowing it was there in reserve, a back-up. I squirrelled it away, saved it. It wasn't even that I was worried about the people I'd leave behind, more that it would have been pointless. It felt like there was nothing left to take.

I went back to my room and cried like I hadn't for a long time. I buried my head in the pillow as I wept and smelt the dust and a faint trace of aftershave and wondered if anyone could hear me – that bloke with the Northern accent had been outside again earlier – and buried my head deeper and wondered if you could die like this, suffocating; then after a while gave even that up and drifted into sleep.

Later, I heard people come back and the shouting and singing start and the stereos go on. Then it went quiet again, and I lay fully clothed on my bed waiting for it to start again in the morning.

The best years of your life.

Chapter Twenty-nine

At least I hadn't been with people from work last night. That was something. I hated it when that happened, when you had that sense of dread all weekend about going into the office on Monday. Only one thing could make that feeling go away: more drink.

It had been happening often enough with Emma – so what now, *without* her?

Without Emma. It had crept up on me and now there it was.

Matt said to me that I'd be a fool to let her go, that she was the best I could hope for.

She was.

I hoped she wasn't too miserable. But she would be. I thought of how my phone had rung once then stopped on Friday evening. I answered but there was no one there. Number withheld. It was her, I knew, going home, thinking about the weekend stretching ahead. 'What nice thing have you got planned for me this weekend?' she'd have asked, if things were normal.

'I'm going to surprise you,' I'd have said. Which always meant: nothing. I didn't care what we did, you see, as long as it didn't stop us finding a pub every now and then for a quick one.

'Don't cry, Emma, please don't,' I'd said, that night in her flat, but she'd just looked at me. Confused, let down. No shouting. Just crying. 'I might as well,' she'd said. 'I'm going to when you're gone.'

I went to the bathroom and tried to piss but nothing came out. I spat and the spit was brown.

I'm killing myself, I thought.

Imagine if I was ill, really ill, then I'd need Emma – or *someone* – more than ever. Then, all the freedom and independence and one-night stands – that was a laugh, what one-night stands? – wouldn't be worth a thing. What if I had some horrible disease? I *was* smoking again. I'd smoked for over ten years before Emma had helped me quit. Imagine that, waking up in some hospital bed and having no one visit. One person just wasn't strong enough to face that sort of stuff on their own. Maybe two weren't, but they stood a better chance than one.

I'll stop smoking, OK. I'll stop today. But what if it was too late? What if cancer had already sown its seed? There already, dormant, waiting until I was really and truly miserable or, worse still, had found a woman and probably had kids. Yes, it would wait until I was settled down and happy, then get me. My wife – and it's funny, I'd known from the second I'd seen her across the bar that she was *the one* – preparing for another busy day and me in the bathroom cleaning my teeth and spitting and there: blood. She'd call out, 'Goodbye, don't forget to do the packed lunches,' – I was on the school run today – and I'd hear the door slam and I'd be in the bathroom with loo roll to my mouth, loo roll with red on it.

It's just a hangover, I told myself. Everyone gets them. Everyone gets this.

But it wasn't just a hangover – it felt worse. Much worse.

Outside my bedroom door there were probably piles of puke, fire extinguishers off the wall, stuff broken, and the manager waiting for me downstairs. He might be used to stag nights, but nothing like this. And brown spit and no piss and the inside of me all churned up and the bruises waiting to brown and no Emma and Mum at home, without Dad, going on and getting through it and me doing this again, again, again.

I went into the bathroom and looked at the graze in the mirror. It *would* scar.

My hair was all standing up in spikes, wet and sticky, with that stale smell of beer and smoke in here too. And I looked so deathly pale.

Emma, look what's happening to me.

Pale and weak and shivery.

Sick of always feeling sick.

Couldn't face breakfast. Couldn't face the others. But I needed to see them. That old boy might be on reception. He might have been there last night when we came in.

I sat up. Dust and faded curtains. Sour polish. So cold. I'd never drink again, I really meant it this time.

Trouble was, I couldn't for the life of me imagine what came next.

I pressed the button on the remote. Nothing happened. I stood up, feeling dizzy, and remembered standing, staggering, in front of that blonde girl last night. 'Thief,' she'd shouted.

The telly spluttered to life and some current affairs programme was on; the chap being interviewed didn't look much older than me. Every time he opened his mouth something sensible came out. He had showered and shaved and probably been collected early by a taxi. It must be nice: being in demand. Getting up early and putting on a tie on a Sunday, staring in the mirror and straightening it and being awake, aware, not scared, not full of the dread, no vomit taste in your mouth. No scar on your head. Mine would be there now for the rest of my life.

I remembered that actor I'd seen on the telly who wrote his own obituary whenever he got depressed to remind him of what he *had* done and all his good points. I got out of bed and went to the desk – just getting there made me puff. There wasn't space for my knees under it, so I sat sideways. A few sheets of headed paper lay on the desk top.

I was shaking.

I tried to write 'A good laugh', but the pen didn't work. I picked up the pencil, which had *Sea View* down one side, and wrote: A GOOD LAUGH.

You couldn't dispute that. I was. Ask anyone.

I wondered what to add. Everything that came to mind seemed to belong under that heading. Drinking too much. Staying out all night. Bad attempts at womanising. Messing around at work. Not exactly a life's work, was it. Besides, it wasn't a good laugh, not really. I only did those things because I didn't know what else to do. And being with me when I was pissed can't have been that much of a laugh for anyone else.

Ask Stevie.

Ask Matt or James or whoever it was who carried me home.

Ask Mrs Married or Demi or that blonde girl who said I took her cigarettes.

Ask Emma.

I wondered if Stevie was awake. I thought of him and that girl with freckles, yes, that's what we'd been arguing about, me saying that stuff about leukaemia, and I thought about him in bed with her in the next room – the start of something special, maybe, or just another one-night stand – and I started crying.

Stevie, I'm sorry. I don't know what came over me.

I wanted to write words like 'reliable', 'honest', 'genuine'. But they sounded strange, almost mystical.

Couldn't even think how 'genuine' was spelt.

I wanted to write 'decent'. But that, too, sounded odd.

There didn't seem much call for these qualities in my day-to-day existence.

Maybe I was nothing more than a good laugh, someone to get pissed with, someone to spend Saturday nights with. Anything other than that, though, and I wasn't your man. When you needed someone to rely on, you wouldn't turn to me.

I started doodling on the top of the paper, but my head hurt and I got bored because I'm crap at drawing.

Come on, there must be something?

What about that weekend I'd arranged a few years before in New York. Everyone enjoyed that. OK, there'd been a a bit of a cock-up with the hotels, but once we all got there and managed to meet we enjoyed it. Forty-eight hours drinking in the Big Apple, was how I billed it. It was a right laugh.

Think . . .

There ought to be headings like 'trustworthy', 'wise', 'considerate', 'achievements' – but where?

OK, there was work, but that was a joke. I only did it for the money, to pay for weekends like this, to pay to go out. It all led back to booze. I was hungover most mornings and pissed most afternoons. I hadn't put any effort into work for, well, I couldn't remember how long. Years. Dad always used to say it was a privilege to be a teacher. How wonderful it must be, to feel that about your job. How nice it would be to do something well – to take pride in a piece of work, to be complimented on a job well done. My boss, out of the blue, had said a few weeks before: 'What's happened to you?'

Hardly an epitaph, that.

I wrote: QUALIFICATIONS. Then under it: 8 GCSEs. 3 A levels and a 2:2 degree. A Bishop Desmond, as we always called them.

There.

But I wasn't bright: I passed everything by rote learning. And everyone had qualifications, all the lads did – except these weren't *all* they had. They had hobbies and talents, things about which they were passionate that the rest of us didn't understand. James was a real war buff; Stevie – believe it or not – loved painting; and Matt was still as much into his old films as ever. Laurel and Hardy had always been his favourites. He'd even joined their fan club, the Sons of the Desert. We took the piss, but he didn't care.

This was turning into a CV, not an obituary. I didn't come on a stag weekend to write a CV.

I wrote the word HOBBIES.

Then nothing.

Rephrased it as OTHER INTERESTS in the hope something would come, but it didn't.

Playing five-a-side football, maybe?

No, the others did that; I turned up afterwards for the piss-up. Sometimes I sat in the pub while they were playing and when they got there I was already half cut.

I remembered that series of Historical London Walks Emma and I had done, and how bored I'd been. It seemed so futile: walking one way and having stuff pointed out to you that you'd forget anyway, then walking back.

Going out drinking was my only hobby.

SOCIALISING, I wrote. MEETING PEOPLE.

What else? I didn't have a passion. Anything would have done: metal detecting or horse-riding or car restoration. Any one of them would have been a start.

I felt truly miserable. Wrote DEPRESSED.

The piece of paper had *Sea View* at the top, A GOOD LAUGH beneath it, then QUALIFICATIONS, HOBBIES, OTHER INTERESTS, SOCIALISING, MEETING PEOPLE and DEPRESSED at the bottom. I underlined DEPRESSED.

I wrote SURVIVED BY, but I had no wife, no kids.

I wrote Emma's name, because I wanted to see what it felt like. It made me shiver.

Next to it I wrote Nicki, Nicki-with-an-i. Then I remembered how she'd recoiled from me when I'd touched her knee, a look of revulsion on her face. Yes, that was it: revulsion.

I wouldn't be survived by anyone.

No one would carry my photograph in their purse or wallet. No one would look at the little boy or girl, ruffle their hair, and say: You're like your father. Not at this rate.

I thought about Mum and Dad; they'd given me as good a start in life as anyone could have hoped for. I wrote underneath: Mother. But that would be strange in an obituary. You shouldn't be survived by your mother. That's the wrong way round.

Claire always said I could be godfather to her first kid, but she was no nearer having kids than I was.

I'd always said I'd get a dog when I bought a flat but I hadn't even got round to that. The flat or the dog.

And it occurred to me I hadn't *done* anything for years.

I wasn't supposed to still feel like this at my age.

The obituary would stop here. School and university and family. Even they weren't mine, they weren't things *I'd* achieved, they were what I'd been given. Stuff like that comes to you when you're too young to mess it up.

After that, all I'd really got to my name was 'a good laugh' and 'depressed'.

I wrote Nicki's name again, and I felt tired, even when I got to the 'k', so tired I couldn't be bothered to write the rest. Too much effort.

Voices in the car park. Maybe they were fellow guests, talking about me? They were laughing, though I couldn't for the life of me imagine what about. The sound of laughter seems so odd when you actually listen to it. I wondered when the last time I laughed when I was sober.

All I wanted was to sleep.

'A good son', I made myself write. As if.

A good drunk, more like.

And I wasn't even a particularly good drunk.

I imagined my photo in an obituary and something came to me from last night: the flash of a camera. Standing, propped between other people. The flash, then falling back down.

At the top of the paper I wrote 'Robert Mark Purcell. 1970–'

I couldn't write the final date.

Sea View, that was a joke. Maybe there was – from the roof. With a pair of binoculars. I remembered that line in *Fawlty Towers* where the old bag complains about the view. 'This is Torquay, madam,' John Cleese snaps, 'what did you expect, herds of wildebeest?'

That made me laugh *so* much the first time I saw it. We'd been in Stevie's room in Halls – he was the only person who had a telly and video on our corridor. It made me laugh so much I'd felt sick.

Until recently, it still could. Well, until a few years ago.

I wrote 'R.I.P.' on the top. Then I went back and sat on the bed.

Later, I ventured out. Made it along the corridor. Nothing broken yet, no irate guests. Made it past reception. It wasn't the old boy, but he was familiar. Had I seen him last night? He stared at me. Into the breakfast room and there they were, my friends, all sitting together on the far side. I went towards them. Matt looked up. 'Here he is,' he yelled. He cheered and the others clapped and cheered. I sat down and, as I did so, felt hands pat my back.

They were finishing their breakfast. They were talking about going for a kickabout on the Moor, about lunch in a pub, about who was supposed to be where at the wedding. Matt cracked a joke in a voice slightly too loud for comfort about a man with a wig on another table.

No one, not even Stevie, mentioned last night.

Chapter Thirty

It wasn't so bad outside.

'We can't leave without having a kickabout,' Matt had said. So we bought a ball, one of those plastic ones kids have, and walked up to the Moor. More than ten years had passed since we'd first played here.

So much for a bit of fun, though. Stevie had persuaded some Geordie lads to let us join in their game, so it was full-on five-a-side. Because James volunteered to go on their side, we got two of them in our team. Matt was our goalie as he'd hurt his leg in the gym. I sat cross-legged in the goalmouth next to him; merely moving was making me feel sick. 'The last line of defence,' I claimed when anyone moaned.

I watched my friends play, saw the fun they were having doing something this seemingly simple. I saw Stevie taking part and realised how integral he was to our group. And I felt like apologising to him there and then, no matter who was listening – what was most important was doing it. Then maybe we could move on, get back to how we were.

Matt squatted on his haunches, doing occasional stretching exercises. I poked the mud in the goalmouth. It had been a hot summer and it was still dry.

'How much of last night do you remember?' he asked.

'All of it. Well, most of it.'

There was a pause. It's coming, I thought. The truth. I smiled nervously. I wanted to get it over. Experience had taught me that it was never *that* bad – I was here, after all, and Matt was still talking to me.

'So,' he said, nodding at my forehead, 'you remember that, do you?'

I touched it; it hurt. 'Yes, I fell over?'

'You could say that. You fell flat on your face in the road. You were lucky you didn't kill yourself.'

'Sorry,' I said, because I couldn't think of anything else.

'Do you remember dancing on the table?'

Of course I didn't. I didn't remember anything in any detail after Mrs Married, whatever time she was, and even she was a blur. Everything before this weekend seemed a long time ago. 'Yes.'

'You nearly got us chucked out of the Anchor.'

The Anchor! Had we gone there?

'Those girls were furious at getting covered in beer. The bouncer wasn't impressed either.'

The word bouncer triggered something. I recalled coming down off a table – falling, helped, or was I pulled? 'Calm down or you're out,' this voice had said. Just the words now, no face. I felt sick. 'If a man can't let his hair down on a stag night, when can he?'

Matt looked at me uncomprehendingly.'You were out of it,' he said. 'Not just pissed – completely out of it.'

Why was it always me who had too much, always me who spilt beer over girls, always me pulled off the table by a bouncer, always me at lunchtimes on Sunday feeling this? Why was it always me asking myself why it was always me?

Shouts drifted down from the other end of the pitch. The ball came to us and I ran, or tried to, but I was shaking so much I could hardly move. Matt booted the ball back up the other end and I sat down next to him again.

'I don't go out that much nowadays, that's what it is, I can't take my beer like I used to.'

'It was the vodka that sank you. You were knocking back trebles like water, do you remember that?'

The word 'vodka' brought back something. Standing at the bar, just facing the bar, shouting for it. Couldn't see what the barman looked like, or who was standing on either side of me or behind me. Lots of people. Pushing. No room. *Vodka*. If I was sinking trebles even three would have been nearly ten. Ten! And all the beer, too. 'I didn't have that many,' I said.

More yells from the others. I watched Stevie, our striker, weave and pass out to the wing and when the ball was crossed back in he jumped and headed it with a resounding thud. He scored.

'Nice one, Stevie,' I called. 'Great header.'

161

He didn't reply. He ran back to the halfway line. He was in shorts and had taken his top off. I couldn't help admiring his physique yet, at the same time, it made me angry. He had to strut around like a peacock, even now.

I wouldn't be acting like Stevie was if I'd got off with that girl with freckles last night. I'd have asked her to eat lunch with me, to share the day with me. I wouldn't treat her as a one-night stand. I remembered the way the freckles on her forehead moved when she smiled. It wasn't fair that she was somewhere else. Gone.

Later, I called: 'Over here, over here,' to Stevie, waving my arms frantically as if he might pass it to me. He didn't, but it might have been because he was pissed off with me or it might, of course, have been because I was crap at football or simply because I was behind him and it would have meant passing backwards and he was taking this, even this, seriously.

Out of the blue Matt said: 'Rob, are you all right?'

'Yes, course. Bit tired. Bit hungover. Bit Sunday morning, you know how it is.'

'You nearly started a fight at one point, trying to get those girls to dance. You tried to manhandle one onto the dance floor.'

I could see myself pulling an arm. She didn't want to come. This was what Saturday nights had become like. Instead of remembering them I heard about them.

'She didn't mind.' It was instinctive, this. Instinct, and practice. Deny and shrug off.

'Her boyfriend did, though.'

'What happened, Matt?'

'Nothing, no thanks to you. You're lucky I did a good job as peacemaker. I apologised profusely – mainly because you couldn't speak – and then carried you off the dance floor.'

'And that was the end of it, yes?'

'Not exactly. The bloke she was with tried to have a go at you a bit later, I was at the bar at the time, but apparently Stevie stopped him.'

Typical Stevie. Throwing his weight around. Knowing that no one would take him on.

'And then?'

'And then you caused general mayhem for another hour or so, collapsed in a corner and we carried you back to the hotel. Not forgetting nearly cracking your head open on the way back, of course.'

162

Thank God. They carried me back to the hotel. General mayhem. Carried back. Collapsed. Nearly cracking my head open. *Nearly*. I'd got away with it. I'd learnt my lesson.

'Thanks for looking after me, mate. I'm sorry about getting so smashed. I'm a prick sometimes – you know that.'

'Your problem is that you never know when to stop. You never know when you've had enough. It's always been the same.'

Always! Did Matt know that three, five, ten years ago? Were my friends seeing things in me even then that I couldn't? I felt flattered, but scared. 'Aren't we all like that?'

'I'll have another pint if I feel like one, but I get to a point where something stops me having any more. You do the opposite. Last night, I was watching you and you weren't drinking socially, you only had one aim and that was to get pissed. You couldn't stop yourself.'

'I was enjoying myself,' I said, trying to justify it, knowing if I admitted that I was wrong, it was admitting that the last ten years had been wrong.

'You didn't look as if you were enjoying yourself. You were just *gone*. You worried me a bit, mate, to tell you the truth. Listen, when I asked you a minute ago if you were all right, I didn't mean in a "how's-your-hangover" sort of way, I meant are you all right generally? You seemed different yesterday.'

James ran towards us with the ball. I grabbed him, tried to bundle him over but I bounced off and it occurred to me I couldn't even take this seriously, but had to try and reduce it to a spectacle.

Matt looked at the ground, and pressed on. 'You seemed, I don't know, not yourself. God knows I've seen you out of it enough times and good on you, we've all done it, but I've never seen you like that before. You didn't care: not about the people around you or us or even yourself. We're mates, right, best mates, so I can tell you this – I've got to – but I don't know if I *liked* you much yesterday.'

Two groups of kids on the next pitch were arguing about who was going to be Newcastle. How nice, I thought, to have a team. I saw the allotments on the far side of the Moor where the old boys went on Sundays and beyond that the city and, in the distance, the Halls where we'd all met and I felt more lonely than I'd ever felt before.

Five or six hours, I thought, and I'll be back in the Star. Things wouldn't seem so bad there. 'I was drunk, that's all.'

'I didn't ask if you were drunk. I asked if you were all right.'

I wanted to explain to Matt how I had felt at the beginning of the evening, as if everything was gone: Emma, and this place and us, the lads.

We sat for a few seconds in silence, then Stevie scored again. He put his shirt over his head and raced to the touchline with his hand up in the air. 'Shear-er, Shear-er,' we all yelled.

We joked about needing oranges.

'A vodka and orange's what I need,' one of the Geordie guys on the other team said.

'So *are* you all right then, Rob?' Matt said, persisting. 'It just felt like we'd lost you.'

Play came back down to our end again; I picked the ball up and hoofed it as far back as I could, which wasn't very far.

'Handball,' James shouted.

'Bollocks. I'm goalie now,' I replied, sitting down again next to Matt. A muscle in my leg twinged. 'Maybe I should move? Get out of London? I'm sure that's half the reason I'm feeling like I do.'

'You weren't like the Rob I knew – the one I used to be at college with, the one I've known all these years.'

He paused, concentrating again, like he was struggling with something. It was an expression I'd never seen on his face before. 'I don't want it to be like it was last night. That's not how I want our friendship to continue, Rob.'

We looked at each other again, me and Matt, and I felt like crying. Something was changing. This, I knew, was new ground.

'I'm upset about Emma, that's all. I needed to forget about her for a night. I'm a liability, aren't I?'

'You're good value,' he said, smiling, and that smile was almost enough to make me forget this and talk about something else – a mutual mate or our next night out or anything, as I had so often in the past. But I remembered how awful I felt most mornings now – the headache and the sickness and how dull, how flat everything was, and how that feeling never went, not even when I started drinking: the drink just stopped it getting worse.

'I drink too much,' I blurted out. 'Not just occasionally – all the time. You don't realise. No one does. I spread myself thin, I go out with lots of people. Everyone thinks the time I get pissed with them is probably my one occasion for doing it that year. But I do it with everyone.'

I considered telling him how I couldn't get through a day now

164

without a drink. How, when I dipped into that filing cabinet beside my desk in the middle of the afternoon, what I was looking for was in a bottle. I wanted to tell him, but couldn't quite do it. 'I'm scared.'

'It's not that bad, is it?'

'It is, Matt. It's got worse. We don't see each other that much nowadays, you don't know.'

I wondered about telling him how on Wednesday night I went for a pint in Victoria Station when I was waiting for a train, and woke up on a bench at one in the morning. 'To tell you the truth, I've been considering drinking a bit less,' I said.

He smiled. 'What, early retirement?'

The early retiring line had never sounded as funny, as beautiful, as it did now. It meant nothing had changed between us. I wanted to hug him, then take him for a beer to celebrate the fact that we were still mates.

'Why don't you try stopping completely for a bit?' he said. 'Go teetotal for a month. Prove you can do it.'

Go teetotal? I was considering drinking *less*. No one mentioned not drinking at all. That wasn't what I had in mind. At the moment it wasn't practical, either. There was the wedding next weekend for starters. And there was the Dublin trip next month, that would be a big one. Even this week would be impossible: I was going out on Tuesday and there was a work leaving-do on Wednesday and Thursday was my quiet night on my own recovering in the Star. Then there was the weekend after next. It would only be my third without Emma, and I didn't have anything planned. It wouldn't be as easy as this weekend, there wouldn't be anything to help me take my mind off her. I suppose there was Monday – tomorrow – but after struggling through the first day back at work after the weekend, I liked to collapse in front of the telly with a few tinnies. I'd do it if all my mates were going to stop. But they didn't have the slightest intention of even cutting down. What was I supposed to do? Go out with them and watch them all getting blotto? A great laugh that would be.

'That's a bit rash, mate. Maybe I'll cut down.'

'Do that, then, but do something. Please, Rob. You could set yourself a limit. Never have more than, say, four pints.'

'Four pints of vodka, that should just about do.'

'I'm being serious here,' Matt said, his expression reminding me of Stevie's just before he slapped me last night – as if this was somehow new territory. Four's not too bad, I suppose. That was workable. Four meant six and that was OK. I'd just have to make sure it was Stella.

'Seriously, why not?' Matt said.

What could I tell him? That it was when I'd had one I wanted another, and then another. If I was going to do it, I'd have to stop completely. Permanently. What would I be like then? I might not always like what I sometimes was now, but without the drinking there mightn't be anything left. I didn't answer.

'Only one thing for it, then,' he said firmly, 'you'll have to pack it in altogether. It doesn't have to be for ever, not to start with – you could try doing it for a few weeks.'

For as long as I'd known him, Matt had tried to get me to drink; now he was trying to make me stop.

'You can do it, I just know you can,' he said, and again I could have hugged him. I love you for the faith you've got in me, mate, I wanted to say, but you don't know me, not when it comes to booze. I wanted to say: I'm not strong enough for this, Matt.

Cars streamed past on the ring road.

'I'd help,' he said, 'we'd all help.'

It occurred to me that Matt was the sort of bloke who *would* stick by me even if I carried on drinking. He stared at me, as if he knew the way my mind was working. 'You've got to try and do this.'

I could hear everyone shouting at the other end of the pitch, but couldn't make out what all the fuss was about.

I said: 'I'd be a much more focused person. Much more disciplined. I'd be a better person, do you know what I mean, I'd work harder and waste less time, all that stuff . . .' I felt the *but* already formed, loaded even before the sentence was started. 'But, but, anyone can do those things. I'd get up earlier for work and be more sensible and not occasionally say things I shouldn't but wouldn't I be just boring? Going out's fun. Getting bevvied's fun. It's better than being boring, surely?'

As I said it, I had a vision of pissing in an alley some time last night, unable to get my flies undone, feeling the warmth on my leg. I'll take boring any day of the week, I thought.

Matt said: 'No one said anything about not going out. It's just the not drinking we're talking about here.'

It had never occurred to me that the two could be separated. But

166

I suppose that was how I'd been about going out and smoking before Emma.

'Listen, Rob, between you and me, that's the only reason I didn't ask you to be my best man, to be honest. Because of the drink. Katie was a bit worried you'd, you know, get a bit carried away and maybe not cope with it all too well.'

So it was Katie's idea. I felt angry at her, then I felt angry at myself for not having made more of an effort to act sober – to seem more altogether – that time I met her. Finally and almost violently, I felt angry with the booze. It had stopped me being Matt's best man. I touched the wound on my head.

'You know what you need,' Matt said. 'You need a hobby.'

'I've got one. Fishing.'

'Since when?'

'Since always.'

I hadn't been fishing for years, though. I was so passionate about it when I was younger, too. Where did that go?

'Well, do more of that,' he said.

Nice idea – but the thing is, if I was sat on the river bank, I wouldn't be in the pub. Maybe one day fishing, one day in the pub to start with? See how it goes.

'You'll have me caravanning and trainspotting next.'

'I'm trying to be serious here. I'm trying to help you.'

Is that what it had come to, needing help?

'It doesn't matter what you do. Play golf, do gardening, go hang-gliding, take up synchronised wanking if you like! Anything as long as it turns you on and keeps you out of pubs.'

I was tempted to say: What turns me on was that girl with freckles last night, but I couldn't remember whether Matt had talked to her, and he didn't look as if he was in a joking mood.

'Try spending a few weekends sitting on the river bank.' He'd got his hand on my wrist. 'You've got to *want* to do this, Rob.'

It struck me how sitting on the river bank was all it would take to keep me out of the pub, and I felt scared. Drinking could so easily be taken from me.

'But weekends are the one time I get to drink properly. Two whole, beautiful days of it. I love it Matt, I can't stop that, I can't *not* do it.'

He drew in closer to me, so close I noticed the flecks of blood on his neck from where he'd shaved.

'Rob, are you . . . are you . . . are you an . . .'

The ball hit him on the back of the head. Matt grabbed it and whacked it back up to the other end. Then he sat down again and I picked at the mud and we stayed like that in silence for a while.

'What happened between you and Stevie last night?'

'Nothing.'

'You sure?'

'Yes, why?'

'There seemed a bit of tension between you.'

Stevie obviously hadn't told Matt. I could give him my side of events now, blame Stevie. But I didn't have a side of events. I *couldn't* blame Stevie.

'Something did happen, actually. I mentioned Vicki.'

'Oops. I wouldn't worry about it, though, I put my foot in it all the time about her.'

'No, but I said a load of stuff I shouldn't.'

I would have told Matt what, but I couldn't remember what I said. And he wasn't listening anyway; he was watching two girls walking past.

'You should have seen the girl Stevie was talking to in the club last night,' he said.

'I *was* there,' I answered.

Chapter Thirty-one

Back in Stevie's room, it was like any other Sunday morning. We all moaned about our hangovers, our stomachs, our bank balances. The headache pills got passed round. I did what I always did: read the recommended dose and doubled it. I wasn't, it turned out, the only one who was off my face last night. James had tried to climb a lamp-post, apparently.

Matt and James disappeared to collect their stuff. I stayed. It was just me and Stevie. Funny, but I couldn't remember ever being alone with him before, although I must have been. It occurred to me he could hit me now.

He sat down in the chair and put his feet up on the windowsill, then stretched back. His shirt strained across his shoulders. He'd showered and I could smell his aftershave: the room smelt how his room in Halls always used to. I wondered where to begin. Setting this right felt like the first step to setting everything right. Would it help if I told him how I'd felt last night? Thing is, I couldn't *remember*.

'Listen Stevie, about last night . . .'

'What about last night?'

'I need to talk to you about what happened.'

'Go on, then.'

'I was a right dickhead.'

'Were you,' he said coldly. 'I wouldn't have guessed.'

'Yes, I was, I was to you. And I'm sorry.'

'One of those things.'

I didn't know if he meant it, he was so hard to read. But I couldn't leave it like this. It would eat me up.

'Thanks for getting me home; Matt told me it was you that looked after me.'

169

'Couldn't exactly leave you in the state you was in, could I?'

The way he said 'state' made me suddenly aware of his Yorkshire accent again. That always *was* one of the words that made it sound strongest. And what kind of state was I in? Was it just the typical Saturday-night state, or worse? Matt would have told me, surely, but maybe Matt didn't know.

'Well, cheers. I owe you one.'

'Don't mention it. I was going your way anyway.'

He said I, not we. Maybe that girl didn't come back with him? Or maybe she *was* with him when he put me to bed. Maybe she helped, thinking all the while about Stevie: He's kind, he looks after his mates. And about me: How can anyone let themselves get like that? After he'd put me to bed, he would have had her all to himself. They could have slept together in here with me comatose next door. And afterwards, they'd have talked, talked as you do with a one-night stand – no shadow-boxing, they both knew the score – and she'd have thought how sensitive *he* was because of how he'd helped me, the drunk bloke. I looked at the bed, then at him, and he knew just what I was thinking.

'Best man's job, isn't it, looking after the guests,' he said.

Best man! Guest! Was he having a dig? I almost wanted him to have a go at me now because if we fell out, really fell out, I might never have to see him again and, awful as that would be, it might prove easier than having to think about this weekend every time I did see him. I wouldn't have to feel so, so always in his shadow. If only I could remember what *did* happen, apart from him holding my shirt, that vein on the side of his forehead pumping, the slap. I still couldn't believe it: Stevie had slapped me.

'I was hoping we could forget about last night, put it down to experience.'

'Experience?'

'Yes, you know, *one of those things*?' How many times was I going to have to say I was sorry? 'Stevie, I'm sorry. Sorry about getting so hammered and you getting lumbered with me and about what happened earlier in the evening, too.'

He didn't say anything and I remembered the sting on my cheek when he hit me. I touched it now, involuntarily, but felt nothing. It was numb like the rest of me. The only thing I could feel was my head: the hangover, gently and continuously beating, and the occasional spear of pain around the cut on my forehead.

Everything was going wrong. Even my mates. *My mates.*

Stevie looked out the window. I did, too. It was the same view as from my room.

'I don't know what else to say, Stevie. I was pissed.'

He ran his hand through his hair again and I remembered burping at that girl. That line about leukaemia!

I wondered what he'd have done if I had hit him. 'What the fuck are you doing, Rob,' he'd probably have said, more surprised than dazed. And what would I have done then? I wouldn't have wanted to hit him again, not Stevie, but a fight's supposed to be about hitting someone again and again – hitting them so many times, so hard, that they can't fight back.

'I'm just so upset over Emma. The last thing I should have done was take it out on you.'

'I said: Don't mention it.'

But I couldn't not mention it. This could be the end of me and Stevie. I'd apologised and I couldn't see what more I could do. I felt bad enough as it was, without this. I knew I wouldn't be able to think about anything else until we'd cleared this up. Until he told me it didn't matter, it was forgotten. Please, Stevie, tell me those things.

'I'm sorry. I'm really sorry,' I said. 'I'd hate it if this came between us. I was upset about Emma. I was upset because I thought that girl was flirting with me. It took me back a bit seeing her with you; I was jealous.'

I waited for him to say: Don't worry, no sweat, these things happen. But he didn't.

I said: 'I shouldn't have mentioned Vicki either. That wasn't me last night, it was the booze.'

What was me? Last night *was* who I was. There wasn't another me. I wanted to put my arm round him, but it wouldn't feel right – not here, not now. Maybe it never would again.

'I'm so sorry,' I said again. I just wanted to go home. Wanted to go to the flat or Mum's – anywhere, really, just as long as it was away from all this: Stevie and this hotel and Newcastle and this stag weekend. So much for making me feel better. Once I was away, I could start forgetting.

So many Sundays now, apologising. How many more would there be? The prospect seemed impossible. I wiped my eyes; I was crying.

171

'What's happened to you?'

I didn't know if he meant right now, this instant, or just generally. When people asked me that, they usually meant generally. Drinking had done that. I had to stop. *Really* stop.

'You've got to sort yourself out, mate, you really have,' he said, coming towards me. He put his arms out and I wondered what he was going to do but he put them round me and hugged me and we stood there in the hotel room for a while like that. And Stevie said: 'Don't worry about last night, not a problem,' and I felt his shoulders and his back as I cried.

'I'm going to stop drinking, Steve,' I said, wiping my eyes. It sounded weird, like someone else in the room was saying it. And what if I couldn't? 'I mean it, none of this would have happened if I hadn't been drinking.'

'You'd better put some TCP on that,' he said, standing back, looking at my head. 'As beer wounds go, that's pretty impressive.'

'Thanks,' I said, laughing, wiping the snot from my nose.

And he laughed – a nice laugh, a Stevie laugh – and I felt a calm wash over me. I realised, too, how much I liked this bloke, how much less of me there'd somehow be if I'd never known him. It was pathetic, the way I'd always been so jealous of him.

'Sorry if I wrecked your evening.'

'You didn't,' he said, going into the loo.

I wondered again if he did get off with that girl. I hoped that he did; that way, his evening wouldn't have been completely ruined. Plus, I'd get to hear about her sooner or later: Stevie was almost as reliable as Matt when it came to giving statutory debriefs. I'd probably get to hear all the gory details next time we were in the pub.

But you're not drinking, remember.

Yes, but I could still go into pubs.

Would a statutory debrief still be funny if I wasn't drinking? I imagined myself standing next to Stevie, listening, with a Coke in my hand, and it was an odd sight, like somebody else.

What if he had got off with that girl and started going out with her? Freckle-face. The girl who looked like Abi. Becky, I think her name was. How embarrassing would that be? I'd die! She wouldn't forget me in a hurry. Maybe that was why I drank? I was just so tired of not being noticed.

But how wonderful it would have been this morning to be the one who didn't get remembered, who didn't stand out, to have been no more sober and no more drunk than anyone else.

Maybe if she did start going out with Stevie, she'd find out what I was really like, that last night was an aberration?

But I was like last night.

I felt dizzy and wished I hadn't come at all this weekend. It would have been better for everyone.

I thought about Becky and whatever it was in me when I first saw her had gone. I tried to recall seeing her when I'd been a bit sober but couldn't.

I wondered why I had been so desperate for her last night. Maybe all the booze had numbed me today. We stags were the important ones now. She was just a girl in a bar. Now, she was somewhere else and I'd probably never see her again; already there were more important things and knowing that made me sad.

Stevie was back in his chair, looking out of the window.

'I'm knackered,' he said.

'So who was the lucky lady last night then, Stevie?'

He ran his hand through his hair.

'You must have got off with someone. Law of averages and all that.'

'Put it this way: I didn't get much sleep.'

I waited for him to give me the debrief – tell me all about the 'bed athletics', as he sometimes termed it.

'I didn't get much sleep because I spent most of the night sitting up with you, mate, making sure you didn't choke.'

It wasn't the first time.

Neither of us spoke for a while.

'What was she like, Stevie, Becky?'

'Nothing happened, Rob. She buggered off; not that anything was going to happen anyway. I've met someone in Bath.'

'I didn't know that, you didn't tell me.'

'That's because it's early days yet. But it's going really well.'

'So is this it: is this finally Mrs Jones?'

Stevie smiled at me. A big grin. *His* big grin.

'I'm really happy for you,' I said.

'Cheers, Robbo. Now let's get moving. Checkout time.'

Chapter Thirty-two

The other two got the Metro down to the pub for lunch, but I couldn't face that, so I scabbed a lift off James. I felt a bit embarrassed about being around Matt, and Stevie as well, to be honest. James was the only one who hadn't said anything about last night.

He turned the key and the Pogues started playing, dead loud. 'Sally MacLennane'. I hadn't listened to it for ages – it just made me sad. I turned it off. 'Bit noisy for this time of day,' I said.

'Don't be such a killjoy,' James said, turning it back on, winding his window down, singing. We drove. I noticed that his head touched the roof; I wasn't sure if I'd ever been in a car with him before. I couldn't believe how much this suburb had changed. It was more like London than Newcastle. I recognised it as the place I knew, yet it was unmistakably different.

'Remember when we went to see the Pogues in the City Hall?' I asked.

'Yes, course I do.'

James stopped singing; the song played. Then he started singing again, shouting at the top of his voice, and I did, too: like that, concentrating on shouting, I could almost not notice the song itself.

James was going to take Anna, but she'd chucked him the day before the concert so he had a spare ticket.

I listened and I wanted it back: this band and the person I was then, the people *we* were then – but it was gone, all of it, gone for good. Somehow it had slipped away over the last decade or so.

'Look at you,' I said. 'All settled down. What would you have said if I'd told you a few years ago that you'd be married with a house and a kid on the way?'

'I would never have believed you. I can recommend it, though,' he said. And he smiled, a sort of I-know-I-shouldn't-be-saying-this smile.

I remember Dukie saying to me on his stag night, about the only thing I could remember from that night: 'If it doesn't work out, at least I can say I've given it a go.' Then he'd added: 'But it will work out.'

I saw the map on the floor, the little notepad on the dashboard, the coins in the coin compartment. It was like someone's dad's car.

James turned the music up.

We were standing against the pillar in the cellar bar of the City Hall. Girls dancing on chairs. Blokes skulking round the edges, getting legless. The support band playing. That aching inside even then, that later would be this. We'd gone into the auditorium with everyone else and I'd known we'd be friends from now on. It was the first gig I'd been to. 'Brillo,' James had said as we piled out. 'Not what I had in mind for tonight, taking you, but wasn't that the business?'

Afterwards, we went to the Onion for a couple and I ended up snogging Rach on the dance floor. That's right: it was the night me and Rach first slept together. Hadn't really thought about her for ages; now I would again. That was all I needed – having Rach, as well as Emma, on my mind. I'd hoped Rach was well and truly in the past.

'Listen,' I said, 'we're going to beat the others to the pub by ages, why don't we take a little detour – why don't we drive over the bridge?'

'Where do you think I'm going?' the Duke said.

We stopped at traffic lights and we sang and two people – students, by the look of them – were at a bus stop; I couldn't take my eyes off them, couldn't get it out of my head that they had it all in front of them. They were still, just, at the stage where there weren't choices. You do something – go to university, say – and know it was the right thing to do and that it didn't mean *not* doing something else, not really.

I watched them; he was lighting a cigarette and she put her head on his shoulder. I felt angry and a little jealous and a little protective, too, wanting to tell them: Enjoy this.

The previous weekend I'd dug out our graduation photos. Stood uncomfortably in those gowns with the mortar boards on, we all looked so young. Claire looked like a little kid. And literally everyone was smiling. There wasn't a single person in any of those photos who wasn't. It made me cry, looking at them. Just because we were like that once, and weren't any more.

'Bloody students,' James said. 'Squandering our hard-earned money on drink and drugs.'

The lights changed and we drove on. Look after yourselves, I thought. Look after each other. They'd go home and there wouldn't be any food in the house and it would be a pigsty and there'd be nothing on telly, so one of them would suggest going out, just for a quick one, and they'd end up in the Sun or wherever the in-place was nowadays and that would be it, they'd be settled in for the night then. Impromptu nights like that always were the best. Exam time, I thought, and they'd be out in their front gardens. Sitting on deckchairs, reading, chatting, waiting for six o'clock to head off for a beer. Just for a break, then back to work. Having coffee together the next morning with hangovers, and worrying about missing a day's revision. Getting a degree anyway. Graduation day. Loading up the car. Hugging their housemates and driving away.

Then this. Like me. I wouldn't wish that on anyone.

I, too, would go home and find there was no food in the flat and it would be a pigsty and there'd be nothing on telly, nothing for me to do.

They would be going home to their shared houses. They'd be listening to loud music from a CD player on the kitchen table and it might not be the Pogues, but it would be *their* Pogues. They'd be feeling what I had that night in the City Hall. These two, and millions of people like them.

Tonight, somewhere, would be the night one of them got pissed and had to be carried home.

Tonight, somewhere, would be the night two people who had been flirting since the beginning of term slept together.

Tonight, somewhere, would be the night there was a fight or someone's car got nicked, or one of them had a phone call saying his brother had been badly hurt in a car smash, as had happened that night to Matt.

They didn't know it now, but I did.

I looked up; we were on the bridge.

'Bloody students,' I said to the Duke.

He wasn't listening; he was on the phone to his wife.

176

Chapter Thirty-three

Rach was with her husband and her son.

She seemed, I don't know, middle-aged. Like a woman version of the girl I'd known. All grown-up. I thought: When did that happen?

We swapped news on mutual friends. Talked about the old days. Laughed. Her husband shifted uncomfortably from foot to foot. Ollie, his name was. She was mine once, Ollie, long before she even met you, I thought. I remembered that black dress she wore on her twenty-first. Her favourite necklace. That time she dressed up as a pirate for a fancy dress party. How turned on I could sometimes get, just being in the same room as her.

Ten years had passed since we'd been seeing each other. Ten years and now I'm seeing Emma, I thought, and there were others between you and Emma – of course there were – but I still remember how I loved you, Rach. I may not love you *now* but I can still remember how it felt. I always will.

We chatted. They lived in Wiltshire. She'd packed up work; Ollie was an estate agent. They were up in London visiting some friends for the day. Emma was in the Star waiting for me. I'd just nipped out to buy some cigarettes. It was a chance in a million, bumping into Rach.

'And what are you doing with yourself nowadays?' Ollie asked, like we were old pals, like we'd even met before.

'I'm in market research,' I answered. 'One of the big firms up in town.'

'You always told me you were going to become a teacher, Rob,' Rach said.

'Yes, I did, didn't I.'

Go, Ollie, piss off for a few minutes so it's just the two – well,

177

the three – of us. He stayed. Your wife helped me go to the toilet once when I was legless, bet she's never told you that, Ollie, has she. Your wife and I had a shower together that night after we missed the last Metro and walked back in the rain because we couldn't afford a taxi. Once, when we were on that holiday in Greece, she told me she'd like to have three kids.

But they were the ones who'd got married and that could never change now. Even if they got divorced, they could never *not* have been married. They'd lived together, had a child, he'd been with her longer than I had. We lasted a little over a year, me and Rach. We'd gone to the café for lunch and I wouldn't have guessed in a million years she was going to dump me.

I was mortified.

I probably should have seen it coming, though. 'I don't want to get too tied down while I'm at university,' she'd said.

We stood on the pavement outside the Star; Emma would be wondering why I was taking so long.

Rach fed the kid an ice cream. That could have been mine, I thought, not bitterly or jealously or thankfully: it was just a fact.

'Josh, meet Rob; Rob, Josh.'

I'd forgotten how she said my name, slightly rolling the R.

I shook the boy's little hand. 'You at school yet then?'

'He's two, Rob,' she said, grinning.

I saw the tiny chip on her front right tooth.

Then I watched her go, Rach and her new husband and her new son, willing her to look back. It was as if I had to explain something to her. Still, after all this time. I wanted to shout out: Rach, wait, please don't go. I didn't want the same amount of time to go by before I saw her again.

I went home and dug out my Sinead O'Connor CD and played it at full volume and remembered Rach in fits of laughter as me and Matt had sung along. She had said how she could see the two of us still best friends when we were old. 'Bestest', was her expression. Then, in bed that night, she said she knew what I'd look like when I was old, too. Me. It was kids' stuff, I guess, saying those things, but she'd said them to me, and I was glad. I was convinced we were going to settle down together. You know, get married and stuff.

I still knew all the words.

The woman in the flat downstairs banged on her ceiling when I turned the music up.

I must have listened to 'Nothing Compares 2 U' about twenty times that night after I bumped into Rach. Emma had gone home in a strop because I wouldn't leave the pub. I felt guilty, playing it, as if I was being unfaithful to Emma; but then I wondered if in a funny way *Rach* was the one I'd been unfaithful to all this time.

I knew things weren't going well between me and Emma and thinking about Rach helped. Once upon a time, she meant the world to me. There wasn't anything I wouldn't have done for her. We made love, once, in the bluebell woods behind her mum and dad's house (neither of us had done it outside before) and she hung onto me as I came, a bluster of uncontrolled young excitement. I'd forgotten that. It was April, the very end of April, and she'd insisted that we go walking there that weekend. 'It's got to be *this* weekend,' she'd said. 'The bluebells are only at their best for a few days.'

Now, she was somebody I bumped into at Wimbledon station. Somebody whose kid I smiled at, awkwardly, and asked: 'How old is he?' Then, for the laugh: 'Or is it a she?'

Chapter Thirty-four

It felt odd, being here and deliberating *whether* to drink. The only deliberation I'd ever done in the Three Kings was over *what* to drink. Yes, I know I said earlier I was going to stop, but that's the sort of thing you do say when you're hungover. And I didn't know we were coming to the Three Kings, then, did I? If I'd known that, I'd have said I'd never drink again *after* today. This was different, this didn't count.

'What do we want then, voddies all round?' I asked. I was joking, I had no intention of having a voddie – at least, not unless the others did. 'Go on, it's a stag weekend.'

'It was,' Matt said, 'and today's the day after it. Today's Sunday.' He sidled up to me. 'Remember what you were saying earlier.'

I did remember, but it seemed ages ago, almost as if it wasn't me saying it. 'Don't be a killjoy. Come on, let's have one for old times' sake.'

I felt the palm of his hand in the small of my back – it wasn't heavy or clumsy, but gentle, like the way you'd touch a child, or something very small. 'Please, Rob.'

The others told me what they wanted and I set off for the bar. Images of last night hit me: glasses, faces, conversations, colours. I steadied myself. Looked around. Took my bearings. Acclimatised. There. That was better. But then I caught a whiff of beer and had to stop, stand still. I almost heaved. I remembered how I'd knelt over the bog this morning and how, after I'd been sick, I hadn't had the strength to get back up for ages.

I wasn't going to have a drink.

I got the round: a pint of Coke for Matt, a pint of orange juice and lemonade for James, a shandy for Stevie and an orange juice and lemonade for me.

The barman, a stocky Geordie lad, glanced at the graze on my head. Probably assumed I'd got it from falling off a mountain bike or playing squash or something sensible. When he put the drinks in front of me, he said: 'Now you go easy with this lot, young man.'

If only he knew.

I went back to the table. Should have had a Coke, at least that would have *looked* a bit like a Guinness. Could always have a real one next round, I suppose. The lads had said they'd only stop for one, but people always said that. They might change their minds – it was Sunday afternoon, after all, what else was there to do?

The others were talking about New Year's Eve: how special it was going to be, what with it being the Millennium. James was taking Sarah to the Lake District; Matt was going to Paris with Katie for their first New Year married; and Stevie had got a cottage with some mates from work. They were laughing as much as they had been last night. My friends could do it sober. Didn't know how, but they could. I didn't have anything to say. I'd got no plans for New Year's Eve. I felt bored. I sipped my orange juice and lemonade: it felt sharp on my gums.

It had unsettled me, Matt saying, 'Remember what you were saying earlier,' when I got the round. Something new and serious in the way he said it.

Soon my glass was empty and then I had nothing to do. I went to buy some cigarettes – sod it, I smoked enough last night, a few more wouldn't hurt – and got that same little hit of excitement as they dropped out the machine.

I offered them round, but no one wanted one. Matt gave me the look he had earlier at the bar. 'Thought you'd given up.'

Who are you, I thought, my dad! 'Stag nights don't count,' I replied, laughing.

I smoked; they talked.

Stay sober, Rob. Stay sober. The fun's over. The weekend's winding down; everyone's going home. Stay sober and I might just be able to put last night down to the excesses of a stag night. But all those drinks behind the bar! Beer and lager and shorts and even brandy.

Me and Matt found a bottle of brandy in the cupboard after we moved into Merryfield Road and had it all one afternoon.

It was like they were already poured, waiting behind the bar for me. They'd put me back on a par with my friends. Close, just a few feet away, was something that could make all the pain in my head go away.

'Right,' I said, 'I'm going to get a proper drink, just a quickie. Who's going to join me?'

The others weren't even halfway down theirs.

Stevie agreed to have a shandy; I called him a Shandy Boy.

'Don't want to make a fool of myself now, do I,' he said.

I turned to the other two. 'Sherry?' I said, hoping they'd laugh, hoping they'd pick up on the line and do that thing from *Withnail and I* where we all say 'Sherry' about five times. But all they did was ask for more soft drinks, halves this time.

I hoped it would be the same man who served me so he knew I was on the pints, but there was no sign of him. I walked towards the bar and knew I'd got away with last night. The lads weren't pissed off with me, not really. Matt had said he didn't like the person I was last night, but that was just then. And that business with Stevie, stuff like that could make you even closer friends. Now I was here, in this old place with three of my best mates, and could have a beer and forget all about it. I could have cried with relief. I watched the lager coming out of the tap and the bubbles in the glass and the slops on the bar and, again, I nearly heaved. But I had known it would be like this, it always was. I also knew it would be better soon. The barman went to put the glass on the bar but I grabbed it from him and had a big swig. Then I put it down there. I lit another cigarette, had a drag, then rested it in the little groove in the ashtray, the way I liked to, and had another sip. Immediately, it felt good.

I felt the badness draining away and something good and familiar taking its place. This is how chemotherapy must work. I took another big swig. There, more chemotherapy. Get better, body, I thought. Heal.

I took a deep drag on my cigarette and blew the smoke out of my nose, the way I liked to, and I knew that this was it, this was *me*. Everything that had come before was readying me for this. I was a natural.

I gritted my teeth, clenched my fists. Felt like shouting: *Yes, this is what I've been missing, this is it. I've found it.*

It was like when you're a kid and after not understanding long division for months, you suddenly just get it. Finally, you *see*.

I took more beer, drew again on my cigarette. This was enough: listening and watching the smoke rising, beautifully blue and

182

gracious. Lost friends, hangovers, illness – any of it was bearable if I could feel like this. The morning cough, the pins and needles in my hands and feet, headaches that could knock me over, I'd put up with all of it.

Anything was possible.

Why had I been denying myself this?

I sat down again. The others were still talking, God knows what about, and I stared at the top of my beer. Took a big mouthful. I put the glass down and immediately wanted more. I had another mouthful, then another and then another. A good feeling rippled through me. Soon, there wasn't any left.

I went to the gents'; they were miles away in here. We always used to laugh that by the time you got back, you needed to go again. It was hard pissing, like I was trying to squeeze something out that didn't want to leave. I remembered, for some reason, Rach's twenty-first birthday: the actual night, the Tuesday, when we came here, not the weekend she had the party at home. I was out of it; she had to help me go to the toilet. 'That's really how I wanted to spend my birthday,' she'd joked afterwards. I'd brought her here for a meal, but we sat in the Sun for so long they'd stopped doing food by the time we arrived, so we had a quick one and legged it back to the Sun for last orders.

Walking back from the loos, I thought: Two won't be excessive; two will be fine; lots of people have two on a Sunday afternoon; I'll be eating and it's a stag weekend; even three would be OK – which made two seem quite restrained.

'I'll get some more,' I said to no one in particular, realising I was smiling.

It was good stuff, this Stella.

Things weren't so bad: that graze on my head would heal, they always had before. In time, it would make a story. My mates had always stuck by me in the past. They liked me as much because of the drinking as in spite of it. There, that was a good argument. Who said my brain was frazzled? So I got bevvied sometimes, who didn't?

'We're OK with these,' Matt said. He – like the others – was nowhere near finishing the one he'd got. 'It's not your round anyway.'

Funny, I thought, he'd spent all morning trying to get me to go teetotal and now he was trying to buy me the stuff!

'I'm going to be skint soon if I've got to buy a caravan,' I said, laughing loudly and putting my arm round him. A couple on the next table glanced at us, and Matt wriggled away from me.

'Let me give you some cash, then,' Matt said. 'If you're determined to have one, I can't stop you, but I don't want you complaining I'm dodging my round.'

He counted out a couple of quid in change. It was leftovers from last night's kitty: shrapnel.

I stood at the bar, counted my money and listened to my friends' conversation. They were talking about a canoeing weekend in the Peak District. 'So, you up for it?' James asked Stevie. 'Too right I am, Dukie.'

They had long since given up asking me whether I was up for anything like that. The conversation went on to sport, restaurants, politics – politics, for Christ's sake! Someone was talking about mortgages. Whose voice was that? I turned round and it was Stevie. Stevie! Not you, please, not you. These people had changed. Everything had changed since we were at college. Then, we used to fit other stuff in the gaps between *us*. Now it was the other way round. We saw each other when we weren't doing other things. I wanted my friends back. The people that these guys *used* to be. It was like they'd been taken over by a strange spirit, a demon. They needed exorcising.

'Maybe next time we all meet up, we'll do some exercise,' I laughed at no one in particular. 'Something energetic. Something exciting. Trainspotting, maybe.'

No one answered. They were talking about the best places to buy sofas. And how much the service charge should be for a flat, whatever that was. I didn't know where or when, but sometime between graduation day and now, they had become *adults*.

Where was the Stevie I knew? The man who slept on kitchen floors and park benches. The man who could quote almost every line from *Platoon*. The man whose favourite expression for years had been: What goes on tour stays on tour.

I wondered how much they'd put up with, how much they'd forgive, because it was me. Everyone had their breaking point. I remembered Matt standing over me in the middle of the night last year – we were in his new flat – and him holding my head over a bucket, carelessly. I could still vaguely remember it lolling around like a vegetable, him saying: 'Not on the fucking carpet, Rob,' as I puked. And the look on James's face that night in Amsterdam when I suggested we went into that massage parlour. 'No, I can't do that,' he had said as we stood in the street outside. 'Don't you think it's a bit sleazy?'

'Precisely,' I'd replied, laughing.

Sooner or later, I'd run out of excuses and they'd run out of patience. They wouldn't want me upsetting the neighbours in their newly mortgaged houses, puking on their new sofas, pissing on the carpets that they had to change nappies on and breaking the table the in-laws gave them as a moving-in present.

Stevie was talking about the gym and I imagined him there. His biceps were big: proper biceps, how blokes' arms were supposed to be. He could have killed me last night. I felt a new anger rising in me, coming out from under the tiredness and the sickness – an anger at myself for not looking like that, like Stevie, for ... for being so pathetic, for what happened last night, for all of it. I couldn't bear it a second longer and if I wanted to get pissed I would, no one could stop me, no one.

A vodka. Sneak a vodka in. Why tell the others? It had nothing to do with them. I checked to see if there was a discreet bit of bar, but there wasn't. I knew we should have gone to the Sun: that place had loads of odd corners and quiet bits out of sight. There would have been plenty of spots I could have disappeared in there. At least, there would have been if it hadn't been pulled to pieces for this so-called refurbishment. 'We've seen enough of that place for one weekend,' James had said, when I suggested we went there for lunch. They opted for here because it was near the station. I complained, but, of course, no one listened to me. Not that I was particularly bothered where we went: I was just relieved we weren't going home. Yes, sneak a voddie in while I was up here at the bar then go back with a soft drink and no one would be any the wiser. Maybe then I'd talk? Laugh? Another one wouldn't hurt. Yes, I know it was a vodka and it was early, but if it was early then I'd have all afternoon for it to work through my system. I was just having a good time with my mates. I imagined myself dabbing the ice with my forefinger, how the lemon would taste, the ice banging against my lips. But you don't have to imagine, Rob. Go on. Go on.

I recalled the night I came here with Matt and all his Hockey Club mates. 'Down in one, down in one,' they'd yelled at me, forcing me to drink from that hockey shoe. And last night – which pub was that? – Matt buying me a short and singing 'Down in one' as he thrust it at me. I slipped along the bar and bought a double vodka and Coke, not too much Coke, and a bottle of still water, and had a swig of the vodka; as with that first ciggie last night, there was something almost sexual in the feeling: succumbing. Like, it's out of my hands now. Just two swigs saw it off and then I went and sat back down with the lads. They stared at the water.

'A body like mine's worth looking after,' I said, flexing the muscles in my right arm and feeling them with my left hand. It was the same old feeling: the sinewy thinness. Then I sat, sipping the water and listening and waiting for the vodka to work. It wouldn't take long. It was nice, listening. It was enough now. I listened to the conversation of these people, my friends, caught bits and missed bits and there was no need to talk. I was a part of it again. Something reminded me of when I was a kid, lying in bed and listening to the faint purr of conversation from my parents downstairs.

Some old boy was asleep on his own at a table next to us. 'Must be my sparkling conversation,' I said to the barman when he came round collecting glasses.

'Don't take it personally, he's always like that,' he laughed.

The brown of the table began to look all soft and honey-coloured. I put my foot up on the footrest of an empty stool: that felt so good. Thank you for all this, I thought. *Thank you.* I made a concerted effort not to look tipsy. Stifled a giggle. I looked at my friends and it struck me I liked knowing something they didn't.

'Still on the wagon then, Rob?' Matt asked. It was like he knew, but he couldn't, I'd stood behind some fat guy to neck it. An image of me lolling around plastered on a wagon came to mind. I burst out laughing.

'Rob says he's been thinking about not drinking a lot recently,' Matt said.

'What?' Stevie asked. 'You've been thinking a lot about not drinking, or you've been thinking about not drinking a lot?'

It was classic Stevie. Hungover and still sharp. I haven't forgotten what you did last night, Stevie. How you nicked that girl off me.

'I'm on the wagon,' I said, laughing, deliberately swaying from side to side, pretending to be on a real wagon. 'Actually, I've been thinking about getting some mates who aren't afraid of a good time on a Sunday afternoon.' I meant it as a witty retort. But it sounded cold. Cold and nasty.

'Don't get plastered again now,' Matt said. 'Please.'

'But you said this morning I had to set myself a limit. You said when I went out I had to drink four. I've only had one. We're supposed to be stags, aren't we?'

He didn't reply; he turned back to the others.

I didn't care. Why was it me who was in the wrong? Maybe these guys with their mortgages and their pensions and their Sunday trips to the in-laws – sorry, the outlaws: ho, ho, ho – were the ones who were wrong. Maybe they were the one-dimensional ones. Matt had joined a conversation about the Millennium Dome. Stevie quite liked Peter Mandelson, apparently, reckoned he was more erudite then Tony Blair. That's the word he used: erudite! What was this, a work meeting? Well I'd got some blue-sky ideas about lager if it was. I'd run with the booze. It was *my* baby, after all!

It occurred to me, as they were talking, that I didn't have one single political opinion. Vodka. It's all so pointless. I remembered being on King's Cross station in the week, going across it, and how I'd had to stop and sit down because it didn't matter, any of it, the noticeboard telling people what time the trains came at, the dirty white tiles on the floor, the pigeons and the people moving, moving, moving. It didn't matter and I couldn't face it, couldn't do it.

Accept it. Have another drink. This is me.

At last, I thought, I can do this more often. Do it without the uncertainty, without the guilt. Just get down to some drinking. Today, and for ever.

'Here's to one-dimensional-ness,' I said, raising my bottle of water. It was Evian and, for some reason, the label made me laugh.

The three of them carried on talking among themselves.

'I want to propose a toast,' I butted in, my voice louder now. 'A toast to Matt, and to Matt and Katie, the couple, and a toast to the institution of marriage. Cheers.' I swigged the water.

The others glanced at me, then started chatting again.

'And to James with his lovely wife and kid and Stevie and his lovely wife – oh sorry, silly me, you haven't got a lovely wife, have you, you're like me: single.'

The three of them looked at each other and it struck me that none of my friends, not one of them, was smiling. That seemed odd.

'Thanks for that, Rob. Touching,' Matt said.

I'd surprised myself, to be honest. But these things happen when you're drinking. It's an occupational hazard.

'I fancy a top-up,' I said. 'Don't suppose there's any danger of any of you lot having one?'

187

Nos, no thanks, no time. Not even a half among them.

'We've got to get home soon, Rob,' Matt said. 'We all have.'

I went to the bar, bought another voddie – a double, yes, course I want a double. 'I'm celebrating,' I told the barmaid. 'Yes, I'll tell you what I'm celebrating, I'm celebrating one-dimensional-ness.'

'Oh,' she said, uninterested.

And I thought again: *So be it. I'm just being myself – if this is what it means, then so be it.*

I watched her pouring it: beautiful – it and her – and paid. I took a sip, the first long, magnificent sip, and didn't want to put the glass down. Not ever.

After two sips, the vodka had gone.

Emma once said that watching me drink was like watching a switch tripping. It was as if the second I had the first sip I couldn't stop until I was wasted. She'd said it one Monday morning after we'd been out on Sunday afternoon. She'd stuck on Diet Cokes, but I'd put away eight or nine pints. 'It's not a crime,' I said the next morning when we'd argued and she cried.

'It would be nice to do something else once in a while than sitting in the pub.'

'I love you,' I'd told her.

'Love you too,' she'd said.

Nobody had ever said that about me before – about the switch tripping – and I'd thought: Here's someone who really knows me. I was embarrassed about drinking in front of her for a while after that. It meant she knew how I felt when I swallowed the first sip, when I walked into a pub, when I saw a small glass with vodka and Coke in it next to a pint glass. Even when I leant against the bar. It was like a switch tripping. I felt embarrassed and exposed. It was supposed to be my secret. It was about the time our relationship began to go down the pan. I remembered the evening we split up, Emma on the doorstep, me outside. It seemed clearer than the previous time I'd thought about it.

'Don't cry Emma, please don't,' I'd said.

'I might as well, I'm going to when you're gone.'

We both knew that *gone* was for good. For ever.

It's over, I'd thought. She'll never have me back now. I've blown it.

I went back and the others were collecting up their stuff. 'We're off,' Matt said. 'Are you coming or not?'

Chapter Thirty-five

My mates had gone, but it didn't matter.

I felt good, I was rocking. What a place. What a weekend. I wandered through the Bigg Market and my feet were light, off the ground. I was floating. I loved this feeling. So what if I drank. All the students round here did, and I wasn't that much older than them. Only eight years older than the third-years.

And stuff like last night happened. I remembered when I'd gone over to Nicki-with-an-i, catching Matt's eye, and how he'd winked at me. And telling that girl who looked like Demi Moore – seriously, she looked *just* like her – how I recognised her from London when in fact she lived in Newcastle. I smiled. Mrs Married, even Mrs Married, what was it she said to me: 'Grow up.' Grow up! I was nearly thirty and she said that to me. It was hilarious. I couldn't help it if *she* was dull. She didn't know me. I was the life and soul, I was the good laugh. You needed someone like me on a stag weekend. A stag. And as for that bloke who got arsey when I actually pretended to be a stag, well, talk about a sense of humour failure. I'd have found it dead funny if someone had done that in a pub. And the blowing noise I made – so what if it didn't sound like a stag, how was I supposed to know what a stag sounds like – it was funny, funny. I know what I'll do, I'll call in at that sports shop and sort myself out a hobby. I'll show them. They've got everything in that shop. I'll buy a golf club and get a football and play five-a-side in the park. I enjoyed our kickabout this morning, after all.

Having a hobby would give me something to do at weekends now I didn't have Emma around.

Look Emma, I'm getting over you. I'm getting hobbies. I'm looking to the future. We split up last week and here am I: having the time of my life.

A bell rang when I opened the shop door. I was tempted to do that stag thing again, stand in the door and do it, then run off. I was the only person in the place and it stank – all sanitised and sterile – not like the Three Kings. The bloke behind the till watched me, staring at me all oddly; he can't have thought I was going to try and nick something, surely.

'Can I help you?'

I concentrated. Sober. 'Just looking,' I said. 'Maybe I'll need some help in a bit.'

'Well just ask if you do, like,' he said. Another local.

I wished I talked like him: not a bit South-East, a bit London, a bit posh, a bit nothing. I went to where the golf stuff was. Looked at the price tags. The numbers were all blurred. This, even this, would make a good story for the lads.

There was a telly on the wall and some bloke was demonstrating swinging. If I'd have been with one of my mates, I'd have said: Is this what happens at those swingers' parties?

'Tee-off,' the guy doing the commentary on the telly said, and I wanted to crack a joke about tea. Making tea. Someone else had come in and was looking at clubs.

'Earl Grey if you're making,' I said. He walked off.

I'd been in here once before, I now remembered, to buy a badminton racket as a birthday present for Claire.

The bloke on the telly was hitting balls in slow motion. It was like when the Six-Million-Dollar Man used to do bionic stuff. And before he whacked them – this bloke, not the Six-Million-Dollar Man – he wriggled. It reminded me of a cat having a shit, and I laughed out loud.

The bloke behind the till eyed me up and down again, staring at my forehead. Hadn't he ever seen a bit of a graze before? 'Playing squash,' I said.

I picked up a club, found a bit of space, tried to do the wriggle. Swung. Swayed. The man came over. 'So, what can we do for you, sir?'

I suddenly realised I was pissed again. Shit. 'Golf,' I said. 'I'm after golf.'

'And which particular bit are you after, sir?'

'I'm after taking it up,' I said. I realised I pronounced it 'teking', echoing his accent. 'I'm a beginner and I want to start golf as a hobby. I could do with some clubs. Maybe some beginner's clubs?'

He pointed to a set in a red leather bag. 'Good starter set these, sir.' He took one out. 'There's a range in here, sir. Woods, irons, everything you need to get you going. Very reasonable price, too.'

I wanted to say I didn't need an iron, it was golf I was after, not neat shirts. And wood, woods, must be a joke in there somewhere ... couldn't find it, though. He held one out to me. I took it and held it in both hands, feeling its weight. 'Nice,' I said, staring back at him, feeling queasy.

Matt's voice breaking back to me: 'I don't know if I *liked* you much yesterday.'

The shop assistant was moving, both his faces were. It was funny, you should have seen him. I nearly burst out laughing. I fished through my pockets and found my Barclaycard.

Ten minutes later, I was on the station with a bag of clubs, a golf coat, a fishing rod, a football and a box of maggots. He'd asked how many maggots I'd needed and when I'd hesitated he'd said: 'A pint or a half?'

Automatically, I asked for a pint.

Chapter Thirty-six

It must have been about midnight and we'd been snogging all the way home: it started in the Onion and carried on when we were on the Metro and we were still snogging when we got back to Merryfield Road. Me and Claire were snogging!

It had been a cocktails night and for once she was more out of it than me. She'd just been dumped by some bloke and was gutted. I reckoned she was better off shot of him – he was a right beer monster, a real git – but I hadn't mentioned that because she was so upset. Towards last orders, though, she'd started crying and I decided it might make her feel better if I told her.

'I never liked the bloke anyway,' I said. 'You can do much better than him.'

What I thought was: Maybe you'll spend more time with us again now.

I couldn't get the key in the door and then Claire tried and she couldn't, and one of us fell into the garden and a light went on in Edie's place and somehow we got in.

We fell on the sofa and after a bit more snogging I put my hand up her skirt. Her tits were bigger than I thought they were. I rubbed them through the bra, then I rubbed her through her jeans. It felt like Claire, and not like Claire.

'Let's go upstairs,' she said.

One of us knocked the table lamp off the telly. We made it up the stairs, fell onto my bed.

I tried to get her bra undone, but couldn't.

She tugged at my trousers, but couldn't undo the belt.

I stood beside the bed, managed to do it, but got them stuck when I tried to get them over my shoes. I climbed back on the bed like that.

'Rob, I'm cold,' she said, pulling the duvet up over us.

We hung onto each other for a few seconds. 'Let's just go to sleep,' she said.

And the next thing I knew there was the smell of bacon. My head was pounding. I walked downstairs nervously, petrified things might have changed.

She came into the living room clutching a spatula. 'I don't believe it,' she giggled. 'You've touched my tits. I let you touch my tits.'

'Don't worry, I don't remember much about it. And if it's any consolation, they felt just like Matt's.'

We both laughed.

We ate breakfast and set off for college, a little cautious round each other. We both knew this had been bound to happen sooner or later; but now it had, we both knew it would never happen again.

'I couldn't go out with you,' I said. 'It would be like going out with one of the lads.'

'Thanks, Rob,' she said. 'You really know how to make a girl feel special.'

'I didn't mean that, I meant—'

'It's OK. It's just that every once in a while it would be nice if you lot saw me as something other than one of the lads.'

'What do you think I was doing last night?'

'Don't know,' she laughed. 'I don't remember much of last night either. Which is no bad thing!'

We walked to college; we had a Contested Countryside lecture. Stevie obviously doesn't see you as one of the lads, I thought. The pair of them had slept together in Freshers' Week.

We sneaked in the back of the lecture hall because we were a bit late, but the others all saw us come in and cheered.

Chapter Thirty-seven

I put the golf coat on. My jacket – a present from Emma – had got lost last night. I stood the clubs up against the wall but they kept falling over, so after a while I didn't bother trying.

I sat and waited for a train, the maggots on the bench next to me.

I lay down, the booze going out of me now. I just felt tired.

Woke up. Maggots by my face. Cold. Looked at the clock – one fifty – can only have been asleep for a few minutes. I retched but nothing came up. Hung onto the cold metal bench then retched again and puke came out. It splashed over the bench and on the platform. Retched again – noisy, like a dog barking. It felt like I was losing my insides.

'Disgusting,' a woman standing nearby said, walking away.

I felt disgusting; and disgusted.

Nothing more inside me to come out.

I wasn't going to drink today. I had promised myself I wouldn't – and now I had. I was pathetic. This wasn't funny, this was sad. Just as well the lads couldn't see me. I felt scared that I might get arrested or something for being sick on the station in the middle of the day, and scared at what I'd done last night to Stevie, let alone what I must have done generally for Matt to say he didn't like me any more. I knew I'd have to drink a lot now, drink continuously, to get through this, to forget, but I didn't have the energy.

I'd felt better in the Three Kings, but now I felt the same as I had this morning. Worse, in fact. The shivering had started. I might as well not have had those vodkas.

Drink, drink again, drink for the rest of the day and you'll feel better, a voice told me.

But something I'd never heard before was at work too. A voice in my head, saying, simply: Don't.

194

Is that what Tiger plays with – woods? The joke I should have thought of in the sports shop came to me but it didn't seem funny. The feeling when I'd seen that man wiggle like a cat wasn't funny now – and the good feeling I'd had walking through the Bigg Market and in the pub, having a laugh with all my mates, a stag weekend, had gone.

So had the headache.

Now it was just this.

Sitting here in Newcastle Central on a Sunday afternoon feeling nothing.

There was a 'Men At Work' sign on the platform. James had three or four signs in his room in the first year: a 'Men at Work' one he got when we were revising, a 'Toilets' one, and another that said 'Way Out' – which someone changed to 'On The Way Out' with a marker pen. I got a sudden urge to go and get it – this weekend's trophy – and I wondered if I could, without being seen. But there wasn't any point. Helen would have a fit if I took it into the flat and no one would be able to see it, propped up in the corner of my room.

My mates had gone.

Some guy said: 'Where are you playing?'

'What?'

'Which course are you playing?' He was overweight and middle-aged.

'I'm not,' I said. 'Just practising.'

He walked off.

One by one, carefully, precisely, I threw the maggots to the pigeons.

I had a hobby.

Chapter Thirty-eight

I went into the waiting room and sat, leaning forward, my head in my hands. The room stank, but after a while I didn't notice. A woman came in; I saw her shoes, her legs, her tights, the red skirt. I thought about seeing what she looked like, but couldn't be bothered. A door opened on my right, then another one. There was a brief silence and then she began to piss. It went on for ages. The pissing noise stopped briefly before starting again for a little while, desperately. Finally there was a flushing sound, then one door opened, then another, and the shoes and legs and tights and skirt walked back past me.

I didn't look up.

I stayed sitting there.

It stank of piss but in a few hours I would have forgotten that. Nothing lasted.

I tried to remember how many people had said to me this week: 'You'll meet someone else.' But I'd lost count. They'd meant it nicely, but what they were really saying was: Emma doesn't matter. Emma's dispensable. Emma means *nothing*.

How could I say to them I didn't want to meet anyone else.

That time she cried at *Titanic*.

The noises she made when she orgasmed. Hearing that for the first time.

Telling her about Dad.

Her expression when I explained to her for the very first time that I didn't always want to do the job I did now. What I wanted, what I really wanted – OK, it might be a pipe dream, but it could happen – was to work with young people. Kids. Teach. She'd looked surprised and somehow pleased, and I liked knowing it was me who'd made her feel like that.

But here I was facing the prospect of doing it all again. Meeting someone new. Spending time getting to know them. I didn't know if I had the energy. I'd done it all before, loads of times. I'd done it with Emma when I'd kind of thought deep down that this time might be the last.

Sleeping with someone I didn't know – at least, sleeping with them sober – petrified me. The leap of faith it took. The trust. And that stumbling towards familiarity, towards real intimacy. The stuff that took time, that could only come with time, all remained to be done afresh.

Back to square one.

What was it Matt had said last night – how knowing you were going to be with someone for the rest of your life was the best feeling in the world? He was right.

How many times was I expected to do this? I couldn't do it once more, let alone twice, three times, half a dozen . . .

What was the point?

Not letting yourself get too hopeful and being called a pessimist. Being optimistic and getting let down, or doing the letting down.

Always one or the other.

Either way, falling off the horse.

All wasted – with Emma and so many others before her.

Was it all for nothing?

I'd done it so many times.

I didn't want to, couldn't do it again.

Even the jealousy I used to feel for Emma – what was the point of that now? Emma could be in bed with someone else right now and I wouldn't have known. A time would come when I wouldn't even care. Hearing about it would be as irrelevant as hearing a weather forecast for a faraway place.

'You're silly, getting so jealous,' she'd once said. 'There's not exactly a queue of guys waiting to go out with me.'

Then, when I didn't answer, she'd said: 'You know I'd never cheat on you.'

And now? Nothing. That jealousy was gone with everything else. Gone with that nervous car journey the first time I went to meet her parents – sorry I made such a fuss about that, baby – the hangovers we saw off in bed together, you always slept on the left, didn't you, the meals out, all that time we spent together, even the silly seemingly unimportant time: the doing-nothing time, the evenings we sat in front of the telly. The sleeping, even. That was *our* time, Emma. And what was it now: gone, dead, wasted, pointless, nothing.

It's not your fault, baby, I know. But it's not mine either.

Maybe we met too soon? Too early? I don't know; I wished I had the answers but I didn't.

A few days ago we could have told each other personal things and now we couldn't even speak. Already, everything we had was being replaced. Waiting for a train at Wimbledon or Clapham Junction or Victoria, having a hangover, even having a cold, for Christ's sake – one by one I'd do the things I did with you, Emma. Except, without you.

Every day now, every moment, you're slipping into the past. Becoming an ex; something sounds so inconsequential about that.

And if we met in a few months' time, Emma, you'd say: 'Wow, very snazzy,' about my new car and I'd think: I've had that for ages. I'd feel sad that you didn't know, that we didn't talk about it, sad that you didn't tell me what colour to go for, what trim you liked.

Soon, if we were still speaking, we'd have to arrange to meet each other like work contacts. You'd say: 'I can do Tuesday and Thursday,' and I'd say 'I can do Wednesday and Thursday,' and we'd agree on Thursday and not know or ask what each other was doing on the other nights.

Soon, we'd have to look up each other's addresses. Soon I'd forget, too, which one of those herbal teas was your favourite, how you liked your shower so much hotter than me and how you preferred toast cold – cold, seriously – and how we liked to make love, too.

It would happen with you, Emma, as it had with the others. And I didn't want it to.

Pointless, all of it.

I love you, Emma.

Soon, though, I won't. Soon, though I will have *loved* you.

There doesn't seem much difference between the two words if you say them quickly: love; loved.

Just a d.

D for dunce.

You'd taken about ten rolls of photos on that holiday we'd had in Devon last month. It was like you knew. I imagined you now, getting two copies made, addressing an envelope to me and posting them. Posting them! It seemed so strange. Maybe I'd go back to Devon many years from now and joke about that holiday. 'Came here with a woman, did you?' whoever I was with would ask, smiling, taking photographs of her own.

I coughed, that rasping cough which you always used to say made me sound homeless. I lit a cigarette and took a long, deep drag.

A woman tutted and pointed at a No Smoking sign, so I went outside. No point *not* smoking now; my body was knackered anyway. It wasn't as if it would be putting my Great North Run attempt in jeopardy. Not exactly as if I was on course for a personal best this year. A PB, as Matt referred to them.

No point not smoking anyway. I come from a long line of short-livers.

There was a girl on the platform opposite me, standing on one leg and poking at the shoe on the foot she was standing on with the other one. She was making delicate little stabbing motions, wobbling as she did it, obviously trying to scrape something off it. It looked like a piece of chewing gum. But all she managed to do was get it stuck on the foot she was trying to get it off with, because she swapped legs and stood on her right and started poking at that shoe with her left one. The same thing kept happening; she kept shifting from leg to leg. I wondered why she didn't just bend down and pick it off. Or just leave it there and forget about it.

I went back in the waiting room; it reminded me of somewhere. Where? Which weekend? When? So much of the past I couldn't remember.

There didn't seem much point in having done anything if you just forgot it, or if you just had to do it again. Nothing was new. Even me saying to Emma: 'I'm going to drink less.' I said it to Rach once or twice too, nearly ten years earlier.

There didn't seem much point in doing anything any more.

All that anguish. All that pain. And for what? To be told – in your twenties and thirties – by people twice your age that you never stop learning. That you never stop making mistakes. That you never get it right. It was pointless. Less than pointless. Minus. Negative.

I didn't want to feel like this; I wanted this to end.

I would carry on going through it time and time again: the same stuff and new stuff in the same and slightly new ways. I would hurt others and they would hurt me. It didn't matter if it was deliberate or not. It only seemed fair to have to do it once. Remember, though, what that teacher I hated in senior school always used to say. 'Life's *not* fair,' he would tell us. And when he did, something in that twelve-year-old want to strike out at him. Because of the way he wore those glasses, because of the way he dropped me from the football team, because of the way he wouldn't let me and my best friend sit together, because I could almost feel a truth in what he said then. Already there was an ache, a confused feeling, in that child's chest that he knew would be there for good now. He felt it tug, like a fish on a line.

And I wondered then, sitting in the train station – as I had wondered as a kid – if I could do this rest of your life thing. There seemed so much.

Just as well, perhaps, we didn't know what was coming. If we knew what we'd have to endure, if you saw the markers of misery lined up like fence posts stretching across the horizons, you'd never go on. You'd just hang up your spurs.

Instead, it came in little instalments. Little phials of misery, peppered with just enough good times to keep you going. Little pockets of hope like morphine to deaden the pain.

And I wondered again if I could do this rest of your life thing, looking along the platform and down the train tracks which led out of Newcastle, seeing the people there, queuing, weary, quietly capitulating.

Chapter Thirty-nine

'Hello Robert,' Mum said, out of breath. 'How are you? Where are you?'

'I'm in Newcastle. Heading home after a stag weekend.'

I'd had a sudden urge to phone her. Tell her that I was well and happy. Laugh a lot, and make her laugh.

'Did you have a nice time?'

'Yes, fine, thanks.'

'Did you see the bridge?'

Mum, I thought, I didn't see anything. I don't remember anything. I was carried out the pub unconscious. Help me.

'Yes, I did, bit tired now, though. I'm just ringing to say hello, really, see how you are; it seems ages since we spoke.'

'Oh, that's nice. I'm fine. Can't seem to shake off this flu, though.' She sounded tired and very small. More than ever, I wanted to see her. It struck me how long it had been since I'd touched her.

'So, did you see all your friends? How are they, how's Matthew? Bet it's cold in Newcastle; still, I expect you found time to call in that pub you took me to, what was it called, the ...'

'The Rising Sun, Mum.'

'That's it, the Rising Sun.'

We'd gone there for lunch when Mum came up for my graduation.

'And how are you, more importantly?' she asked. 'They're not working you too hard, I hope?'

'Who?'

'Work.'

'No, course not. How are you doing, Mum?'

'I'm good thanks. There was a programme on telly about Falmouth last night, don't suppose you saw it, did you?'

'No, I was out, wasn't I.'

'Oh, yes, well it showed some of the places we used to go to – the beach and that pub that used to do those massive shepherd's pies. You remember Falmouth, don't you, Robert?'

'No, not really.'

I did though. We used to go there every year on holiday when I was a kid. We always stayed in the same cottages. Dad dragged me out walking most days. What good would it do either of us to talk about that now?

'What have you done this weekend?' I asked.

She told me that Auntie Barbara had popped in for tea last night, that she'd cooked a big lasagne with the top all browned off, the way I liked it. I took a drag on my cigarette; she coughed.

'Anyway I can't talk now, Mum. I'm in the train station.'

'OK, Robert,' she said, 'I'm about to have my dinner anyway. Thanks for ringing.'

She put the phone down.

I thought of her alone at that table. Putting a place mat out for herself and arranging the cutlery. Opening a bottle of wine, pouring herself a glass and putting the bottle back, gently and precisely, on the mat beside her plate. Chewing. Feeling, perhaps, a bit tipsy and wanting so much to be held, to be hugged. Then tonight, climbing the stairs to an empty bed.

I realised that my dad had been dead longer now than I had known him alive. I realised, also, that I couldn't really remember all that much about him: what he looked like, what he *was* like. Just occasional things remained: like lying in bed that time listening to the clink of glasses and him laughing with friends downstairs. He was rarely drunk and rarely noisy, and it occurred to me how nice it was to hear him like that. It was one of the few occasions I did.

Sometimes, people still reminded me of him nowadays. Richard Briers. Johnny Morris. Leonard Rossiter. There was something about them all. A photo of John Updike in a shop window once stopped me dead in my tracks; something about his expression was just like Dad's; there was something boyish, mischievous even. Endearing qualities in a man that age. Fifty-something. The age Dad would always be.

Odd things reminded me of him, too. Jazz on the radio. Flecks of grey in a man's hair. Seeing someone in a patterned jumper like the ones he used to wear. 'Sweaters', he always called them.

I could go days, sometimes weeks, without him even crossing my mind, then something would make me remember. Yes, I'd want to shout, *that's* what he was like.

And the last time I saw him, ever, I had come back from fishing and he was sitting on that old white sofa, looking pale and drawn. Thin, somehow, and he wasn't a thin man. Mum was sitting next to him with her hand on his arm. She was breaking an orange into pieces and passing them to him, looking into his eyes.

For Mum, now, being alone wasn't temporary. I could always find someone new; she couldn't. Eventually you can't – or don't want to – get back on the horse.

She had me, I suppose, but I wasn't much to shout about.

Or maybe there would be someone else for her? I assumed there wouldn't because if it was me in that situation I'd never have the balls to pick myself up and dust myself down. But Mum wasn't me.

Funny, in many ways I hoped there would be. Anything, as long as it made her happy.

I used to worry about her when I first went away to Newcastle, what with her being on her own and me so far away. But she'd never been one to sit around moping. She kept going after Dad died, made herself go out, forced herself to do things and see people in a way that I knew I should – but couldn't – do in Freshers' Week.

She didn't sink, my mum, as it must have been so easy to do in that situation. The strength of character – the resolve – it must have taken was quite beyond me.

She'd been ill last Christmas and had got out of bed only briefly each day for soup. It had occurred to me then that there would come a Christmas when she wouldn't be here. 'Pensioners flu,' they called it on the telly and I thought: No, that can't be right, Mum's got it. Then I remembered: she *is* a pensioner. You saw it in the wrinkles around her eyes and the colour of her hair but there was more to it than that. She was changing shape. She was getting smaller, shrinking, bending. It was as if she was being pulled gradually back to the ground.

Emma used to end every phone call to her Mum and Dad by telling them she loved them. 'They're not going to be around for ever,' she'd say to me.

I should tell my Mum how much I loved her. Tell her that, no matter what, I would always be there for her. I wanted to see her now and look into her eyes and tell her. I'd say whatever else did or didn't happen, that was one thing she needn't ever worry about.

I dialled her number again. It was so familiar now, that number. It seemed inconceivable that a time would come when I didn't ring it any more.

She answered, as I knew she would.

'Hi Mum, it's me.'

'Hello, Robert,' she puffed. 'I wasn't expecting that to be you.'

'I know we only just spoke, but I forgot to mention I was hoping to come and stay on Wednesday night if that's all right. Only I'm working in Hampshire on Thursday and it'll give me a head start on the traffic.'

I wasn't working in Hampshire at all. I just thought she might like to see me. I'd have to ring a sickie on Thursday.

Yes, I'd ring a sickie on Thursday and then go and spend it in the Star.

But I wasn't going to drink, was I.

'Course you can come; it'll be lovely to see you. Bring some washing if you want.'

'Yes, don't worry, I'll do that. How's Chop?'

'He's lovely. So noisy though. Every time I leave the house he starts barking. It must drive the neighbours mad while I'm out. I should walk him more, but my knee's been playing up again.'

So typical, that. Not to make a fuss. Her knee, I imagined, was probably half crippling her.

'And how's the house?'

She told me how she'd cleaned it from top to bottom last week-end. Started at the front door and worked in, that had always been how she'd done it. Got some man in to do the carpets with one of those machines – didn't realise how dirty they were until after-wards. 'You won't believe the colour they are now,' she said.

Mum, I thought, I'm being sucked under.

'And do you want something to eat on Wednesday?'

'I don't know. I'll probably be quite late. Maybe just a sandwich.'

'What about a frozen meal? Or a salad, maybe? Shall I get you a salad?'

I didn't ring up to talk about food, I thought. I called because it's all gone wrong. Because everything's falling apart.

'Look I can't natter because my train's about to leave. I'll see you Wednesday.'

'Yes, look forward to seeing you Wednesday, Robert.'

My forehead stung, really stung.

I coughed again, so much it made me retch and I pulled the cigarettes out of my pocket and screwed them up, and the instant I felt them crush in my hand I thought: What's the point in doing that, I'll only end up buying more. It might not be today or tomorrow or even next weekend, but I will. It was a waste, if nothing else. Mum taught me that; she hated waste. All her generation did. I threw them in a bin, and wondered quite how many times I'd thrown away half-full packets of cigarettes before.

I'd spoken to Mum and nothing had changed. My head hurt, inside *and* outside, and I wanted it to stop. I needed a drink, but I had to stop myself, too. Stood up. Nothing to do. Touched my head again: no feeling, but blood on my fingers. Started throwing more maggots, then couldn't be bothered to stand any more so I sat down on the floor.

A woman dropped a coin by my feet.

How would Mum feel if she saw me like this?

I'm trying, Mum. I'm trying to sort myself out. I'm trying to get over Emma. I'm even trying to get a hobby. I'm trying but, I don't know, just don't seem to have any enthusiasm for any of it any more. And I knew I'd never use that golf stuff. Couldn't face it: the people and the club house and the golf society dinners and me not drinking there because I wasn't going to after today, was I, and all the other people there, they'd all be knocking back the booze, and watching them do it might be bearable if I could, but I couldn't. And golf, it was silly, it *was* ridiculous – standing all serious and hitting a ball as hard as you could. *Why?*

I wanted to be at home now. Home-home. With Mum. There'd be something to eat, something hot and fresh. Mum would busy herself and within a few minutes there'd be a meal on a tray in front of me. She would ask if there was enough on my plate, then give me more anyway. She'd tell me about the food, the sauce. It wasn't nouvelle cuisine or anything, it was simple, good food. She'd give me wine and, as she only ever had one glass, I'd end up finishing the bottle. The heating would be just right, the sheets would be clean; there'd be fresh milk and loo roll. I could just sit and sleep and Mum wouldn't know – thank God – what I'd been doing or where I'd been twenty-four hours before. I'd watch telly and she'd potter around, and wouldn't look at me the way other people did on a Sunday. When I was younger and went there, the phone would always ring for me but it didn't now and that was nice. I could sidle off early to bed and sleep.

I pressed redial on my phone. Mum was there.

'Hi Mum, it's me again.' I didn't have anything to say – just wanted to hear her.

'Hello again,' she said. 'Everything is all right, Robert, isn't it?'

'Yes, course, why?'

'Because I've had three phone calls from you in the last ten minutes, and I'm usually lucky to get three in a month.'

'I'm sorry. I'm really sorry, Mum.'

'Don't worry, Robert, I'm only pulling your leg. It's always lovely to hear from you, you know that.'

'No, not about the phone calls, Mum. About, about ...'

Then, just to stop the silence, I said: 'Did you join that Bowls Club in the end?'

'Yes,' she said. 'We had our first game there last week.' Then she told me about how they had to buy the white clothes, her and Auntie Pat, and how she wasn't very good, but reckoned she could get into it, it was fun, a real laugh, and listening to how cheerful she was made me feel worse. 'So tell me about *your* weekend,' she said. 'I love reunions.'

The last time I'd seen her – it must have been three months ago – she'd just come back from a college reunion. She'd smiled a smile I hadn't seen before, and seeing it made me warm inside. 'It was over forty years ago we'd first met,' she had said. They had stayed up talking 'til three in the morning, apparently, then slept in the halls of residence. Bill got drunk and fell off his chair. 'It was funny, Robert,' she had said, 'Bill was always the one who got drunk.'

I didn't know what to say. All that came to mind was: I wish you'd had a chance to get to know Emma better. Instead I said: 'I'm tired, Mum, really tired.'

Something in me longed to tell her what had happened last night and how it kept happening. She'd know what to do; mums always did.

'It's called a hangover,' she said. 'And you will get them if you drink like you do.' It wasn't said with any malice; it was just a factual observation.

I wondered how she knew. I'd never been drunk in front of her, not for years anyway. I waited, hoping she'd ask me about Emma, because if we got onto that subject she'd probably have some comforting things to say about that, too, but then I remembered again: I hadn't mentioned Emma to her for ages, so she probably assumed we weren't seeing each other any more and didn't want to embarrass me. I coughed.

'Robert, are you sure everything's all right?'

'Yes, I'm just tired. Feeling a bit low, you know. Maybe it's work, I think I need a change.'

'Yes, well, remember what I always told you – you can do anything you want if you want it enough.'

Her simple, unshakeable optimism made me shiver. If only that was true, Mum.

I was tempted to say, as I'd been tempted to say to Matt earlier: There's only one thing about me you don't understand, Mum. The booze.

What I want is to *not* to be a big drinker, what I want is to *not* be a smoker, what I want is to *not* be the arsehole I've become.

'The train's nearly here so I best go. Take care.'

'We'll talk properly on Wednesday. Look after yourself in the meantime.'

I rang off again and I remembered that obituary I'd written in the hotel room. The cleaner would have been through there by now. She'd have screwed it up and thrown it in the bin and emptied that into a dustbin sack with the rubbish from all the other rooms at *Sea View*: the tissues, the condoms, the tampons. She'd be in a rush, probably; she'd have her own life. And it occurred to me that living the way I did could kill me. People like me dropped dead without warning in their thirties. Collapsed of strokes or heart attacks. Until now, death had always been something that happened to other people – but I had *become* another person. I stepped in front of buses late at night, I lurched down sets of concrete steps, I wobbled, precariously, on the edge of railway platforms. People like me ended up with fractured skulls, broken pelvises, stab wounds; we died quietly, bubbling in our own vomit in car parks.

And the people upstairs on that bus going home wouldn't know they'd hit something or, believing the driver had misjudged the corner and taken out a railing or a bin, would curse and sneak in a fag and cheer when it started moving again, oblivious to the ambulance lights moving away. Or that train driver, afterwards, would shake his head and say it was almost as if I was trying to take a short cut, the way I darted out diagonally in front of him. He wouldn't have seen anything, just a shadow. Then he heard the thud and had known. Or, 'It looks bad,' passers-by would say after I'd fallen, watching me not moving, making whimpering noises – noises they hadn't heard before. Someone would put a coat over my chest and I'd die, somewhere between Wimbledon and a hospital, or on the pavement outside the Star. The next day the wind would blow McDonald's cups across the spot where I'd fallen, then that night they'd get swept away.

You could only get that drunk so many times without something really bad happening.

And my mum would be left to bury me. Relatives and friends would come in for coffee and offer to stay longer – overnight, if it would help – and then go. She'd see out her years, all those years, with a deep, enduring private grief. A grief that comes at night, at one thirty am when you wake from a troubled sleep and know you won't sleep again. When you know you'll never sit grandchildren on your lap and give them soft encouragement and teach them the difference between right and wrong.

She would roll over, cold, but there wouldn't seem any point in rearranging the duvet. Why do that, she'd think. My boy's gone.

She'd lie there, images of the funeral flashing into mind. Friends of mine she knew, friends she had met that day for the first time. One of the hymns she tried to sing, but couldn't. What was said in the service. Always the life and soul. Always a good laugh.

I could die, and people would still be passing through here. Newcastle Central. Queuing up for soup, blowing the heat from it, hurrying across the little footbridge, glancing up at the timetable board and ducking their heads when a pigeon flapped up in front of them. They'd still be going about their business, oblivious to the fact that I was dead. They'd be dodging the litter and doing up their coats, thinking, 'It's getting cold,' and passing through my favourite station. They'd be running for trains, collecting a paper, flicking a look at the top-shelf magazines in Menzies, guiltily buying a bar of chocolate and heading home. To warmth, and the people waiting for them. Lads, calling in that pub on the corner for the first pint of the evening. The shunting of taxis out the front, the growl of buses.

Except I wouldn't see or hear it. It wouldn't be for me any more. I'd be dead.

I didn't want to die,

I was too young, too unfinished, too incomplete.
Too scared.
I didn't care whether I was a good laugh.
It was a good son I wanted to be.

Chapter Forty

We were round Magnus's house.

Us kids swarmed round him. He was Welsh and fixed punctures and sometimes gave us money. I felt I had a special claim on him: he lived next door.

Magnus had a red face and used to call out to me when I was on my bike and laugh a lot somewhere behind his red beard.

'He likes a drink,' people said disapprovingly, and being a kid I used to imagine him with a big glass of squash, somehow doing something he shouldn't with it: gulping it or burping or wiping his mouth on his sleeve or even spitting some of it on the floor.

I used to feed his cat, Malt, when they went on holiday and once, exploring the house, I found a bottle wrapped neatly in a sock at the back of a drawer. Whisky.

'I don't want you round there any more,' my mum said, when I told her.

I was heartbroken: Magnus had said he'd make my bike the fastest in the road. 'We'll show them,' he said, but he never told me exactly *who* he'd show.

Truth was, he was in trouble with my mum long before then. 'Come in here, young Rob,' he'd called out to me one day. 'We'll make your bike special.'

And he'd taken the back wheel off and put on one from some little kid's bike that was at the back of his garage. I watched his huge hands as he worked and I noticed how delicate they were and how yellow his fingers were.

When I rode it up the street, it made me rise then fall, rise then fall. Magnus laughed uncontrollably behind his red beard. 'Fuck me,' he howled, 'it's a penny-farthing.'

My mum was furious when I told her, although I didn't know

whether it was because of the bike or because he used the F-word. 'His wife must have the patience of a saint,' was all she said.

Another time, we saw him one night yelling in the garden, yelling at the fence with his arms in the air. 'He's not himself,' my mum said. 'It's the Scotch.'

'I thought he was Welsh,' I answered.

His real name was Alan, but we called him Magnus because everyone reckoned he was dead clever and Mum always said he should go on *Mastermind*. Eventually, all she'd say was, 'Such a shame, such a shame,' with a look on her face I'd never seen before.

Later, Magnus moved. Later still, I learnt he killed himself, leaving – I found out when I knew the meaning of the words – a widow and a mother-to-be. It was supposed to be their new start, that baby, so his wife told my mum. Some new start. We fell out of touch with her and I never met the kid. It would be a teenager now.

Maybe he or she drank?

It is, some do say, hereditary.

Chapter Forty-one

I always said I'd bring you here, didn't I? To Newcastle. Promised myself and promised you, too. But you've gone. I've lost you. A handful of decisions *do* define a life's course. You were one of them, Emma. We could have got married, but we didn't. Simple as that.

Now, though, I couldn't bear not knowing whether it was the right or wrong thing to have happened. In one way it was definitely wrong, because I couldn't stop thinking about it. Do you see?

And were you somewhere else, maybe wondering about me? Where I was, how I was?

I'm in Newcastle Central, Emma, feeling shit, feeling shit and missing you.

I'd sort of half planned to bring you here for your next birthday or maybe my thirtieth, but we didn't get that far, did we?

I want to be on the sofa with you, Emma. Just next to you would be enough. Your hand on my knee. The remote between us. Even hearing you slurp your tea would be enough.

I remembered the first time I'd gone back to her flat and how I'd seen the wedding invite on the bookcase and – teasing – I'd said: 'This looks very posh, who's Miss Emma Peters?'

'It's me, *silly*,' she said.

And the way she said 'silly' could have made me hug her. Instead, I'd asked for a drink – it was way past chuck-out time – and we sat on the sofa and after a few minutes, when the booze got me back up there, I kissed her and she seemed OK with that and after a while and a few refills and some fumbling on the sofa she put me to bed.

Emma. Baby.

The clock said quarter to two. Fifteen minutes to the train.

What came next? Tomorrow and the next day and the day after

that? I'd managed not to think about what came after this weekend all weekend. But Sunday afternoon really had come. I was on my own now. I had to go back to London and the flat, no Emma, and sit there tonight not ringing her. Sit there feeling like this. All I wanted was for this weekend to go on a bit longer.

Please.

I felt like stamping my feet, shouting. But I was too tired.

I shivered. I'd get a cold tomorrow as I always did after a big sesh. I had a cold most of the time. I'd be on the max-strength Lemsips every night this week if I was to have any chance of sleeping. I knew I'd cough all night, too, always did after smoking. Emma always used to nag me to go to the doctor's about it. 'Just to put your mind at rest,' she said.

The only time I'd felt good today was when I was walking to the bar in the Three Kings. Walking up there knowing that in a few seconds I'd ask for a drink, say the words, and then have one. The anticipation. But it lasted precisely that long: the length of time it took me to get to the bar and say it: A double vodka and Coke please. And afterwards, well, afterwards *this*.

Ten minutes 'til the King's Cross train.

I was cold, but it was better to be here and cold than on the train warm and going back. Once I was on it, the weekend was over. When I got back to the flat, I'd exchange a few words with whoever else was in then crawl to my bed and fail to sleep. I never did on Sundays. It would either be boiling or freezing in my room, it was always pot-luck which, and I'd lie there feeling sick and drained and sorry and trying to forget last night – and all the other last nights – and wondering what Emma was doing and knowing that eleven days before, we'd made love. We'd made love knowing that it – us – was about to end. I'd sensed she was building up to something. And knowing that we were on the way out, and still doing it, made me a little ashamed now. It wasn't something Emma did lightly, making love, but she did it with me that night and we were fierce, frantic, desperate in a way somehow almost not sexual. It was more basic than that: like we were trying to go beyond sex.

She must have known she was going to chuck me the next night, too.

Again, I remembered those brown eyes that shone like marbles – in the early days when she was excited and then, towards the end, when she cried. I'd lost them.

I'd lie there tonight knowing this weekend had been different for me than for the others. Again, the drinking had been different. It was like that last sex with Emma: abandoning myself to it, trying to find something that wasn't there. It simply hadn't worked.

I wasn't a teenager any more. Then, it was just booze and it was funny. It stayed funny at uni, too, everyone got rat-arsed, although there was something even then, I now realised, in my drinking that there wasn't in other people's. There was a recklessness in me that I didn't see in my mates. A recklessness and a purpose. They sometimes got drunk. I made sure I did. I had to.

Seven minutes.

I took a deep breath, hoping the fresh air might make me feel better, but it didn't, it just made my throat and chest itch. It was autumn, and already getting cold. 'Don't forget to pack your balaclava,' Mum had said when I told her I'd been accepted by Newcastle. And then she'd given me a big hug and told me how proud she was of me; and I felt all tingly inside, knowing I'd made her that pleased.

I couldn't imagine tomorrow. Even the rest of today. More weekends like this? More no Emma? More drinking?

No, no more drinking. I meant it this time.

I need to know what'll happen after today. I need some direction. I need some answers.

When did it all go so flat? What had happened to how it used to be? When did I become someone who nearly kills himself in the street, jokes about leukaemia and starts fights with his friends? Some sad old perv who gropes girls' knees in nightclubs. Assault, that's what that was. I assaulted her.

I could learn to be a better person. No, not learn: *remember*. I could do it. Sober.

Sober, I could be reliable, honest, genuine. Good. A good son. A good boyfriend. A good friend.

I was like that once. When I first came to this place.

Trouble is, it seemed such an uphill struggle. Such a fight. I didn't know if I had it in me.

The King's Cross train pulled in and then out again.

I'd made my mind up. I was going to the Rising Sun.

214

Chapter Forty-two

Claire burst into my room crying.

'The bastard, the fucking bastard,' she said.

I shut the door and she sat on the bed. I'd been revising for our Globalisation exam the next day. I thought she had been too but, seeing how red and puffy her face was, I knew she'd been crying for a long time.

She didn't have a bloke on the go at the moment, so I didn't have a clue who she could mean. 'Who?'

'That bastard dad of mine,' she said, sobbing uncontrollably. I went to her, put my arm around her. 'What is it, Claire?'

'He's done it again.'

I sensed the conversation I was about to have would be one I hadn't had before. I'd known her for a year, but this was new territory. I stroked her hair.

'He's hit my mum again, Rob,' she said and, as if saying it made it worse, she started crying louder, harder. 'We thought it had all stopped. He hasn't done it for years, but she's just rung, she's in a right state. He's broken her fucking nose. He's broken my mum's nose.'

I said nothing. It was the first time I'd ever seen a girl cry in real life, you know, other than kids, and it shot into a part of me I'd never felt pain in before. I knew, somehow, seeing a girl cry would always make me feel like this: scared and sick and a little guilty, and like I wanted to hug them very tightly. I stroked her hair more.

'It's the drink,' she said. 'He's only been back on it for a few weeks and already it's started. Mum can't go through all that again.'

Then Claire stared straight ahead, like she was looking way beyond me, my room, the Halls, even the whole city – into somewhere only she knew.

'How is she?' I asked. Stupidly.

'*How is she?* How do you fucking *think* she is, Rob!' she screamed. 'She's got a broken nose and a fucked-up marriage and a fucked-up life and a tosser of a husband who cares more about alcohol than he does about her.'

It was odd, hearing her swear like that. She swore all the time – more than most of the blokes we knew – but it was never directed *at* anyone. It scared me.

'She's got a tosser of a husband whose idea of a good night out is to have ten pints of beer then beat her senseless. That's how she is, Rob.'

I still didn't know what to say. I just wanted her to stop hurting. It struck me quite how unimportant – quite how ludicrous – our exams were, how ridiculous us all getting so worked up over them had been, when there was stuff like this going on.

'One night he hit me,' she said, turning to me, hugging me. It was as if she couldn't bear me looking at her. Along the corridor, I could hear someone playing hockey, the ball bouncing off the walls.

'He beat me because I stayed out late with a boy. I said I'd be in at ten and it was midnight, so he hit me. He was sitting on the stairs waiting for me. When he stood up I knew he'd been drinking because he wobbled and then as he came towards me I could smell it, he stank.'

She kept crying. Kept hugging me. Tight.

'He hurt me so badly, Rob. Why do you want to hurt your little girl like that? Why do you want to hurt anyone that badly?'

She touched her cheek. Flinched, as if something there still hurt.

'He kept calling me a slut. I was fifteen, Rob. He kept asking me if I'd been out fucking on the street, he said no daughter of his was going to become the town whore. Every time he called me the town whore, he hit me.'

She touched the side of her face again.

'I wasn't even doing anything. I was with this bloke and his mum and dad. We were having a barbecue in their garden.' She laughed, blubbing like a baby, wiping the end of her nose. 'I wouldn't make much money as a whore if I spent all my time at barbecues, would I.'

Then she cried. 'I went to a barbecue so he sees fit to hit me,' she said, her tone becoming angrier. 'I shouldn't have had to grow up round a man like that. It wasn't until I was about eleven or twelve that I realised it wasn't how all dads were. Now he's doing it again to my mum, and I won't have that. She's too old. If the bastard's drinking again, he's got to go.' It struck me that Claire, while she often got tipsy, never got really pissed – other than that night we shared a bed – and I wondered if her dad's drinking was the reason. 'He's had his chance.'

That night – exam or no exam the next day – Claire drove home to her mum. She set off about ten and collected her mum and, by all accounts, told her old man once and for all what she thought of him and where he could go. She helped her mum pack and drove her to her sister's where she stayed for a while to get her head together. And I realised, then, what she'd meant when we'd been talking that time a few months after starting at Newcastle; she'd asked me about my dad and I'd told her he had died, and she'd said simply: 'Mine too.'

Claire ended up staying for three days; she missed two exams, but got passes on account of her excellent course work. The little swot. Then she came back to college and everything was normal. We went round together in the same old gang; exams finished and we had a glorious week of doing nothing, drinking and relaxing. We went to the coast at Tynemouth and played football on the beach and Claire, as always, moaned about getting put in goal. She joked about how she'd discovered the perfect way of getting out of exams. Stevie got thumped one night in the Bigg Market for making a pass at some girl whose big Geordie boyfriend was behind him at the time. We all sorted out houses for the second year. It was hot, and we waited nervously for results.

After we'd all been out one night, Claire came into my room. 'Thanks, Rob,' she said, about nothing in particular. 'You're a real friend.' And I got more of a buzz out of hearing her say that than I think I had about anything ever before.

'How are things now?' I asked.

'Mum's moved out for good,' she said. 'She's gone back to Nan's. She's getting her life back together, she's strong.'

I dug out a can of beer, the only one I could find, so we shared it, half filling the two pint glasses I'd nicked that night from Caesar's.

'When I was fifteen,' she said, 'I swore I'd never have a drink. Ever. I hated everything about it so much. But then I realised, I'm not my dad. We're our own people. You know, Rob, it's funny, but when I went back home this time I saw how pathetic he really was.

I'd always remembered him as this *big* man. Him standing up that night on the stairs and wobbling and coming towards me is an image I've never been able to get out of my head. I thought: If he falls, he'll smash the whole house. But I saw quite how vulnerable, quite how pathetic he was this time. He seemed small, Rob, small and old. I'm not scared of him any more. That's all.'

Chapter Forty-three

It still disappointed me.

Never mind that I came in here yesterday and the day before, I still couldn't see why they had to change it, this of all places. Suppose it was only a pub. But it wasn't only a pub, it was the Sun.

I sat at the table nearest the stairs up to the balcony bar. A few people watched as I bundled in with all my stuff but the old place was pretty empty. Then I wondered what to do next. I mean, I hadn't come here for a drink. Seriously, I'd come here *not* to. If I had one now, even one, I wouldn't get home. That was why I came. Do it here, I reckoned, and I could do it anywhere.

Tomorrow was the deadline for a big project at work, one me and the boss – OK, the boss – had been working on for months. Waking up in the Hotel Where We Spew knowing I'd missed it, feeling like I did this morning – but alone, none of the others around – would have been too much, I couldn't face that. And all the time I was sitting here not drinking seemed like some sort of minor victory.

James came in here once dressed as Superman. We told him we were going to a fancy dress party and he spent the whole evening in the outfit.

The night Stevie double-booked and two of his girlfriends turned up.

Matt offering to wash up for an hour if he could have a free beer.

Me, asleep one night under the table.

Five minutes, and I hadn't been to the bar. Do that again and again and soon the afternoon would have gone and I wouldn't have drunk. Later I could go home.

I felt like some sort of equilibrium had been reached. I wasn't heading home, which was good and bad; but I wasn't drinking, which was good and bad; and as far as I was concerned I wasn't staying here tonight, which was good and bad.

I sat. Just one drink would have decided it now. But it would have felt good. That first sip. I could almost taste it, almost hear my voice ordering it: 'A pint of Stella and a vodka and Coke please.'

Besides, I'd got nearer to *not* drinking in these last few minutes than I ever had. I'd thought about it, been honest, realised I did drink too much and had resisted for a while. That was a big step in itself. If I drank now, the next time I felt like this I'd be even nearer to stopping. This weekend's drinking wouldn't have been wasted.

But drinking and getting drunk and staying here tonight would be too much. It was too final a step, too much of an answer.

But the lightness in my feet, the way the edges would become soft, the way that nothing would matter, everything funny ... Mum ... think about her .... The flashing of a blue light outside Wimbledon station. A passer-by saying, 'It looks bad'; then walking on. Yes, stay sober. Stay like this. Another five minutes. And all the time I was sitting here like this, I could do either: drink or not drink. I still had the choice.

The old place was filling up. And outside, Merryfield Road. A hundred and four paces to Number 65. Matt, of course, reckoned he could do it in under ninety. James, with his legs, could do it in nearer eighty. Some music came on. I wondered if the juke box was still in the alcove round the corner. I went and checked but there was no alcove – no corner, even. Just a promotional poster for Bacardi Breezer on the wall. Bacardi Breezer, who drank that! Some of the people in here were little more than kids. Fewer students than there used to be, too.

I used to know everyone in here. A satellite student union. How many pub crawls did we start or end here? Literally hundreds. We met here, drank here, ate here, we even revised in here. That was Matt's idea: 'Sun brainstorming sessions,' he called them. The idea was to work together over a pint. Of course, we never talked about work for long. There were more important subjects.

The best days of your life.

I said the words to myself. Whispered them. *A pint of Stella and a vodka and Coke please.*

Then I made myself say another word, too: 'Death.' Because I didn't want to die and it was a long way home from here if I was wasted. A lot of bus routes, a lot of concrete steps, a lot of train track.

But one more night's drinking – what difference could that make? Just one. And I'm only talking about having a quiet one on my own before setting off. One for the road.

Remember last night, Rob. Your face pressed against that carpet, people tugging at your arms and legs. The roughness of the carpet, the red on your cheek. Dusty. Feeling like you were falling, disappearing, you and the carpet and whatever was beneath that.

I touched my forehead; it had started bleeding again.

I didn't know what to do. I wanted to ring Mum, but I'd rung her three times already and she'd think it odd.

I wanted to ring Matt, James, Stevie – anyone so I could hear their voices, but what would I say? 'Please help me.'

Hardly. They'd think I was pissed or taking the piss.

I could ring Claire, but I knew what happened next was down to me.

It was my choice. And it was a simple one.

Stay or go.

Stay sober or get drunk.

Lose your friends or keep them.

Carry on killing yourself slowly, or stop.

I felt angry that the choice had become so polarised. Who had let it become like this when all I wanted to do was have a pint and go home? And I felt more frightened than ever before.

Matt would be back in Manchester soon, the city he now said was his favourite place. He'd be opening the door and calling, 'Hi, it's me,' and finding Katie curled up on the sofa, smiling at him. She'd have been waiting, looking forward to seeing him, wondering what sort of state he'd be in. Looking forward to looking after him.

The prospect of never seeing Emma again seemed an unimaginable one. Fine, if it was just for today or this week or this month, even, as long as I knew she'd be back after that. But *never*? I couldn't do it, no way. It was like saying I'd never drink again.

But that was what I had said.

Both those things were what I had to do.

A shaft of sunlight was spearing through the window and I watched the dust particles in it: hundreds, thousands of them. I tried to concentrate on one, any one, but couldn't. There were just too many.

I grabbed an empty pint glass from the next table and put it in front of me. And I held that pint pot at the bottom, the way I liked to, with my fingers wrapped around it, squeezing it gently. It was empty, completely empty, but when I lifted it and put it – almost – to my lips it felt good like it always did.

After a while, two girls and a boy – students, I reckoned – came and sat at the table I'd taken the glass from. One of the girls had blonde hair: lovely and straight and shiny, it came halfway down her back. She was wearing a blue rugby top with the number 7 on it.

'Just one, right,' she said as they settled in.

Having spent the morning clearing up after last night's party they'd decided, apparently, they deserved a break. They talked about the party and their new house and who was going to do what – 'pink jobs' like cleaning for the girls and 'blue jobs' like putting out the bins for the boys – and a bit about their courses, then went back to talking about the party. Everyone had got paralytic by the sound of it.

So much for that one, too, they'd had a couple within half an hour.

Once in a while, one of them would glance at me and my empty glass. I wanted to tell them that I wasn't boring or tight or the sort of person who never has more than one in the afternoon. That was bound to be what they were thinking. It sounded like they lived in Merryfield, too. I tried to hear which number in case they lived in our old house but it was obvious I was listening so I picked up the paper someone had left behind and pretended to read it.

The lunchtime crowd disappeared and the afternoon lot drifted in.

A barman wearing a themed top with a name badge on it came over at one point. 'Are you going to have a drink?' he asked. 'This is a pub, not a waiting room.'

I wondered what happened to Den Watts. Frank Butcher.

'I know,' I said. I could have just a Coke. I hadn't thought of that. 'OK, I'll have a Coke.'

'It's not a restaurant either, the bar's over there,' he said, pointing.

I felt like telling him I was coming in here when the bar used to be in the other corner – when he was probably still at school.

In the old days it was mostly students worked here. They'd serve us even if it was a few minutes past last orders, they wouldn't rush us out as they had me and Matt on Friday and they'd turn a blind eye to the everyday stuff that happens in pubs: breakages, the odd game of cards, the occasional drunkard – usually me – upsetting the other punters. They knew we were good customers. Broke students, but big spenders. Like these three.

I walked to the bar. I stood there and thought: Coke, or vodka and Coke. Coke, or vodka and Coke. Someone I didn't recognised asked me what I wanted.

Stay sober or get drunk.

Lose your friends or keep them.

Carry on killing yourself slowly, or stop.

'A Coke,' I said, and this massive sense of relief washed over me. Like how it was after all that work when I saw on the results board that I'd passed my degree.

'Ice and lemon?'

'Er, yes, I suppose so, yes.'

I sat back down. Weird. I couldn't remember ever coming here and having a soft drink before. All those times, and I'd never had one. And here I was, doing it. It didn't feel much different.

I'd forgotten how Coke tasted without vodka in it. Sweeter, somehow.

The students were playing that drinking game where you name someone famous, then the next person has to come up with someone whose first name begins with the same letter as the previous person's surname. It was ages since I'd played it.

'Jeremy Paxman,' the blonde girl shouted.

'Peter Mandelson,' the other one added.

'Michael Schumacher,' the guy said.

'Susan Sarandon,' the blonde girl said, and the game changed direction. I'd forgotten that: how play changed direction if you said someone whose first and second name began with the same letter. You could gang up on someone, keep sending play back to them, making them drink. The buggers always used to do it to me.

I felt OK really. I wouldn't be able to eat, but there was nothing new in that. Other than that and the flashbacks and the feeling cold and the shivering and the worrying that I'd upset all my friends, I felt pretty good.

The girl nearest me was trying to come up with a name beginning with C. There were loads: Carol Vorderman, Chris Cristofferson, Chris Eubank, Charlie Chaplin. Two of those would even have changed direction.

She couldn't think of one.

I shouted: 'Chris Cristofferson.'

Seriously, I shouted it at these people I'd never as much as spoken to before.

'Who?' she said, surprised. She must have forgotten I was still here.

'Chris Cristofferson,' I said. 'Singer. American.'

'Never heard of him.'

'There is one,' I said. 'Trust me.'

'You can't have that,' the lad next to her said. 'It's got a K.'

'What, his Christian name or his surname?' she asked.

'Both.'

'Are you sure?'

'Sure I'm sure, my dad likes him.'

Typical, I thought, there's me convinced I'm going to change direction – and I'm doubly wrong!

'OK,' I said, turning back to the blonde girl. 'Try Chris Eubank.'

'We've had him,' she said.

'Carol Vorderman.'

'I've had her.'

I nearly said. 'Wish I had.' If I'd had a drink, I'd have said it. If I'd had a drink, it would have been funny. 'Charlie Chaplin then.'

'Like it,' she said, smiling. 'Charlie Chaplin,' she called.

'No, not allowed; no helping. Come on, two fingers,' the bloke said, pushing her glass towards her.

Leave her alone, I thought. Then: No, let her drink.

She had a swig of her drink and I had a swig of Coke and play started again and went on for a bit. I sort of watched and whenever one of them downed some I had some Coke and they argued a bit about whether you could have soap stars and whether you could have STEPS and when they got bored with the game, they chatted.

'Sorry to interrupt,' I said, looking at the boy, 'but did I hear you say you were Merryfield Road?'

'Yes, why, you're not here for the rent, are you?' Something about the way he said it reminded me of how Stevie had sounded that first day I'd met him. I could just tell I'd like him.

'I used to live there. I was at the uni. Are you lot students?'

'How did you guess,' he said, smiling at all the empties on the table. One, indeed! They must have had three or four each. 'When were you here?'

'I left in 1991.'

No one answered. This lot would probably still have been at primary school then. The only thing that had stayed the same was having this place, and even it wasn't the same.

'This old place has changed a bit,' I said. 'It used to be a proper pub. More spit and sawdust. They used to have bouncers on the doors throwing the drunks in.'

The blonde girl nearest to me laughed and I thought: *You're pretty*. Even now, feeling like this, Sunday afternoon, I noticed that. Her. If I knew I was going to get off with you, I'd have a few, I thought. You'd make it worth it.

'I used to live in Merryfield,' I said again, only this time to her. Her hair was shining in the sunlight. The sun never used to shine in here when there were net curtains up.

'Which number?' she asked, glancing at my forehead then looking away.

'Sixty-five,' I told her, touching my head; it hurt, but at least it wasn't bleeding any more.

'We're fifty-two.'

'You all share?'

'Yes, us three and Webbo – but he's at home working.'

The boy shouted: 'The lightweight!'

It reminded me of how Stevie had once said he wasn't going to do any work for the first two years. Only later did I realise quite *how* clever he was.

'You look as if you're visiting,' she said, glancing at the golf clubs, the fishing rod and the football. I felt ridiculous.

Just as well I didn't bring the maggots.

'I've been up for a stag weekend. My best mate's getting married.'

'Must be really weird coming back. How often have you done it?'

'This is the first time for three years.'

'I often wonder what it'll feel like coming back. I haven't even left yet and I'm worried about that. Crazy, isn't it.'

'No, not at all. What course are you guys on?'

The bloke was doing Applied Maths and the two girls were doing something complicated-sounding with computers. I might have been tempted to say they were boffins, on courses like that, but they quite obviously weren't.

'Did you have a good time last night?' the boy asked.

'Yes, I guess. Suffering a bit today.'

225

'You don't look too bad.'

He must have assumed I'd done my head before this weekend. If only he knew.

'Don't you believe it. I'm like a swan' – and I was going to say something about appearing better on the outside than the inside, what is it they say about swans looking nice above the water – but I couldn't remember what and I felt stupid for having mentioned swans, so I left it at that.

'Where have you got to get back to?' he asked.

'London,' I told him, remembering throwing my arms in the air and beer going everywhere when Nicki had asked me the same question last night. 'I didn't fancy getting on the train earlier. I needed a bit of time to clear my head.'

'A train's not a good place to be hungover on, is it,' he laughed. looking at the other two knowingly.

I remembered the time I chucked up on the train; the time, too, I wet myself on the Underground. They weren't amusing stories. They were sad.

'I wondered what you were doing sitting there on your own. I figured you must have been waiting for someone.'

'I came in here for a few minutes to get myself back together before setting off.'

'You're in the right place to recover,' he said, smiling again at the glasses. 'Nothing like this stuff for setting you straight.'

I swigged my Coke and wondered about buying a round, a proper round: a pint for everyone and a vodka, as well, for me. It wasn't as if I was short of cash and, besides, I deserved a drink. I'd been here for nearly two hours and hadn't had one. That must have proved something. I'd had about twenty-seven Cokes since I'd been sitting here.

I could leave, I guess. Go home. But the idea of leaving for no reason seemed an alien one.

That was another habit I'd have to break: never leaving a pub until it closed.

226

Chapter Forty-four

I was walking round, trying to get home. But it's not that easy, is it? Not when you've got to get past the Star. Not when there are about a dozen pubs between the station and home. Not when it's only seven o'clock on a Monday and these places are all open for another four hours.

I'd been out for a few with the guys from work and they'd all buggered off, the lightweights, so I'd got the train back, but I didn't want to go home to the flat. Five pints wasn't enough tonight.

I knew I shouldn't have any more. Not on a Monday, not with my annual appraisal at work tomorrow (my excuses would be better without the hangover), but I couldn't go back to the flat, either, not just yet, so I was walking in circles round the Star.

I'd gone out at the front of the station and turned left. It was sort of going towards home, even though the back way was quicker. But walking this way meant going past the Star. It bought me more time to make up my mind. It gave me the chance to see the pub, if nothing else.

As I approached I could see the light spilling out onto the pavement. Beyond it, darkness. Keep walking, Rob, just keep walking. Keep your legs moving and get past. But what about after? The music and the light would be gone, as would the sweet smell. Just noise and traffic then. The steel of cars. Moss on the tiles in the underpass. Darkness.

I walked. A man was selling chestnuts on the pavement, cooking them over embers in a barrel. Yes, that's what chestnuts smell like, I thought, as if I had been wondering. It was the first thing I'd really smelt for days, weeks. Christmas soon. I imagined Christmas Day, the sherry coming out at ten, the beer at eleven, then wine and more beer and eventually spirits. I remembered Christmases from when I was a kid, that sense of excitement: lying in my bed on Christmas Eve, unable to sleep and listening for the clonk of hooves or the scratch of a sleigh on the drives and gardens. Now, Christmas meant a week off work and an excuse to get slaughtered in the mornings. The prospect of that was exciting.

Emma had said something similar to me not long before. She complained how I never wanted to do anything any more – she'd suggested, one Saturday, we went and saw a film or visited one of the museums or maybe Madame Tussauds, but I hadn't been up for any of it. 'We've been seeing each other for well over a year, it would be nice if we actually *did* more stuff together,' she said. 'The only thing you ever get excited about is going to the pub.'

I got to the Star. Looked in. It was good in there. Warm, and safe from the outside.

I stood.

I knew the people in there were different to me, just as the guys from work had been. They could meet for one, for a chat, and when their pint was gone they could put the glass back on the bar. Me, after I'd drained the last mouthful, I held onto its round base like I was clutching something precious. One more, one more, was more important than anything else in the world. More important than anything that could happen tomorrow. And when it came, the new beer, and I had a whole pint and lit up a cigarette – well, that was the best of all.

Don't go in, Rob. Think of tomorrow and that black feeling all day and puking, quietly, in one of the cubicles at work. Please don't.

I'd had five already. One more wouldn't matter.

But work? Work!

One more, just one.

It wouldn't be just one, would it?

I managed to get past. Dark and cold. Nobody much here. I walked on. The flat would be empty and cold. I'd sober up and feel drained and sick and sit around worrying about how bad I'd feel tomorrow and what was going to happen with me and Emma and all I wanted was one more drink, which wasn't unreasonable.

And then it occurred to me. Even if I kept walking, I wouldn't have to go home. I could slip in the back exit and go through the station again and out the front and turn left and there, again, would be the Star. The people would still be in it. This wasn't the end of the evening. I needn't go in, not necessarily. I could always walk past a second time, and that still wouldn't be it, the end, not like last orders. I could keep walking for ages.

I came round again quickly. Standing outside the Star I heard the same noise, smelt the same smell, felt that warmth. People were pouring out of the station, going home, going out. I could go in there and fall over and all they would say was: 'It's Christmas.' I'd wake up tomorrow and feel awful but I'd get through the day, as I always had done before, and the next time I did go in, even if it was tomorrow, the people – even the bar staff – would be different and no one would know me.

You could get away with anything in London.

Then I remembered how one of the secretaries at work the week before had said: 'It looks like you've got sick on your shirt,' and laughed, then stopped, because we both realised it *was* sick.

For the second time, I walked past.

I kept walking. I'd keep going home but there was always that back entrance. And even if I did turn into it, that didn't mean I'd definitely go in the pub. I could go round again. By the time I'd got round it would be ten minutes later, ten minutes' less drinking. I'd have done it twice, now, that was twenty minutes – a pint less than I would otherwise have had. Maybe a short, too. I deserved a drink for that.

The third time I walked round, 'Fairytale of New York' was playing on the juke box.

I stood, paralysed. I couldn't walk any further. I couldn't go in.

Always reminded me of the first Christmas Eve I spent in a pub, this song. Must have been about seventeen. Mum had to put me to bed that night.

I saw Shane MacGowan on telly once sinking half-pints of Martinis at eleven o'clock in the morning. I only wanted a pint.

I stood outside a door. People manoeuvred around me. A few tutted. I was moving, now, but I just came to another door.

Music drifted out, that line about having your dreams taken from you.

Don't, Rob. I tried to get walking again, but my legs wouldn't work. Please, don't give out on me now.

But in ten or twenty years' time, I'd come back here to visit and think: that was my local. When I was working in London, I'd say, that had been the pub I went to all the time. I'd probably have a family then: stuck in some suburb, respectable, boring, not having smoked or got pissed for years. I'd want something to look back on then, to remember. And the people inside couldn't all be wrong.

Who cared about a hangover? I'd survive. Fuck it, I said out loud: Fuck it, fuck it, fuck it.

And I got this surge of excitement. Like, yes, I'm going do this. Like having a drag on a fag when you're a kid. Like buying your first porno mag.

Like, no more fighting. It's over.

I felt a tingle in me, like something about to happen. Yes, this is what I'd been waiting for.

I felt like I was about to start crying with exhaustion or relief. And I turned left into that bubble, that world, that me.

Chapter Forty-five

It was OK here. Talking to the students was all right. I felt comfortable. These three didn't get all anal about alcohol, nor seem fazed by the fact that I was hungover. They came out for a quick one on a Sunday and stayed all afternoon. I liked that. I liked them. They were nice.

This lot could easily have been my friends. If I'd been a few years younger, I could have been in their year. Things wouldn't have been all that different, they'd have just happened a bit later. I could have been going back to their house tonight. It would have been *our* house, mine and theirs. Living at 52, not 65. They, not my friends, would be the ones I'd have spent the weekend with. Four second-year students having a piss-up in the Sun on a Sunday afternoon.

The second year was by far and away the best. None of the stress that blighted the start of the first year, and finals still not yet even a distant prospect. I'd live in Merryfield now, not London. It would have certainly made getting home easier tonight.

But, if that was the case, I wouldn't have known Matt or the rest of the lads. I wanted my friends, I didn't want to be the older one, the old one, here. I didn't want to know that these guys would leave this city, know that they'd load their cars and hug as they slammed the boot in Merryfield Road. They'd stay in touch, but things would change, would get difficult. Muddled. Sometime, they'd stop believing that you make things happen, discovering instead that they happened *to* you. It's true what they say: your years at uni are the best years of your life.

Not that you know that at the time, of course.

I was a decade older than these three, but it didn't help. It hadn't done me any good. I was the one sitting here alone trying to relive the past when I should be going home and getting on with the future.

I was the one hungover and depressed, I was the one who'd made a dick of myself again last night and who'd spent the afternoon fighting, fighting not to have vodka in my Coke.

It wouldn't go away either, this feeling. I knew it would be with me now for a long time, like a weight. It might not always be as bad as today – but always there, like an itch on your toe when your leg's in plaster or how it must feel to have a rucksack on your back.

I took a big mouthful of Coke. It seemed a long time since I'd introduced myself to anyone, certainly feeling as sober as this. But I could do it. There were butterflies in my stomach but not the burst of fear I was expecting. It was easy with this lot – it felt like I'd met them before.

'My name's Rob,' I said, putting out my hand.

They all shook it: Nathan, Laura and – the one nearest me, the blonde one – Mel. One of my favourite names; I'd been wondering what it was and now I knew.

I checked how she was sitting; if there was anything going on between her and Nathan, but if anything it was Nathan and the other girl who were an item. They were sharing one of the Sunday supplements.

'So, got any suggestions for my best-man speech next weekend?' I asked Mel.

'Oh no, you're the best man, are you? Are you nervous?'

'Petrified,' I said. 'The trick, I imagine, is making my speech appeal to everyone. Suppose it's all in the', and I paused for ages, absolutely ages, then added: 'timing.'

When she laughed, she got all these wrinkles across the bridge of her nose. I didn't normally go for blonde girls, but it was like Stevie always used to say to redheads: 'I don't usually go for girls with red hair, but I'm prepared to make an exception in your case.'

When I saw those little wrinkles, something reminded me of that day I'd seen Emma on Waterloo Station. She didn't know I was on the next platform; it was just a coincidence we'd both been there. It was rush hour, loads of people, and she was walking along reading. She wasn't looking where she was going, she was glued to her book, and she walked straight into this railing. I nearly cried out: Emma, be careful. She looked up and kept walking, kept reading, and went down the stairs to the tube and I ran after her but by the time I got to where she'd been, she'd gone. It wasn't that it struck me as particularly dangerous or funny or even cute, it was that I felt this incredible *closeness* to her at that moment. Anybody else in the world could have bumped into a railing on Waterloo Station and I wouldn't have felt quite what I did. That *involvement*. Funny, how I remembered that now, sitting here in the Rising Sun, for the first time in, what, a year? What I'd forgotten was how it made me *feel*. But now I remembered exactly: I felt so lucky it was me she was going out with. And I remembered, too, which book it was. It was the book I'd been trying, half-heartedly and unsuccessfully, to read this weekend. *Captain Corelli's Mandolin*.

'Have you got your speech all ready then?' Mel asked.

'No, I'm going to wing it,' I said. Then, without intending to: 'I wish I was still a student.'

'You enjoyed your time here then?'

'I loved it. Wish I was still here now, to be honest. There's so much to look forward to when you're a student.'

'There's always things to look forward to – however old you are – just depends on whether you're an optimist or a pessimist.'

'You reckon?'

'Yes, I do.'

'You know what the definition of an optimist is, Mel,' I said, getting a little bloom of excitement from using her name. 'An optimist is someone who's not in possession of all the facts.'

I hoped that she'd like my line – see me as the older, worldly-wise, cynical but sensitive sort.

'That's not true. It's the half-full, half-empty thing. It just depends which you are.'

'Right now, I guess I'd have to say I'm half empty,' I said.

'I'll tell you what the difference is. An optimist is someone who thinks their life is as good as it can get. A pessimist is someone who *knows* their life is as good as it can get. Course, I think they're both wrong: life can always get better.'

Her unabashed optimism reminded me of Mum. *Always look on the bright side. Chin up. Every cloud, Robert, every cloud.* And that expression about optimists and pessimists was one, I was pretty sure, that Mum had used. I'd certainly heard it somewhere. It was simple, but true. I liked it – and I liked what Mel had said afterwards, about how life can always get better.

If I had my time again, I thought, I'd be more of an optimist.

'I do wish I was a student again, though.'

'Sounds like you've got your rose-tinted spectacles on. You're

233

forgetting the exams and what it's like to have no cash and all the crap bits.'

'Yes I know, you're right, it's just then when I was . . .' I nearly said 'your age'. 'When I was here, I had so many plans, I was so full of what I was going to do, it wasn't until I left that I started realising I wasn't going to do them. I was even planning to buy our house in Merryfield Road. I wanted a little piece of this city to be mine for keeps – does that make any sense?'

'We keep saying we're going to do that – buy the house collectively and turn it into a commune and have mad weekends here with our husbands and kids in ten years' time.'

'I could have been your landlord if I'd stuck to my plans.'

'You couldn't have been any worse than the one we've got,' she laughed.

I remembered how the cooker had broken in our flat at Easter in the third year and Mr Breach – Mr Leech, we used to call him – still hadn't fixed it by the time we left.

'You could always go back to college you know, become a . . .' and she smiled at me, 'a *mature* student.'

I nearly said: 'I couldn't – you don't know me.' That's what I would have said to Emma.

I nearly said: 'I couldn't – you're young, you'll learn.'

I nearly said: 'I'm too old now.'

But instead I found myself smiling. And it was the weirdest thing, but I genuinely thought: You're right, I could.

'Less of the mature,' I said.

I'd been on a few websites recently, checking out about PGCEs. They did it here, in Newcastle. I'd obviously missed this year's intake, but I'd certainly be in time for next year. Autumn 2000. If I did that, I could teach after a year. Once I'd even got as far as trying to find out how to apply but the boss had come round reminding me of something I'd forgotten to do, so I had to stop. I meant to look again later that afternoon but I had to shoot off early because I was meeting someone, and the next day I was so hungover that making a cup of coffee was enough of a challenge, without considering resigning and moving to a new city to start again back at college.

Besides, something else had occurred to me while I was in the pub that night: that I'd miss the Star if I left London.

Say what you like about my current job, but at least I knew what to expect and could get to the pub twice a day, most days.

If I went back to college, I'd soon be skint again, too. I'd forgotten that, how depressing it is to have to worry about money. Trying to decide whether to go out or get a few tinnies and a video. Knowing you shouldn't do both.

And what if I couldn't do it, academically? I remember doing my dissertation – I'd really got into all that stuff about urban regeneration – but I felt so *stretched*, and that was after I'd been a student for three years. Teacher training would mean being dropped back into that world again.

Maybe wanting to teach *was* just a pipe dream? We all have things we want to be, but can't. I'd asked Emma once if there was anything she'd given up on – you know, dreams she'd sort of had to put to one side. 'No,' she'd said emphatically. Then she'd given me that funny look she sometimes did, and added: 'Not yet, anyway.'

Plus, if I left market research, it would mean the last seven years had been a complete waste of time. It would mean admitting that.

But they had.

Going back to college would mean starting again. A first-year. Freshers' Week. Hello, my name's Rob, I'm from Surrey and I'm doing Geography.

Hiding in my room and walking the streets.

My name's Rob, I'm from London and I'm doing teacher training.

It wouldn't be easy, but it's what I wanted to do.

Emma always said: 'Go for it.'

Likewise Mum.

Even Physical Phil, now I come to think of it, had once suggested a career in teaching. A lot of Geographers do it, he said. Not because they can't do anything else, but for exactly the opposite reason. Because, as well as understanding things, they're often good at *inspiring* that understanding in others.

I remembered seeing my dad once in front of a class. I must have been about ten and had walked to his school, which was pretty near mine. I stood looking through the glass, transfixed, amazed by the looks on the children's faces, the expressions of wonder and excitement. They were riveted, absolutely riveted. That's my dad, I'd wanted to shout. My dad can do that. 'I'm going to be a teacher like you, dad,' I told him, going home in the car. 'You'd make a good one, Robbie,' he said.

Chapter Forty-six

'What did you study when you were here?' Mel asked.

I was taken off guard by her restarting the conversation, almost as if she *wanted* to talk to me. It was like a lifeline. 'Geography,' I said.

She asked me how it was and which were our favourite pubs; as she listened, every now and then she got the wrinkles on her nose. She told me she was worried about course work, she didn't know how she was going to keep up with some of the modules. She had money worries, too. She seemed young – really young. I thought: If I get off with you, I would be taking advantage. Stevie would have ripped the piss something rotten if he'd known!

Not, incidentally, that I had the faintest chance of tapping off with her. She probably had the pick of any of the blokes on her course. And like I say, I'm not exactly Brad Pitt.

She was probably only twenty. A second-year. I was half as old as her again. It would be cradle-snatching.

Bet her dad was worried about her. He'd want the best for her and that wouldn't be me. She didn't know that, what with only having met me a little while before, but I knew what I was really like. I had no right to try and get off with her, to kid her. If I'd just got tipsy last night and had a pint with my lunch and been going back to a great job – a job I loved – then maybe. But not like this.

Besides, I wasn't exactly sure I wanted anything to happen. I was enjoying talking to her.

Mel told me how she'd got legless the night before and had to be put to bed by her friends and before I knew it I said: 'Me too.'

Then she explained how it wasn't the first time, it had happened a few times, and listening to her I felt a sense of calm, the sort I usually only felt with alcohol. Like, yes, it's OK, everything's going to be fine. People get drunk. It happens. Nothing bad happened last night. And I had a sharpener at lunchtime today – so what? I felt so good I wanted to have a lager, but there didn't seem a lot of point. I was getting on OK without one.

Then, just as quick, the panic came. What if I had messed up big time, hurt – seriously hurt – my head and God knows what state the inside of me is in and one day soon something bad will happen, it has to, and Stevie slapping me and Jesus, Jesus, I *will* get arrested if I go on getting in that state. Me in court, saying, 'Sorry, this isn't me ... it was, it was the, I don't know what it was ... I'm one of the good guys, please don't send me to prison.' All those ways I could die and Mum on her own. I mean, here I was on a Sunday, talking to three total strangers 350 miles from home – home, that was a joke, the flat – and I wanted a drink, I did so want something to make it all go away, to make it all seem less, somehow, *imminent*. Work; Emma; Matt; never drinking again. It felt like I was being sucked under again. All I wanted to do was fade into the background, not have to face any of this, disappear. And a drink would calm the nerves: nerves like you wouldn't believe. Half of what I was nervous about, I realised, was wanting to – and not letting myself – drink.

I couldn't breathe. Help me. Matt, Mum, Stevie, Mel, anyone, help me, please.

I told Mel I needed a piss and went outside. The evening light on the red-brick walls filled me with sadness; no nerves now. Even the walls themselves looked sad: so many the same, in that Mediterranean red, doing nothing and pointless. Why build them in the first place? They'd fall down eventually. The yellow M sign for the Metro, weakly lit, so sad; sadness in the parked cars, the cold metal, and inside the seats would be cold when people got into them. People died in cars. This place, and London, my so-called home 350 miles away, and hundreds of thousands – millions – of people living their lives here and there and everywhere in between, independently, interdependently, getting on and getting older and getting together, once in a while, to hang onto the outside of each other as it gets dark and cold and the world, unimaginably huge, spins on through the universe.

Chapter Forty-seven

I went to the loos again. This Coke was going through me like water. My bogs had stayed the same as they always were. Standing there, I could almost imagine that when I walked back out it would be the same out there as it always was. The lads waiting for me. Laughing that I'd missed the deadline for an assignment. Me, shrugging and getting another round in. Knowing I was a student, that I was supposed to get plastered, supposed to hand assignments in late, supposed not to have a serious girlfriend.

I went back and Mel smiled at me.

These three had no idea what I was like. If they'd seen me last night, it would have frightened them. I mean, I wouldn't like to run into myself when I was pissed. This is how I'd got away with it for so long: people didn't expect it of me. I didn't *look* like a big drinker.

Trouble was, different people wanted different me's. Drunk me; sober me. Sometimes I got them confused. You know: who I should be showing which one to and which one I should be at any given moment and which one – if either – was really me. Mel would probably want to see both. But maybe more the sober me I was now.

Maybe I should show her drunk me? Maybe she'd like that? I'd been this me for a couple of hours. Now, maybe, it was time for the other one. The one that doesn't mind getting slaughtered on a Sunday afternoon. The spontaneous one. The outgoing one, the funny one. The good laugh. She'd like that if she was a student. I'd like it, too. If we started going out, she'd laugh about it in times to come and say, as Emma had at first: 'I didn't know what to make of you the first time I met you – you were so out of it.'

At first, I'd liked the 'big drinker' tag Emma had given me. She had me down as a boozer, a good-natured boozer, and it seemed

238

funny. I used to think we'd look back, me and her, and see it as a stage I went through, like drinking too much at college had been. But I wasn't at university now and Emma wasn't here any more.

She probably imagined it was something I needed to get out of my system, something I'd stop sooner or later – especially if we got serious. I guess I did, too. But it hadn't happened like that. She seemed fascinated by that story Matt once told her about how much he'd knocked back that week we went on the Isle of Wight field trip. She glanced at me as he was telling her and I just knew what was going through her mind. She was thinking: See, he used to be like that, but isn't any more.

I remembered how I smelt this morning when I woke up, the smell coming from my hair and my hands and the clothes I was still wearing, and after I took those off and lay in bed with nothing on how it continued coming from inside me: out of my mouth and nostrils and through my skin. Toxins. My body, weak and knackered as it was, was still fighting for me – going to work on what it found inside itself, sweating it out, rejecting the poisons. I was freezing and yet the sheets were soaked with sweat. How could I do this to myself time and time and time again?

'Fancy a top-up, Rob?' Mel asked, going to get a round.

'No thanks.'

I sat. Stayed. They didn't seem to mind. After a while Nathan bought some cigarettes – Marlboro Lights – opened them and offered them round. I said no, but was glad Mel had one. She looked slightly unsure, which made it even better, then took one anyway. When she lit up the smell made me feel sick but watching her smoke reminded me what it was I liked about girls smoking and about how some of the girls I'd gone out with had smoked and how Emma hadn't.

One wouldn't hurt, I suppose.

But it wouldn't be one, would it? It was about fifty last night and earlier today and if I had one now I might as well drink. It was both or neither. If I could sit here and not drink, then I could certainly sit here and not smoke.

I breathed in Mel's smoke; it smelt even better after she'd blown it out – sweet and good and hers, though it made me feel light-headed, too. Sick, in fact. That would be charming, wouldn't it. Make a story, though, for the wedding next weekend. Imagine telling the boys that one. After I left you lot I went to the Sun and got talking to these students and I felt so bad I chundered. Right there and then on the table in front of them.

'It's a long time since you've done that,' Matt would say.

But it wasn't: I'd done it a few weeks before; I just forgot to tell him about that one.

If I ever got married, there'd be plenty of stories for my best man. I imagined my friends in their suits, smiling, as they tucked into the food, and me at the top table and them thinking: 'I never thought I'd see this day'; and me and Matt catching each other's eye – as we'd done last night when I went to talk to Nicki-with-an-i – and smiling. I felt the calm feeling again. Yes, it's OK. I've got my friends, they like me, they like me for what I am, they're there for me. Maybe me and Emma just weren't *meant* to be. Maybe I *would* meet someone else. Miss Right. My life partner. I wondered what her name might be. It might be Rebecca or Alison or Louise, names I'd always liked, and I felt a twinge of excitement. There would be other girls. You can walk through central London and see hundreds – thousands – of women. They can't all be married. When I see them, it *is* simple – I know then I just haven't been out with enough women yet and after a few more I'll find one and it'll feel right. Emma will too, she'll find a bloke who'll be good for her and good *to* her. Sooner or later there'd probably be a woman at work I started fancying. I'd start getting that rush of warm, embarrassed pleasure if she smiled at me. I'd be on the train in the morning wondering what she'd be wearing, whether we'd speak. I'd learn to use chat-up lines, flirt again. Things would get better.

Then the panic.

None of that stuff could ever happen unless I stopped drinking.

And what sort of person can possibly imagine chucking up on a table in a pub with three strangers on a Sunday afternoon and dismiss that as one of those things? What sort of savage?

Me, I suppose. The drunk me, anyway.

Not that I was going to be sick. I'd been sick in the hotel and on the station and twice was always enough.

And what if I did lose my friends? I couldn't bear that. I couldn't get up every day and for it to be me, just me. I wasn't exactly good company.

And what if Matt never wanted to talk to me again? Who would I ask to be my best man, then, if I ever did get married? I'd end up asking someone I barely knew, someone I got along with well

240

enough, but had only met a few months before. When I asked him, he'd sound surprised and try and look flattered and accept uncomfortably and that night tell his friends, a lot of whom I wouldn't even have met, that you'll never guess what: this guy at work or who drinks in the same pub as me has only gone and asked me to be his best man. 'I barely know the bloke – but what can you say,' he'd tell them. And he'd probably make a decent enough job of it, whoever he was. My relatives would introduce themselves to him and shake his hand and ask if he was another Newcastle person and wouldn't really follow when he said: 'No, I know Rob from the Star.'

If I was lucky, he'd tell a good enough story. But there'd be something missing. It'd be obvious in his speech when he recounted tales that were second-hand, mentioned characteristics of mine that he'd never noticed, drunken incidents that he didn't actually see.

He'll tell a good enough story, but it'd be somebody else's. Matt's.

Matt would have been brilliant at it.

Matt still *would* be brilliant.

I had to get back on the horse before any of that could happen though.

Worrying about wedding arrangements in the meantime was rather putting the cart before the horse.

Chapter Forty-eight

It got to six o'clock. I really had to head home. Strange, I still thought of Mum, when I thought of the word 'home'. Her opening the door for me when I was loaded down with luggage. Her asking me if there was enough food on my plate, then giving me more anyway. Me sleeping hungover on the frayed sofa where Dad had been fed an orange the last time I saw him.

A couple of Nathan's mates had joined us and the girls were talking about some guy who'd been at the party. 'Did you see the state of him?' Mel asked. It took a few seconds to register that they weren't talking about me. 'He was all over me. It was disgusting.'

I preferred the way she looked earlier when she felt guilty about having a fag, when she introduced herself, smiling, when she asked about my degree and about my best-man speech and her nose wrinkled and she looked interested and concerned. I didn't want her looking like she did now, repulsed, about me.

I wondered what my friends really thought of me. What they said when I wasn't around. It wasn't the sort of thing you asked, was it? You hardly called in one afternoon and said: 'Hi I was just passing'; then, when they were making tea: 'But do you really *like* me?'

The acid test, I supposed, was how they'd remember me if I did die. Then we'd see. It wouldn't be enough for them to think: Things won't be the same again, because they never were when someone died. What they should think is: Things will be *worse* now.

I needed to be more than someone who could be relied on for a piss-up on the increasingly rare occasions they fancied one. I needed to be more than just someone who didn't take things seriously: the person who'd never settle down, never forge ahead in a career, never buy a flat.

And I couldn't see why they would, not as things were.

As it was, they'd get in their cars after my funeral, get on with their lives and remember me briefly from time to time – less often as time passed – when someone ordered a round of shorts, in certain clubs, at parties, birthdays, wedding, stag dos.

I wanted them to remember what I'd been before the drink: how excited a book could make me; the buzz I'd got volunteering in that school after we left college; the way I could stand and stare for ages at the Tyne Bridge. The stuff before booze took over.

But soon I'd just be the dead friend. The bloke they knew who died, who they told girls about when they got to the tipsy get-to-know-you stage of a second date. And the girl would look upset when one of them – Stevie, say – described the funeral and me, and some of the things we had done together. *Sensitive*, she'd think about him. And she'd listen, thinking about Stevie: This is one of the big experiences of his life, this is the stuff that made him. She would be flattered he told her and sleep with him that night.

Would Emma be there? At my funeral? Would she think that I was the one for her, as she had once said? She'd probably cry, and not know what to think. And then – like the rest of them – she'd shake a few hands and climb into her car and head home. But she wouldn't be there, even if I died tomorrow. You don't go to exes' funerals, do you. And besides, no one knew her number apart from me.

And in the Sun and the Star, the piss-heads would come and go as they always had. Appear and drink and smoke and then one day never be seen again. And both places would probably be refurbished again and again – nothing stays the same – and new people, younger people, would come and make them *their* pubs. That was assuming they even stayed as pubs. They could just as easily be turned into a Starbucks or a Tesco Metro or a cinema or a car park.

Once, my two favourite places in the whole wide world.

Chapter Forty-nine

They were planning another party now and Mel was still sitting next to me. She'd been to the toilet and come back and been to the bar and come back and even been and bought some cigarettes and come back but she was still, still, sitting next to me.

'So you lot in here for the duration tonight, then?' I asked.

'We're supposed to be going back to the house, we've got some mates coming round for dinner. This was just supposed to be a quick loosener before they arrived.'

She looked at the sea of glasses and bottles covering the table, embarrassed. I looked at them enviously.

'You'll be pretty loose by the time you get back at this ... I didn't mean loose, like, you know, you know what I mean.'

'Don't worry,' she said. 'I know what you mean.'

We both laughed. Why are you being so nice to me, I thought. She lit another cigarette. This all *so* went together. I felt peculiar, talking to her and not drinking and smoking. I had a sudden urge to touch her – stretch my arm out and touch her shoulder, like I used to with Emma. Feel the strap of her bra under her rugby top. Number 7. I wanted her to touch me, too. But I couldn't get it out of my head how young she was. How would her dad feel if he found out she was sleeping with a thirty-year-old? And one like me, too.

Although he was probably like Emma's dad, like my dad, like all dads I suppose. All he'd want was for his kids to be happy.

That's certainly how I'd try to be if I ever had children.

Her parents were somewhere on the other side of the country – Lancashire or Cheshire by the sound of her accent. She spoke a bit like Matt. They'd have been worried sick last year when she went to uni. Their little girl moving to the big city. But they'd probably got used to it. They would have met some of her friends and that would have made them feel better. Her mum would probably have disapproved of some of their clothes, but she'd met enough people to know who she trusted and she trusted these people. Mel would have told them about how brilliant it all was and they would have been so proud. This was the sort of daughter Emma would have wanted: clever and funny and *together*, the sort of daughter Emma still might have.

Mel's dad might not like me now, but I hadn't always been like this. I *wouldn't* always be like this.

I tried to imagine her dad, but all I could see was Tony, Emma's dad. I wondered if Emma had told her parents we'd split up. Something very final about that. What would they think of me now? They had come out to the porch to welcome me, shaken my hand, asked me if I'd got enough food on my plate and given me more anyway, just as my mum always did, and no doubt thought: She seems happy, let's hope it works out this time.

I just met her too early, Tony. That's all.

Seeing his daughter upset was the last thing Tony would need right now. He'd been ill. Emma was probably putting on a brave face, but he'd know. He wasn't stupid. He would probably hate me now. No, not hate me, just not want his daughter to be hurt any more. A few months ago, he could have been the grandfather of my son; now he was just an old man I'd never see again.

He had always welcomed me into his home. Patted me on the back. Said: 'Rob, please, sit down.' Asked me about market research. Told me about his garden. He wanted me there because his daughter did. His little girl. He showed me the shed he was converting to a playroom for all Emma's nephews and nieces. 'It's like a plague of locusts when they're all here at the same time,' he said, smiling. Ten days before, he would have stood up for me. He'd have given me money and not begrudged a penny – money that he had accrued slowly, painstakingly, over his successful years in business. He had his own accountancy business, a real self-made man. He ate Sunday lunch with me, laughed with me over brandy and slept me – the very first time I stayed – in the room next to one of his grandchildren.

He would be sad that it didn't work out. Sad that Emma was upset again. Sad that he might never see her married, not because getting married was important in itself – times changed – but because a wedding would have meant she'd found the right person. Her Mr

245

Right. Her life partner. He didn't like the idea of his little girl crying – not when she was ten and fell off her bike or twelve and scared of school or sixteen and angry with a boy, not ever, but especially not now. Not now she was thirty and deserved more.

He didn't have the faintest idea I was a big drinker.

It wouldn't be long, I imagined, before I drove back past Tony's house. I had a friend up there who had parties all the time and seeing the road signs and the place name, I knew I'd get that sudden urge to call Emma. I'd wish that we were going to the party together, and that we could go to see her parents the next day. Play chess. Have a roast. Doze off in front of *EastEnders*. I'd always made a fuss about it, but I loved that stuff. I wouldn't ring Emma when I did go back there, though. If I did, all I'd have to say was, I'm passing your mum and dad's house and just rang, I don't know why, it wouldn't have seemed right not to, do you see babe, I can't explain, and we'd put the phone down and I'd remember how we had sex in front of the fire that weekend we were housesitting. I'd forgotten that. Always when you think you've remembered everything you remember something else.

Chapter Fifty

Mel tried counting how many she'd had, but got confused every time she got to five. 'Wine always does this to me,' she giggled.

'I reckon you've had five,' I said.

She kept trying to count them, trying to remember who bought what for who in what order, and in truth it annoyed me a bit. It was hardly a big deal: five. I had twice, three times, four times that last night.

But then I imagined her in the kitchen later, boiling pasta and mixing up a sauce and hoping her friends liked it – it was important that they did – and dipping her finger in the sauce to taste it and thinking how good it was, then going back to her friends in the living room to find her glass topped up. I'm going to be a wreck tomorrow, she'd think, then she'd say, 'I shouldn't,' and drink it anyway.

Enjoy it, I wanted to say to her. Tonight, and all this.

Never mind how young she was: I wanted her.

But I always wanted the women I didn't have. I always fancied my girlfriend's friends or my friends' girlfriends or my workmates' wives or anyone other than the woman I was actually *with*. It would never stop being like that. I either had to resign myself to permanently moving between women, or *trying* to, or accept it. I had to start appreciating what I had.

I remembered how, for weeks after Emma told me about that business with her ex, I kept telling her, jokingly, that I was going to do the same. You know, sleep with mine. I didn't mean it, I didn't even particularly want to – most of the exes couldn't bear the sight of me – but I kept saying it. It made me feel better than I had when I thought of her with him. What a smart arse I'd been. What a prick. Never really giving it a chance and knowing, deep down, that it

247

wouldn't last. Planning, too, what I'd say when the time came for me and Emma to split up. I had my lines all ready.

If she'd said: 'Grow up,' I was going to say: 'Why? It's not all it's cracked up to be.'

If she'd said: 'Why are you doing this?' I'd have said: 'Me? *Me?* It takes two to tango.'

As it was, I wasn't prepared for what she did say. A bolt from the blue that was.

'You do realise not everyone lives happily ever after, don't you,' she said.

And how do you follow that?

All you can do is walk to the door and say: 'I don't want to hurt you.'

How childish I'd been. How pathetic. Planning my answers like that. Me telling *her* – I can't believe I said this – that there were two of us in the relationship. It was me who needed to be told that.

Another answer sprung to mind now too, except it was one *Emma* once used. The answer she gave me at the end when I said that there were two of us in the relationship. 'Yes, you and the booze.'

However many people there had been, now there were none. It was just another fuck-up.

Emma's words echoed back at me from the night she dumped me when I'd looked surprised and asked what had suddenly brought all this on. 'Nothing's *suddenly* brought this on. I've tried to talk to you about it loads of times. You don't listen to me any more. You don't make me happy any more.'

It wasn't, I now realised, that she wanted us to move in together and I didn't; it wasn't that she wanted to get married and I didn't; it wasn't even that she wanted to have babies and I didn't. More simply than that, it was that I put alcohol before her.

And that was a disgusting thing to do.

I watched Mel push her hair back behind her ears. I remembered how jet-black Emma's hair had been and the way it stood up when she put mousse in it. I remembered, too, the deep, deep brown of her eyes and I cringed, recalling how I'd once told her they were the same colour as Newcastle Brown Ale. *Broon*, as they called it in this part of the world. I saw her every day and I kind of forgot how pretty she was. She looked like – well, she just looked like Emma. Everyday. Normal.

I let the fact that she didn't surprise me any more mean that she didn't interest me any more.

Why didn't I tell her how gorgeous she was, how much she meant to me? Even if we'd still split up, at least she'd have known. She could be with someone in a bar right now – some slimy bastard – and *he* could be telling her.

I watched Mel laugh and her nose wrinkle. If I was going out with you, Mel, I would be different. If I was going out with you, I'd work at it. I'd been lazy, OK, but I couldn't do anything about that now. That was the past. I couldn't change that. I could only change the way I was with my next girlfriend.

Imagine, it could be Mel.

Yes, I'd make more of an effort to appreciate the women I had. Stop looking at girls in bars, hungrily wondering what their nipples were like. Stop wondering how and where we'd split up and where I'd meet the new one. I'd appreciate what I'd got, appreciate the woman I was with for who she was, not for what she meant, temporarily, for me.

Next time, it would be different.

Next time, I'd be different.

Your dad might even like me if I was like this, Mel. I'd come here – to the Sun of all places – and not drunk and not tried to get off with his daughter or get her drunk (she'd done a pretty good job of that herself) or seen her, simply, as a sexual target. That must count for something.

My dad would be more proud of me like this – although, I could never recall a time when he wasn't.

Yes, I'd make more of an effort. Think longer-term.

When you're drinking, the whole world revolves around you. Sober, I now saw, it didn't. It revolved around everyone: Mel and the others in here and all those girls last night and all my mates that I was so lucky to have.

Stevie could have felt every bit as strongly about that girl who looked like Abi as I did. He might have had his own Abi. I didn't have a monopoly on feeling upset and let down. This wasn't just about me.

Maybe me and Emma would get back together. Give it another go. I'd be up for that. But Emma wouldn't. I knew what she was like once she'd made her mind up.

I had to forget her. Move on.

But what if I bumped into her in ten years' time and felt she was *the one*? Too late then. 'We make a good team,' Emma had once said to me.

I was convinced Rach had been the one for a while. But maybe it's different when you're young. When I think about that time I spent with Rach at college the intensity of it could still make me catch my breath. But we were never going anywhere. There was no way she was going to settle down. She wanted to travel. She wanted to see other men. I was her first, you see.

But if I encountered Emma again and felt the same, I'd know we'd have missed everything: the house-hunting, getting engaged, married, having kids, watching them grow up, us getting older. Or she might have done it, but not with me. Too late then. Ten years' time and I'd be thirty-nine. And you, Emma, you'd be a year older, wouldn't you. Well, eleven months and three days.

Emma. I wondered where she was, what she was doing. It seemed odd, not knowing. She always liked to know – even when we first started going out together – exactly when we were going to see each other again. 'I like having you to look forward to,' she once said.

Chapter Fifty-one

Nathan downed what was left of his pint – that made six – stood up and said: 'There's plenty more where that came from back at home.' He thrust his hand towards me. 'Nice meeting you.'

I shook it. 'Good luck with your course,' I said.

Mel asked: 'Are you going to be all right, getting home?'

I wondered if it was her way of telling me to get lost or if it was a come-on, but it was probably neither. She was just concerned, that was all. 'I'll be fine.' I knew getting home would be easy enough sober.

She put her coat and hat on; she was a bit wobbly.

'You're only going round the corner, you're not going to the North Pole,' I said, and she laughed out loud. A panic, similar to the one I always got when the bell for last orders goes, ran through me. *Please stop them going. Someone, please.*

'Bye then,' she said. 'Good luck getting back to London. Don't leave it too late setting off for home.'

'Good luck yourself,' I said. 'Enjoy Merryfield.'

I put my hand out and she paused for a second. 'Don't be so formal,' she said, bending down and kissing me on the cheek. She smelt fresh and sharply sweet, I liked it: it was make-up, I guess, but smoke and gin and a little bit like Emma, too. And the urge came over me to hug her tight then sit with her on the sofa, drink tea and watch telly then get an early night and curl up in bed and feel the soles of my feet on her legs and sleep, sleep away the tiredness and the hangover and what was left of the booze working its way out of my system. When I woke up all that would be gone but she'd still be there. Mel. Invite me round now, Mel, go on. I'll miss work tomorrow, I'll drink again tonight – be the drunk me, the silly me – I'll have a hangover, I'll do that for you, Mel, because keeping you, hanging onto you for a few more hours and maybe after that, is more important than anything else.

But she didn't. None of them did. They went. Mel was pretty wasted by now – she was pushing at a door you have to pull – and it crossed my mind that she shouldn't be using knives later when she cooked this meal. Then I watched them walk out of the Sun and I was left alone at the table beside the stairs that led up to the balcony bar.

I read the paper they'd left behind but got bored.

I put Nathan's empty glass in front of me. Did the same with Mel's. Tried looking around.

Tried remembering all the bar staff who had worked here in the old days.

Tried remembering exactly what Den looked like. Den who became Frank Butcher.

Tried concentrating on anything but the fact that I'd got to go back to London.

And now I had something else to make me depressed too: the fact that I'd never see Mel ever again. I should have asked for her number; she's a student, that's the sort of thing you do when you're a student. I knew where she lived. I could get bevvied, then turn up at 52. 'Mind if I join you, I've missed the train?' I'd say, as she opened the door. And she'd answer, smiling: 'Sure.'

All I wanted was to prolong the conversation, spend a bit more time around her and her friends. Soak up some of their youthful optimism.

But she probably wouldn't find it funny, me turning up unannounced. There wouldn't be enough booze to go round or her mates wouldn't like me or I wouldn't like them or her boyfriend would be there, yes, that's what would happen, and I'd stand around clutching a can like some sad case, getting wasted, wondering what I was doing there but incapable of going because I was too pissed to get out and there was nowhere to go now, it was too late. And they wouldn't want me staying, either; all the floor space would already be taken, and I'd leave about midnight, too late then for a hotel, really out of it, knowing Mel was in Merryfield Road in bed with her boyfriend, whatever his name was, and no Emma and just walking, walking round in circles – following the route of the Metro or the ring road or across the Tyne Bridge above that deep, black oily water time and time and time again.

I'd be upset she hadn't talked to me at her house, upset that she didn't seem to care if we as much as even saw each other again. But why should she? We'd shared a few hours together in the pub on a Sunday afternoon. That was all. We had nothing in common. 'Where have you been?' was what she'd said, when I told her I'd never heard of Shanks and Bigfoot. Never heard of either of them, in fact. It might have sounded funny – endearing, even – today, but it would soon wear thin. Where *had* I been? I was ten years older than Mel; half as old again.

I felt ancient.

Matt was right: I didn't want to end up forty, still sharing some crappy flat. It was like I'd gone into suspended animation. I was stagnating.

Look at me: nearly thirty and getting dumped again. Nearly thirty and another dressing-down about drinking too much. Talk about déjà vu. At least try and come up with something original, I'd been tempted to say to Emma when she'd shouted at me. But she was in tears, and so was I because seeing her like that was tearing me apart.

No, Mel and her friends weren't like me. I grabbed my glass, held it tight, and as I did so I realised where the people like me were: the people who pretended they liked socialising when in fact it was nothing more than an excuse for getting drunk. The people who, if you had one, had two; if you had two, had four; if you had five, had ten. The people who had their own vocabulary as far as booze was concerned. The people who knew what the inside of a pub looked like at eleven in the morning – the same as it did at eleven at night: silly and bright and blurred and home. Home. The people who just followed when someone, anyone, suggested a hair of the dog. The people who always had to have more, just one more.

Right now, they'd be sitting round together on small wooden chairs, taking it in turns to climb, shakily, to their feet and begin: My name is Rob, I'm an alcoholic.

This was why I'd always felt the people I'd been with had never been like me. Because they hadn't been, not completely. But I guess you're never like anyone completely. It would be the same with alcoholics as it would with anyone – just that alcoholics would understand one part of me *better*.

An alcoholic. Is that what it had come to?

I looked around the old place. Blokes supping pints; women with tall, full wine glasses. Everyone, absolutely everyone, was drinking.

I felt rudderless.

I'd thought that I might have been drinking enough to affect my health, that it was making me make a dick of myself – that was par for the course – I'd thought I might be spending too much money on it, losing my job because of it, losing my mates, pissing my life away on the stuff – even, for Christ's sake, dying as a result of it. But I'd never thought of drinking as making me an alcoholic.

Alcoholics are people you see drinking outside in the winter. They drink cider, shorts, wine or anything they can get their grubby paws on – they're dirty and smell and shout at passers-by and most of them are mad.

I wasn't like that. But what's the expression? One's too many and a thousand's never enough.

That's *exactly* how I felt.

Like a switch tripping.

You knew, Emma, didn't you.

What was it you once said: 'Maybe you should try talking to someone who knows about these things.'

You knew, and yet you didn't. You were like the rest of them for a long time: fooled. You knew I drank too much sometimes, that I drank far too much on Friday and Saturday nights – but you didn't know quite *how* much or quite how *often*. I was cunning. When we were together, I'd sneak off – at first to buy cigarettes and then after you'd helped me quit smoking, I'd go to the loo – and neck a quick one on the way and often on the way back too.

What you saw, I guess you put down to weekend binge drinking. And lots of people did that. At least, lots of the people I knew did.

For a long time, you just had me down as sociable. I was forever telling you I'd been invited out for a quick one by one of the lads from work, or an old mate had called up out of the blue and suggested we met up for a couple, or that I'd bumped into someone I knew walking home and we'd gone for a few beers. I was Mr Popular, as far as you were concerned. And why would you have disbelieved what I said? You *were* forever bumping into people you knew; your phone *was* forever ringing. I was dead jealous; you had the ideal excuse to go out every night of the week if you'd wanted it.

Besides, you weren't one to take the moral high ground, were you, Emma? And it wasn't as if you were teetotal or anything. Remember that time soon after we met, I virtually had to carry you home? Afterwards, you put it down to nerves, said you were terrified of meeting me. Ironic, thought, that I had to carry you home when I could barely walk.

That was the only time in two years I saw you like that. Just recently, I'd been doing it to you all the time.

I looked around. There must have been twenty or thirty women in this pub and I didn't want a single one of them. I didn't want Mel, either. I wanted me and Emma to be walking home from Wimbledon station. Eating ice creams in Hyde Park. Her singing along to 'Dancing Queen' at a party. Picking strawberries that day we drove out into the countryside. Complaining about the state of my car. Any of it. All of it.

I wanted to shout out now, thinking about that stuff, at the injustices of it all – the injustice that lets things and people change, that lets important things become, over time, unimportant.

I wanted to shout: *I'm sober, I'm sober in the Sun and I'm putting things back together and I'm not going to mess it up again.*

And maybe it was not drinking in this place, maybe it was having spent the afternoon with those students, maybe it was that business with Stevie or what Matt said or just another long, hard weekend, but something in me had finally snapped.

I couldn't go on as I was, I saw that clearly now.

Chapter Fifty-two

It wasn't as if it had always been like this. I never used to get pissed in the day. Not even in the evenings in the week, not that much. I'd save it until the weekends. I'd feel so full of self-loathing on Monday, I could stay off it for a few days, even right through until Friday if it had been a big weekend. I'd sit in Starbucks and sip coffee with my work colleagues on Monday and they wouldn't have a clue, not a clue. I liked it like that. It kept the two separate. My life was compartmentalised: work, drinking. I knew what I should be doing at different times. Drunk me; sober me. It gave me a sense of order.

Somewhere, sometime, the alcohol had gone from a part of me to all of me, had become the means and the end. And right now, it didn't even feel like an end. It felt like nothing.

I looked around the Sun, but there was no one here I knew. I moved on my chair, but felt no different. Then I squeezed the glass, just to see if there was still feeling in my fingers. Just. I wondered if this is what alcoholism was like. This feeling nothing.

I tried to remember leaving that club last night.

Nothing.

Tried to remember getting back to the hotel.

Nothing.

Going to bed.

Nothing.

It wasn't like I did this every few months or even every few weeks. I did it all the time now. I *was* an alcoholic.

I felt the reality of that near me, on me, in me, like the way you feel the cold from a bottle of beer on your fingertips, the way you feel the warmth from rum in your chest on a cold day.

I should have known when it got so that another drink was the best way – the only way – to cure a bad hangover. It happened first on that boys' holiday to Tenerife and it was a bit of fun, lager with breakfast, something that had to be done once. But back at home, I carried on doing it – occasionally at first, on Saturdays or Sundays. It was with friends then, and they found it funny. It was a big joke. Later, as the evening sessions got bigger, so did the morning-after ones. At some point, my morning tipple changed to vodka. It tasted so clean, so pure, so wholesome. It made everything so much better. Before long, I was doing it in the week. Vodka didn't smell, you see, and that was important when you had to go to work.

I should have known that night last Christmas when I walked in circles round the Star. At the time, I'd known I shouldn't go in, that I was different to the people who were in there – but I hadn't taken that one step further and worked out *what* that meant.

I should have known when I started drinking at my desk at work. I couldn't wait for the evenings. One day I must have figured it wouldn't matter if I had a small bottle of something in the office, just to pick me up – and now here I was, with a bottle of vodka wrapped neatly in a file and hidden like treasure in the back of my desk.

I should have known.

Magnus, I guess, never knew he was becoming an alcoholic. It must have crept up on him. He didn't look like an alcoholic that day he put the penny-farthing wheel on my bike.

It had probably crept up on him.

It had crept up on me.

Now I knew.

Chapter Fifty-three

If only it was an hour ago. No, not even that – fifteen minutes. Those students still here, that was the best, the moment before Mel kissed me on the cheek when I knew she was going to, but hadn't yet.

Yes, I thought, this is why I drink. Because I feel this *wanting*. The feeling that there was something out there, just beyond me. Alcohol quelled that feeling of being different, of permanently missing out on something. Wanting girls to fancy me, wanting to do well, wanting to be someone else, wanting that teacher to not always say to me: Life's not fair. I'd had that feeling all my life. Drink made me forget what I wanted. It made me want less.

And, of course, it stopped the invisible feeling.

'I'm the invisible man,' I used to laugh to myself as I walked to the pub. Then, when I'd got a drink in my hand, the second I took the first sip, I'd think: Not any more. Not any fucking more. I'm invincible now.

But it didn't help knowing this. I still wanted a pint.

I wondered how difficult it would be to keep this up. It wasn't as if it was just one decision. That would be easy enough. However hard it was to do at that precise moment, you only actually had to do it once. Trouble was, I'd have to make that decision time and time and time again: every time I went past a pub, every time I saw Frank Butcher on telly, every time Emma flashed into my mind – dancing round the lounge to Abba, laughing about how she once took her pet rabbit to bed as a child, looking up as she sank to her knees in front of me. The decision to stop anything was actually dozens, hundreds, thousands of decisions, repeated over and over again.

It wouldn't be so bad if I could just forget about the booze now, move on, be normal – other, of course, than for the fact that I didn't drink. But once you've felt like I had this weekend, something changes.

I'll never not have felt how I did this weekend. Never not have been sick on the station. Never not have sat on the platform and watched the trains then gone to the Rising Sun and realised: I'm an alcoholic.

I sat tight. I hung onto that Coke. Thought: I'll see what comes beyond this feeling. See what's on the other side.

If I miss the train, if I miss work tomorrow, it won't matter, not if I haven't drunk. What's the worst that can happen? They'll sack me. I'm going to leave anyway. If I wasn't drinking I could do anything.

Nothing lay beyond this feeling, nothing seemed to be on the other side except more of the same. Wanting. Uncertainty. A faint flicker of optimism.

Mel and her mates would still be in Number 52 getting pissed.

Emma would probably be at home, too. In the flat where we'd split up ten days ago.

Stevie would be home now too. He'd be feeling fine, he never got hangovers; he'd probably already be arranging to go out tonight or maybe doing a bit of work and I remembered him saying something late last night. He was sitting on the edge of my bed holding up my head, and said: 'It'll be all right, mate, it'll get better.'

Matt and James would be home by now, too. Back with Katie and Sarah. This time next week, Matt'd be married. Imagine!

I was glad he'd picked Stevie to be best man. He'd make a better job of it than I ever could. He'd even been on that best-man website, picking up some pointers. And it didn't really matter.

What mattered was that he'd asked me when he was originally trying to pick the date, both for the stag trip and the wedding, which weekends I was free on. 'I want you to be there,' he'd said.

What mattered was that on, I don't know, Tuesday if I was in the flat on my own and couldn't sleep and was tearing myself to pieces about Emma I could ring Matt up and he'd talk to me and cheer me up and not ask why I was calling at such an odd time, but know.

What mattered was that I'd do the same for him in the future, as I had in the past – something that the pessimist in me couldn't help thinking, despite his excitement about the wedding and his undoubtedly obvious love for Katie, could happen again one day.

259

The optimist in me, though, the half-full glass, knew that he'd met the woman of his dreams and that they were perfect for each other, just as the optimist in me – the half-full glass – knew that today I'd started drinking in the Three Kings and then stopped, something I'd never done before.

I'd flicked the switch *back*.

Outside, it got dark.

I sipped my Coke and read the paper and thought a bit more about drinking – and didn't – and a bit more about smoking – and didn't – and a bit more about last night and a bit more about my friends and a bit more about Emma, but that was it. Nothing really happened. I was just sober.

Drink or not drink.

I could do either.

A simple enough choice.

Easy, really. Perfectly black and white. Perfectly clear cut. The weekend *had* ended.

I stood up.

I made that choice.

Epilogue

Midnight, and Claire's saved my life. I more nearly had a drink a few minutes ago than I have all week. 'Fairytale of New York' came on and I almost cracked. It's almost as if I can't *not* drink when I hear that.

Almost.

And besides, Claire saw. Claire knew. She dragged me onto the dance floor and wouldn't let me leave until it had ended. Matt and Katie were having a slow dance; her in her dress, him in some bright pink hat he'd grabbed off one of the girls.

I love that bloke.

I'm never going to let that become *loved*.

We had a sort of slow dance, me and Claire, but the others all cheered so we stopped. She felt odd, not being Emma. My hands fell naturally to a different place on her than they did on Emma, not that me and Emma danced all that often – or at all, now I come to think of it. These are the things, I now see, that will be difficult about getting over her sober: the detail.

Then the DJ played some crap by Westlife and it wasn't a drink I wanted, it was a power cut. Claire must have known the urge had passed, too, because when I was back at our table and looked out at her on the dance floor, she was smiling at me, all pleased.

Later, when some of the guests are drifting off, she comes over and sits down. 'When did you realise about the drink?' she asks. Just like that. Out of the blue.

'Last weekend,' I tell her. No embarrassment. No shame. No nothing, now. Merely facts. 'It was only then I finally knew.' It's the conversation I started having with Matt on the football pitch last weekend. His words of then come back to me, drown out the music. *It felt like we'd lost you. You worried me. I'd help, we'd all help.*

261

'I guess it's always been there to a greater or lesser extent,' I say.

'Yes,' she answers. 'I've always thought that.'

I look at her, wondering how she knew.

'My dad, remember.'

'Oh yes,' I say, embarrassed at having forgotten that. And then I remember that night in Halls eleven years ago when she burst into my room crying and I feel ashamed, not at the fact that I'm an alcoholic, just ashamed at how it's made me forget about other people. Friends.

'Once in a while, Rob – it only happened every now and then – but once in a while, you'd look so like him it terrified me.'

I can't imagine what she means; Claire's dad had always been away when we'd stayed at her house. 'What do you mean?'

'It's hard to explain. Maybe not *like* him, but you had the same look as him. Just sometimes. He always had that look once he'd started drinking; then afterwards, when he was hungover, he looked hopeless. Helpless. You've always been the same, Rob.'

'Why didn't you ever say something?' I ask.

'I did. I tried loads of times, but it was as if you weren't ever listening.

'That's what Emma said.'

'I suppose you never wanted to hear. Now you do.'

'I'm sorry,' I say, 'this is the last thing you need at a wedding. How to spoil a night out in one easy step: confess to being an alcoholic. It sounds silly, doesn't it.'

'It doesn't sound silly at all.'

She puts her hand on my knee. Nothing sexy. Just contact. It's good though. The light catches her face and I notice she's grown her hair since we last saw each other; it makes her look older, it suits her. And I realise, too, how pretty she is.

'I should have gone out with you, you know,' I say.

We both smile. It *would* have saved a lot of hassle. If me and Claire had got it together at college, we could have been married and settled down with kids by now. This could have been our wedding tonight. We still could. Like I say, I *am* going to be a better boyfriend next time.

Thing is, though, I don't want to spoil what we've already got.

'I'm going to go to one of those groups.'

'I'll come with you if you want,' she says.

'Nah, it'll probably be dead boring: lots of old winos in a room together, smoking themselves to death.'

'You'll be surprised,' she says. 'I went to a lot with my dad.'

I never knew she went to AA meetings with him. I've never really talked to her about her old man or, for that matter, mine – other than to tell her that he died, and I wish I had now. One day before too long I will, I decide.

'You know what the difference is between a drunk and an alcoholic,' she says, smiling. 'A drunk doesn't have to go to all those awful meetings.'

Then I talk, and Claire listens. I tell her how upset I've been over Emma since we split up, and upset while we were still together, too, because I knew we were going to split up but would rather that than stop drinking. It's a fortnight now since it happened and I don't know how to refer to her. Can't quite bring myself to say ex yet; but saying her name hurts. And I tell her how the drink numbed that, and how strange it feels now, not knowing where she is.

Always the good listener, Claire.

'He's going to be a lucky man who snaps you up,' I say, laughing. But I mean it, I really do.

She smiles, too. 'Try telling them that.'

And it occurs to me that Claire, too, has had her fair share of relationship troubles lately.

Then she talks, and I listen.

I find I like it, too. Listening.

I know I couldn't have done it without her this weekend and I know, too, that she won't always be around. One of these days, some bloke is going to snap her up, and it won't be so easy for me to ring anytime then and natter for hours. It wouldn't be fair to intrude on *their* evening like that. Not that Claire would mind, she's like Mum: always got time for other people. Matt's the same. Sometimes, when I think about how lucky I am to have him as a friend I feel dizzy and slightly punch-drunk. I go and find him and his bride, and I shake his hand and kiss Katie.

I might not have got straight back on the horse, but a bit of time on my own would do me good now. Time to lick my wounds, to heal.

And Claire's right, what I really need is a new challenge. First thing Monday, I'm going to make some calls about PGCEs. The year 2000 sounds a good time for a fresh start.

Matt's got the mike and is singing along to 'Angels' by Robbie Williams. For a few seconds it goes quiet and some of us listen and some of us join in and we've all got our arms in the air now, waving in time; it occurs to me that I never knew Matt could sing.

He's not Elton John, but he's not bad.

I wonder where and when he learnt and I know you never know anyone completely, not even your best friend, and I know we've a lot still to learn about each other, all of us, and I like that.

It's enough for me to be here. More than enough. With my friends, all in the same place, for the first time in a long time, too long.

Claire asks me if I want to dance again; I take her hand and we join the others, throwing ourselves around and hugging each other and generally making dicks of ourselves. It's a real laugh. No one notices me, in particular; yet everyone does. And being surrounded by these people makes me feel big, strong, somehow more than myself. As if anything's possible.

This is what it feels like to be invincible.